NOT JUST A DOG

LAURA THOMAS

Tiny Mammoth Press

NOT JUST A DOG
Laura Thomas

www.laurabama.com

ISBN (Print Edition): 978-1-66782-724-7

ISBN (eBook Edition): 978-1-66782-725-4

For all the dogs who have changed my life, especially:

*Cody and Izzy, whose unfailing love reminds me
every day that dogs are the best people.*

*And Torres, who taught me that dogs can
unlock all the magic in the universe.*

CONTENTS

JUNGLE

Dawn, Day Two

STELLA KNEW THE beast would probably eat her, but she didn't have the energy to get worked up about it. Drenched and shivering, she lay in fetal position at the base of a tree, head tucked into her knees.

A chorus of jungle frogs almost obscured the sound of the beast's paws padding across the earth. In darkness, the paws approached, then retreated, then approached again, close enough for her to catch a moldy stench.

The downpour had tapered and howler monkeys wailed overhead, shaking branches, releasing cascades of droplets.

Stella's damp sweatshirt clung to her skin, its dirty yellow fabric heavy from mud. Her fingers ran across the hem of the sweatshirt's sleeve, frayed from overuse, having rarely left her body since her father gave it to her almost three years ago.

If he were here, her father would tell her to keep her wits about her, to look the beast in the eye. But her father wasn't here. He was long-dead, and she was lost in a goddamn rainforest with a predator circling her.

Dawn's first grays strained through the tangled canopy, but still she couldn't see the animal clearly. It was large—half as large herself, or larger. A jaguar maybe, or a wolf—were there wolves in Costa Rica? No, she didn't think so.

Jaguar, then. She visualized her death—the cat would pounce, grip her throat, her mud-colored irises would roll back in her head, her limbs would flail. It would be painful, but hopefully quick.

Willing the sun to rise, she fixed her gaze on the shadowed animal crouching a few body lengths away.

She clutched the pocketknife that Alé, the taxi driver, had given her yesterday. *I won't need it*, she had told him. *Take it anyway*, he'd said.

It seemed impossible that she'd said goodbye to Alé *one day* ago—that she'd been lost in the rainforest for less than 24 hours. Wrecked by fear and fatigue, she felt like she hadn't seen another human in weeks.

Slowly, details became discernible in the gray. Mosquitoes swarmed, their buzz rising above the shrieks of frogs.

On Stella's hands and neck and face, clumps of insect bites throbbed. But she forced herself to stay still, resisting the urge to swat the bugs away. Predatory instincts no doubt ran strong within the beast that lurked just outside her vision, and any movement might provoke it to attack.

She trembled, as much from fear as from the chill of rain-drenched clothes.

Something lay on the ground two or three feet away, between herself and the beast. Though she couldn't see it clearly, it looked like a small animal. Furry, rabbit-sized, immobile. She imagined it charging her, biting her, rabid. Maybe *this* was the thing that would kill her. Would rabies be a preferable death to a jaguar attack? No, she decided. It would be slower. More painful.

Should she find a stick, poke it, scare it away? Was that what her dad would do right now? Or would poking the thing just provoke it to attack? She squinted at the smaller animal's eyes—there was something strange about them—they gaped hollow, as if…

With relief and disgust, she realized that the small animal was dead. It resembled a big rat, but not like the dumpster rats that roamed Austin's restaurant back-alleys. This one had longer legs, rounder ears. A little like a rabbit, but not quite. Eyes glazed, its rigid arms strained forward, dried blood clumped on its temples.

Stella's eyes shifted to the larger animal behind the carcass, its fuzzy shape obscured by a tall fern.

A wolf—it *did* look like a wolf, but she knew it couldn't be. There were no wolves in Costa Rica. She didn't know much about animals, but she was pretty sure of that. A coyote, then? Were there coyotes in Central America? She'd seen plenty of coyotes in Austin, but this animal was different. More mottled, darker brown, with black spots and splotches. And its fur was shorter than a coyote's, its ears flopping forward at the edges.

It was a dog.

Stella rolled her eyes. *It's just a fucking dog.*

She'd never liked dogs.

"Go away," she said, her voice frail.

Crawling into a small clearing in front of the fern, the dog held her gaze and lay down, pressing its belly to the ground.

The mutt's skin sagged from his bones, with no fat to cushion him and very little muscle. He couldn't have weighed more than 30 pounds. Maybe less.

"Go away!" She raised her voice a notch louder.

Lifting its torso an inch off the ground, the dog crept toward her, bone-thin shoulders poking up over the landscape of its back. Its eyes locked on hers.

Was the dog rabid? Would it bite? Trembling so violently that the mosquitoes took flight, she tightened her grip on the knife, fingernails digging craters in her palm.

Reaching one paw in front of another, belly now pressed to the ground, the skinny mongrel shuffled two steps closer, holding her in its sights.

What should she do? Stand and kick it?

Alé's knife quivered in her hand. The small blade wouldn't do her any good from this distance.

She swiveled her eyes, hands trembling as she felt around her for a long stick, anything to shield her.

The dog shuffled two steps closer, gaze still trained on hers.

She wanted to cry out, to yell at the thing, but her voice caught in her throat.

Unable to restrain herself any longer, her free hand swatted a mosquito from her forehead, and another from her scalp, desperately scratching a line of bites on her right arm, raking up chunks of her own skin until the bites disintegrated into bloody scabs.

Two shuffles more, and the wide-eyed dog arrived at the dead rodent, just a few feet away. Spitting distance.

Sniffing at the carcass, the animal finally tore his eyes from hers. Then, it stood and turned to slink back to the stand of fern, a large pair of testicles dangling between its legs. The wrinkly sway of the balls disgusted her.

As the dog sat down facing her beneath the fern, she scratched at more bites on her left arm and shoulder, also blotched and dripping.

"G… Go away." She sat up straight to make herself look stronger, more confident.

Her head throbbed and she wanted to close her eyes, but she kept them open, focused.

Again, the mutt stood and walked low and slow toward the dead rodent, pointy shoulders rolling through each step. He sniffed the carcass and looked up at her. Lowering his body, he pressed himself stiffly onto the ground. His black eyes didn't hint at his intentions.

Was she hallucinating, or was the dog trying to *give her* the rat? Lowering the knife to her side, she spoke softly to avoid provoking the animal. "You want me to take that dead thing?"

The dog sniffed the rodent again, staring at her.

She waved an arm at the animal. "Get out of here."

As soon as she said it, she felt a bewildering sadness. Dogs were gross. Fact. But this animal seemed like the only thing in this terrifying place not purpose-built to kill or maim her.

Still, she didn't want it to come closer. Even from this distance, the dog's stench overwhelmed her. Bald patches marred his face and body, and his ribs protruded. This was not a healthy animal.

Stella picked up a soggy stick in her left hand, while her right still gripped the knife. The dog flinched at her movement, darting into the undergrowth.

Her vocal cords now warmer, she called after him, "Hey!"

The dog stopped scurrying, looked back, and she softened her tone. "You don't have to leave. I'm sorry."

Stretching the stick out toward the dead rodent, she poked it, rolling it onto its back. Its rigid arms reached for the canopy, taut bloated belly begging for a predator's jaws. The smell of decay filled the space around her, and she retched, nearly vomiting.

With the stick, she shoved the dead thing a few inches toward the dog, who tracked her every move.

After a few beats, the dog's shoulders lifted over his torso, and he skulked forward. Eyes and tail lowered, abdomen scraping the ground, he crept toward the rodent. She thought he would pick it up and take it away, but he crept past it, continuing a few inches closer to her, then pausing.

Stella held her breath. He was so close. Shouldn't he be afraid of her? Maybe he used to live with a human. Maybe he was lost, and a family somewhere out there was searching for him.

No, this animal had been on his own for a very long time. It would take years for a dog to look as haggard as this one. Nobody was searching for him.

He moved closer still, now just a couple feet away, head down, no eye contact. When he crawled within arm's length of Stella, he turned his back to her and flopped onto the forest floor, taking a deep breath in and out. His fur quivered with fleas. An open wound seeped on his left hind leg, maggots squirming in the pus.

Looking away from the animal, dizziness and exhaustion crashed over Stella. She hadn't slept all night. Hadn't eaten since yesterday. Her head throbbed, and her whole body itched. A chill had deepened into a constant shudder, despite the mild temperature of the morning.

She needed to get the hell out of the jungle, but she couldn't do that in her current state. She could barely move. Suddenly, all she could think about was how desperately she needed to rest.

Her gut told her that she could trust the dog. Was this wishful thinking? Her dad used to say that dogs were great protectors. *If you've got a dog*, he said, *you don't need a gun.*

But this wasn't *her* dog. It was just a filthy feral mutt.

At the very least, it would alert her if anything dangerous approached, right? Lying on the wet earth just a few inches from the animal, she sank into a dreamless sleep.

TWENTY-TWO HOURS EARLIER

JUNGLE

Day One

STELLA WASN'T EXCITED about the hike. She'd come to Costa Rica for the surf lessons and densely-hammocked youth hostels and bars where she could have a margarita right on the beach, toes sinking into the sand as the sun settled red and boiling toward the horizon. During her month in the tropics, she intended to bask in the freedoms of a new college graduate, living by her whims, spending every last penny.

When she returned to Texas next month, she would have to dive into the world of jobs and bills and responsibility. But before she stepped onto that intimidating path, she'd have an adventure, a real adventure. With a thousand miles between herself and all the terrible shit that had happened in her life, she would remember what it felt like to be truly happy. It's what her dad would've wanted her to do.

Her father had always encouraged her to *spend more time outside* and *be open to adventure*. He had adored the natural world. At any given moment, he would have preferred to be outdoors rather than inside any building—and this had always baffled Stella. She found nature to be dull and uncomfortable.

For the first nineteen years of her life, she had pouted her way through forced camping trips, griping about bugs and cold and boredom. *The bugs won't be bad this year,* he'd always said. *And besides, mosquitoes don't like short people. Their blood's too thin.* He upheld this lie even after she learned there was no scientific basis for it.

Despite the forced camping trips, her father had been her hero, her compass. He'd made her laugh, and love herself, and look toward her future with optimism. But now, she had difficulty conjuring the feel of sitting next to him in the car, or the smell of his cheap aftershave. She could barely remember the patterns on his balding head, or the exact shade of brown in his eyes.

He'd been dead for almost three years, and every day he seemed farther away.

He'd been taken from her when she was only 19 years old. As a replacement for her father, she'd inherited six thousand dollars, and the money had sat in a bank account, untouched, carrying the weight of death. But after graduating from college, she'd decided to spend some of the "death money" on a trip that would make her father proud.

She'd thought that traveling to Costa Rica might make her feel closer to him. He had always fantasized about going to Costa Rica. In his thick southern accent, he said that the country's Corcovado National Park was supposed to be "one of the most beautiful goddamn jungles on the planet."

She had decided she would go to Costa Rica, fulfill his dream, experience the wild splendor of Corcovado. She would spend one day of her vacation wandering the jungle, in deference to her father. Maybe she would sense his presence there. Maybe it would feel like he walked alongside her. Maybe she would hate it. Probably she would hate it. But still, she'd be spending time with her father.

So, at the end of her second week in Costa Rica she rose at dawn, tossing her water bottle and favorite sweatshirt into her dirty daypack, and stumbling into the taxi driven by her new friend Alé.

"Hola, Alé." She raised a sleepy arm.

"Stella! Buenos dias, amiga!" As always, Alé's teeth flashed wide and bright.

By the time the taxi bumped off the paved road and onto the dirt road leading to the trailhead, Stella was asleep in the back seat.

At the trailhead, as she stumbled out of the car half-awake, Alé called after her. Rolling down his window, he held out a pocketknife and raised his eyebrows, speaking in lightly-accented English: "Take this."

She squinted in the bright light of the morning as she smiled at his kind eyes. "I won't need it."

Something screeched in the treetops and they both looked up, seeing nothing but leaves and branches and fierce blue sky.

Alé extended the knife farther. "Take it anyway. You can give it back to me tomorrow."

As she took a big breath of muggy rainforest air, she nodded. "Thanks, Alé."

"Stay with the guide," he said with urgency. "You can't find your way through the jungle alone. The Corcovado swallows people, and nobody sees them again. Trust me, mija, I was a guide in Corcovado for many years. Americans think they smarter than the jungle. Nobody is smarter than the jungle. The jungle is smarter than you. Don't forget this, okay?"

"Got it," she said, "Jungle's smarter than I am. Jungle swallows people." Flashing a grin, she held up the pocketknife. "Anyway, I've got this!"

"Yes, you do!" Alé waved goodbye through the open car window, and she sidled across the dirt-packed parking lot to meet the rest of her group: a scrawny guide named Jorge with a face full of measles scars, and two college-aged girls, Brittany and Taylor, wearing teensy cutoff jeans shorts.

Before they'd even left the parking lot, Stella knew that this day trip had been a mistake. Armpits already soaked and stinking, she sweated in the early morning heat, swatting away mosquitoes three times bigger than Texas "skeeters."

As they stepped out of their flip flops and tied on sneakers, Brittany and Taylor babbled about a party where a girl called Lola had banged not one, but *two* cabana boys, and they felt certain that Lola probably had an STD now, or maybe all the STDs, and why was Lola such a slut.

Stella shook her head, peering down the path that they'd soon be taking. She couldn't see twenty feet into the thick undergrowth.

Raising a disconcertingly large machete in his left hand in a motion that seemed vaguely war-like, Jorge motioned into the jungle, hopping toward the trailhead. As the girls followed, he cleared branches and vines from the path with wide, swooping whacks of his knife.

The rainforest felt quiet and lifeless—no parrots flitting overhead, no monkeys swinging from branch to branch. Trees with wide glossy leaves and giant ferns, five feet across, painted the forest with a primeval brush. The air hung thick and still.

Stella wondered aloud, "Where are all the animals?"

"They are far from people and roads," Jorge answered over his shoulder, whacking through a low-hanging vine. The trail forked, and Jorge stepped onto a thinner, but still well-trodden, path. "We will take a trail with less tourists, more animals. You will see them soon."

With each step, ignoring Brittany and Taylor became increasingly difficult. The girls were *soooo hungover* and they *couldn't wait* to have another *Bahama Mama* at the bar later; it was going to be *a killer night* and they were going to look for those hot Australian boys, *yay!*

The way she and Taylor talked, waving their hands like they were clearing cobwebs, reminded her of the pretty girls who made fun of her in middle school because she didn't wear Abercrombie t-shirts and 7 For All Mankind jeans. Not only did Stella lack the acceptable tween couture, she also was about as average-looking as a girl could be, without a single feature that strangers could easily call "pretty." Even her weight rested on the heavy side of average.

For everyone at Stella's school, even those at the top of the food chain, middle school was a bloodbath. Every eleven-year-old scrambled for some kind of power, good or bad. The pretty bitches discovered that power easily, making Stella feel small and ugly because it made them feel slightly less small.

When she told her father that Kayla and Leigh Anne had thrown her school shoes in the toilet during recess, his face reddened, and he clenched his teeth. "Next time they pick on you, you tell those girls exactly what you think of them," he said.

"Like what? What am I supposed to say?" Stella bit her lip so he wouldn't see it quiver.

"Look, Squirrel…" He'd called her Stella Squirrel for as long as she could remember, and the nickname made her feel special. Magical. "You're smarter and funnier than they are. Use that to your advantage. Why don't you dare that girl to pretend she's more intelligent than a poodle?"

Wiping the tears from her eyes, Stella laughed. The thought of saying that to Leigh Anne filled her up like a balloon. Her mind raced. "Maybe I could tell her to put a tampon in her nose?"

Her dad snorted. "That's real funny. You might consider staying away from tampons, but yeah, you're getting the point. That's my girl."

After that day, her father had put notes in the bottom of her lunchbox every day for the rest of sixth grade: *"You're the strongest person I know,"* or *"I can't wait to see you tonight,"* or just, *"I love you."*

Now, ten years after the middle school bloodbath, Stella wandered through a rainforest with Brittany and Taylor, who might as well have been Kayla and Leigh Anne.

She visualized herself body-slamming Brittany and Taylor to the jungle floor, flexing her biceps in glory. She figured she could summon enough energy to take them down. She might be only five-foot-three, but people always underestimated her strength.

For the next twenty or thirty minutes, she peered up into the canopy as she walked, watching for wildlife like her father would've done if he were there.

Stepping into a depression in the ground, her left foot caught on a thick root and twisted sideways at a grotesque angle.

She dropped to the ground. "Shit!"

Brittany and Taylor turned around and gaped down at her, big-eyed, as if they'd forgotten there was anyone else in the jungle. Brittany tied the bottom of her tight white tank top in a knot, exposing her tan belly. With a giggle, she looped her arm through Taylor's and picked right up where she left off: "I think I'm gonna wear the little blue dress tonight? The one with the slit? Or does that one make my thighs look *gigantic*?"

Lowering herself to the ground, Stella lay down on her back and braced her hands behind her knee, lifting her foot off the ground. She'd twisted her ankle dozens of times in roller derby. She knew how to wait out pain.

Jorge jogged over to her. "Okay?"

She nodded. "I just need to sit here for a few minutes."

Taylor turned and swished farther along the trail, nonchalantly swishing through a fern. "Fuck that, we're gonna keep going."

Jorge shook his head. "No, you stay here. We will all wait here until Stella can walk. You will not go without me."

Brittany shrugged, bobbing down the path toward Taylor like a duckling.

Slack-jawed, Jorge looked down at Stella, then back at the girls disappearing into the shadows, calling after them: "WAIT!"

Stella sighed, slapping a mosquito on her neck. Reaching around to pull her water bottle off the side of her pack, she came face to face with a spider as large as her hand. Six inches from her nose, its spindly legs splayed out on a web dangling between two thin trees. If she'd sat any farther to the right, that thing would've been on top of her.

Shrieking, she scuttled away from the spider on her hands and knees. She'd never been afraid of snakes or rats or other nightmare critters, but spiders filled her with dread. Breathing heavily, she couldn't take her eyes off of this one. "That's the biggest spider I've ever… Ow!"

A mosquito dug into her eyelid.

Exasperation worsened the pain in her ankle and the sting of the bites. She hated the jungle. She wanted to be back at the hostel.

Pulling the mosquito repellent from her pack, she showered herself with the toxic spray, addressing her guide through the cloud. "I can't do this hike today, Jorge. I'll just walk back once my ankle stops throbbing. We've only been walking for like 30 minutes. I'll stay on the trail. I'll find my way back, no problem, and I'll hire a cab at the trailhead."

A bird cawed overhead, and Stella looked up to see if she could spot it. Nothing moved in the treetops. Not a bird, or a leaf, or a dangling caterpillar.

"No." Jorge shook his head. "You will get lost."

Stella took a few more deep breaths, relieved by the decision to bail on the trek. "Not a chance. You already cleared the path. I'll be *fine*."

"Dammit." Jorge wiped his face with both hands, cursed again, and pulled a bulky satellite phone from his pack. "I will call Gerald. He lives in Puerto Jimenez. He will come get you. You *will not move from here* until he arrives. Okay?"

Stella nodded, wanting this day to be over. "Okay."

She wondered how far away Puerto Jimenez was. How many minutes she would have to sit here. She tried to remember if she and Alé had driven through Puerto Jimenez this morning on the way to the trailhead, but the car ride was a blur of bumpy naps.

Frantic, Jorge dialed Gerald, rattling off an anxious diatribe in Spanish.

When he hung up the phone, he squatted face-to-face with Stella. "You really cannot come with us?"

"I can't," she said. "I'm really sorry."

In truth, her ankle already felt a lot better. It wasn't a major injury. She could muster the hike if she wanted to. But this jungle… in addition to the physical torment of this wilderness, something about it filled her with an existential sadness that she couldn't explain. It did remind her of her father, but not in a comforting way. The rainforest filled her with regret, and desperation, and anger. Why did this place make her so *angry*?

The last traces of Brittany and Taylor's babble disappeared somewhere down the path.

Stella needed to get out of that suffocating web of trees, back to the beach. Toes in the sand.

"I'll be fine. Go get them." Nodding at Jorge, she waved an arm down the path.

"Do not move." Jorge held up a finger. "Be careful. Wait for Gerald. Promise me."

She nodded again, mustering a smile. "I promise. I'll be okay. I'll see you in Puerto Jimenez tonight. I'll buy you a beer."

He stood, his expression anguished, and jogged after Brittany and Taylor.

For the first few minutes on her own, Stella felt buoyed. As she sprayed herself again with insecticide, the rainforest's flutter of green dazzled her.

Trees stretched so far overhead that she couldn't see their crests. Beneath the giants, smaller saplings struggled upward, catching the light on leaves of every shape: thick and papery palm fans, flat leaves as wide as her torso, long thin leaves shooting out of longer thinner trunks. Most of these trees she couldn't name, but she imagined there must be a hundred species within eyeshot.

Fat woody trunks, some of them ten feet around, met the ground with a splay of roots, spilling out on all sides like noodly rivers. A thinner trunk, suspended six feet above the ground, reached for the earth with stilted roots fanning out like a teepee.

A stand of ferns, each almost as tall as Stella, crowded around the teepee roots.

In the quiet, away from the chatter, she understood how some people could find comfort in the beauty of this jungle: prehistoric and pristine, unmarred by humanity. At the same time, the remoteness of the place made tiny hairs stand up on the back of her neck.

Soon, she'd be lounging at a beachside bar, reading her book and drinking a piña colada. The thought of the piña colada sent her stomach soft with joy.

A coati, raccoon-faced and slinky, climbed onto a branch twenty feet in front of her. Just yesterday, she'd learned what a coati was when one crossed the dirt road as she and her surf instructor flip-flopped down to the beach. And now here was another one, right in front of her. Slowly, she retrieved the cell phone from her jeans pocket and snapped a blurry photo. The coati stared at her for a few seconds before leaping into the dim. She grinned. Dad would've loved that. She'd never been so close to a wild animal in Costa Rica. Except that goddamn spider.

Something akin to happiness overtook her. Her body felt like it was floating. Was this what her Dad had wanted her to experience? Maybe she'd achieved the thing he'd craved for her, finally, without subjecting herself to the drudgery of an eight-hour hike with Brittany and Taylor. Mission accomplished. Now she could go back to day drinking and surf lessons.

She held the cell phone above her head. No signal, of course, and only 23% battery remaining. She shut it off to conserve the battery.

Lifting her ankle off the ground, she rolled it in a circle, confident that she could walk the distance back to town. Barely aching now, the ankle clearly wasn't even sprained. Shame washed over her, popping the balloon of happiness that she'd just been holding. She should've sucked it up and finished the hike. Her dad would be disappointed in her. She was disappointed in herself.

Should she run after Jorge and Brittany and Taylor? No, that would make things worse. They'd left her more than twenty minutes ago. And although she could walk now, she probably shouldn't run, not on this uneven terrain. And what if she came to a fork in the trail? She wouldn't know which way to go. Anyway, Gerald was on his way to find her, and she'd promised Jorge that she would stay put until Gerald arrived.

The silence of the jungle took on a disconcerting timbre. She'd always imagined that rainforests teemed with life, with beauty and danger and noise.

Another half hour passed with no sign of Gerald.

Still sitting with her hands propped behind her, she pressed her heel into the ground to test its strength. Only the faintest hint of pain. Maybe she should just get up and trek back to the car by herself.

Slapping a mosquito on her arm, she was cursing at it as a small man appeared on the trail in front of her, brandishing a machete.

"Gerald?" Her voice fell flat and weak in the dead jungle air.

Something told her this wasn't Gerald. He hadn't spoken to her as he approached. He was just staring at her. Gerald would've spoken to her immediately, right?

A chill ricocheted through her as she looked at the rusty machete in his hand. She reminded herself that Jorge, too, had carried a machete. Lots of people carried knives out here, since vines ran wild over the paths.

Beneath the man's boyish pimpled face, a stained, dark green t-shirt fluttered as he moved toward her. The whites of his eyes flashed through the low light. He mumbled something in Spanish, not clear or simple enough for Stella to grasp.

Clearing her throat, she raised her chin toward him. "Gerald?"

His expression didn't change.

"Are you Gerald?"

He took a step toward her, his eyebrows set hard.

She forced herself to breathe slowly, not wanting to appear afraid.

The man spoke to her in accented English, his tone emotionless: "Problem?"

"No," she said. "I… my guide and I are hiking with my friends. They're all just over there." Controlling the tremble that tried to creep into her voice, she pointed down the path. "They're looking at a sloth just on the other side of that fern. You should go check it out." Looking down at her phone, she dismissed him. "Have a good day."

She felt his eyes scrutinizing her face, her hands, her posture: she sat with knees raised, feet on the ground in front of her.

He squinted down the path, searching for this group of people.

Should she jump up to her feet? She felt vulnerable, sitting on the jungle floor. If she called for help, nobody would hear her.

Forcing herself to turn back toward him, she stared him down, straightening her posture to make herself bigger, like a prey animal caught in a predator's sights.

"My guide Jorge can show you the sloth. Just over there." She pointed again.

Shrugging, the man ambled down the path, looking down into her open backpack as she moved her feet out of the way to let him pass.

Stella swallowed hard. That man was obviously not a tourist.

She didn't like the way he'd looked at her. Generally, she had pretty good instincts, and she sensed that the guy was shady. She needed to get the hell out of there. She couldn't just *sit around* and wait for Gerald. It no longer felt safe. And besides, she would be able to find her way back to the parking lot with zero difficulty. Somewhere along the path, she would run into Gerald and they'd finish the walk together.

Lifting herself to hands and knees, she chewed on the inside of her cheek as she rifled through palm fronds and leaf piles, searching for a walking stick, finding nothing remotely suitable. In Texas there would be a dozen ready-made walking sticks in any patch of woods.

Bracing herself on the fat trunk of a tree, she stood on her good ankle and then slowly put pressure on the tender one. Barely any pain. She could do this.

Still rattled, she limped onto the path toward Puerto Jimenez, favoring her right ankle. With each stride, she felt stronger. Every few steps, she looked back, but the man didn't seem to be following her.

Five or six minutes into her journey, the trail forked. Her gaze bounced from one path to the other. Neither seemed more trodden than the other. The left one? Did the left side look more familiar? Yes, it did. That must be the one. Should she wait here? She couldn't do that, could she? That man could be following just out of earshot.

A *crack* emanated from the forest behind her, followed by brisk footsteps. She whipped around. Something scurried in the gloom, but she couldn't see it.

"Hello?" she muttered.

Nobody answered.

She waited, listened. Nothing.

Was the man following her?

She couldn't just STAND here. She had to get out of this jungle. The path on the left was the one. She was sure of it.

Scuttering onto the left-hand path, she reminded herself that she could always double back if it didn't feel right.

She stepped softly so the man wouldn't hear her if he were nearby.

Dark clouds swept swiftly across the sky, sucking brightness from the day. Sunlight struggled to find passage through the snarl of branches, giving the impression of early dawn even this late in the morning.

In this darkened world, Stella could only see a few feet in any given direction. She admonished herself for feeling spooked; only children were afraid of the dark.

As she watched her feet to avoid tripping again, the path narrowed, forcing her to slow her pace. Had the path been this narrow when they'd passed through here earlier? She hadn't really paid attention; she'd just followed directly behind Jorge, looking up into the trees, fixated on looking for wildlife and on the mosquitoes and the mounting heat.

This has to be the right path, she told herself. She was able to press forward without clambering around overhanging vines and encroaching bushes. So this *must* be the path Jorge cleared earlier.

Increasingly, knobby roots and mats of moss obstructed the trail until it didn't look like a trail at all.

She stopped and looked around. She'd gone the wrong way. Hairs pricked up on her arms and neck, and her cheeks flushed hot.

This isn't a big deal, she told herself. She would walk back to the fork and take the other artery.

Turning around, she assessed the path. In the murky light, it didn't look well-trodden, but she was able to discern which way she'd come.

Stepping around a fern, her foot plunked into a puddle of turbid water, sneaker soaking through. Her other ankle started throbbing again, and she lifted it from the ground like a flamingo, taking a moment to assess her surroundings. Vines as thick as her arm slung down from the canopy, nearly blocking her path. This didn't feel right. Was this the way she'd come?

Her heart raced and sweat stung her eyes, but she forced herself to keep moving. If she continued in the same direction, she'd find the main path soon.

As she trudged forward, branches scraped her bare arms and pulled at her jeans. She stepped over a knotted root system and the path narrowed again, though fallen leaves still showed signs of a track tamped down by feet. As long as there was a path, she would be fine.

Five minutes passed plodding through the jungle, then six, ten, twenty… She made her way through a clump of ferns, eyes glued to the ground so she wouldn't lose sight of the route where debris was more finely crushed. At the far side of the fern clump, she stopped and looked around. Sun still obscured by clouds, the jungle air pressed in like a fog. Squinting back to look for her tracks, she couldn't make out exactly where she'd come from, even twenty feet behind. Her path through the ferns had vanished.

She was fucking lost.

Her socks, sopping with mud, rubbed blisters on the backs of her heels.

Some kind of animal shrieked overhead, startling her.

In every direction, the jungle looked the same. Trees and vines and ferns, trees and vines and ferns. No geological features broke the monotony, no boulders or openings in the canopy. No trace of a trail.

Her heart pounded hard against her ribs, and she lowered herself to sit on a root.

At some point—she wasn't sure when—a shrill hum of cicadas had arisen around her. Otherwise, the jungle stood still.

What the fuck had she done?

This looked like a place where no human had ever set foot.

Pulling her phone out of her back pocket, she turned it on and held it overhead, searching for service.

Nothing.

Fifteen feet above, something caught her eye. A furry basketball dangling from a tree. Reaching out a lanky arm, the basketball unfurled, revealing spindly limbs and googly eyes. A sloth.

For nearly two weeks, she'd wanted to see one of these. Now here it was, its Brillo fur shining olive-brown in a sideways slant of gray light. Slow as sunrise, the animal reached its claw toward a leaf and pulled the prize to its mouth, taking a lazy bite, chewing gingerly. For several minutes, it mouthed a single leaf, tearing off small bites with its lips like a toothless infant. It reached for a new leaf, limbs drifting like the Tai Chi ladies at the community center.

The tranquility of the animal calmed her.

When it moved out of sight behind a leafy branch, she stood on shaky legs, panting. She had to get back to the trail.

She tested her ankle tenderly, putting all her weight on it. It felt mostly fine. She was fine. She would be fine. Once she found the trail.

Overhead, tropical trees formed an impenetrable ceiling, obscuring the cloud-challenged daylight.

She couldn't panic.

Gerald would call Jorge when he didn't find her on the trail, and both of the guides would come looking for her, right? Should she stay put, or keep trying to find her way back? She had to keep moving, right? It seemed clear that she was nowhere near the trail at this point. Nobody could find her out here. She would keep moving.

Should she scream? The only person likely to hear her was the machete man, and she wanted to stay far away from him. No, she couldn't scream.

She'd never felt her heart beating so fast. Bracing against a tree trunk, she tried to slow her breathing to a normal pace. Panic gurled up inside her but she shoved it down.

Scanning right to left, she cleared her mind. She could figure this out. Which way had the group had been heading—West? No, maybe north?

One path seemed a bit more open than the other, so she stepped cautiously in that direction, trying in vain to minimize the noise of her soggy squelching sneakers.

Nearly tripping over a root, she grabbed a vine as thick as a baby's leg. It swayed with her weight, barely keeping her upright. She looked up; the vine looped so far into the canopy that she couldn't see its origin. Green tangles swirled around her, making her dizzy.

Shaking her head, she slapped herself lightly on each cheek.

Forced to split focus between her stumbling feet and a constant evaluation of her surroundings, she stepped in root holes, twisting each ankle multiple times.

After forty-five minutes searching for the fork in the trail, she began to hyperventilate and her body trembled like she'd been thrown in an icy lake.

Was she going in circles? Her mental map was scrambled. The jungle had swallowed her.

Cheeks flushed, no longer hushing herself to avoid the man with the machete, she yelled into the soft sway of trees: "HELLOOO?" Her voice evaporated quickly into the leaves and bark and mulch.

She sucked in and bellowed again: "HELLLLLLLLP!"

Turning in a slow circle, she waited, listened. Something squeaked, maybe a small monkey, or a rodent. Leaves whispered in a faint breeze.

She was nowhere.

Closing her eyes, she tried to conjure what her father would tell her do. He would tell her not to panic, she knew that much. He would tell her to trust her instincts, but her instincts had gotten her into this shitstorm, so her instincts could go to hell.

She would just pick a direction and walk straight. If she walked straight, she'd get somewhere eventually. Right?

To her left, a giant tree had fallen on its side, clearing a wide swath of jungle. A hundred white mushrooms grew from the trunk like tiny, delicate umbrellas. The fallen tree bisected a fairly well-trodden trail that she hadn't seen before.

Stella stepped onto the open swath, to the left of the tree. Behind her, the sun peeked out from behind a cloud. She would head away from the sun until she reached something or someone.

For several hours, she huffed forward, searching for the trail. When she didn't find it, she changed tactics, tramping in increasingly widening circles, and then figure eights, at times certain she was on the right track, and then certain she was nowhere near the track. A blister burst on the back of her heel, sending a shooting pain up her leg every time she took a step.

Every few minutes, she checked her cell phone; still no service. Battery now at 16%.

Exhausted and hungry and desperately thirsty, she unzipped her pack, pulling out her water bottle, paralyzed at the realization that it held only about a cup of liquid. She'd been drinking from it all day with no thought of rationing.

Her hand shook as she unscrewed the cap, took one sip—not nearly enough—and then screwed the cap back on tightly.

Alé's words rattled through her head: *Nobody is smarter than the jungle.*

Her legs ached from fatigue by the time the day's scant light began to wane. It would be dark soon, and she didn't even have a flashlight aside from the one on her cell phone.

Squinting, she stepped around a thick tree and over a clump of ferns. In front of her, a giant tree lay on its side, a frill of delicate white mushrooms rising from its rotting bark. A shiver crawled over her body. This was the tree she had come across hours ago.

Sobbing, she fell to the ground and curled into fetal position. She cried harder than she had at her dad's funeral; harder than when her mom had missed her college graduation last month.

FUCK Brittany and Taylor, she thought, her body convulsing from the sobs. If they hadn't been drilling holes in her brain with their vapid conversation, she might've bucked up and stayed with Jorge.

Why had she even gone on the hike? To do what, *hang out with her dead father*? That didn't even make sense. Why did she give a shit what her father would want her to do? He was *dead*. And even when he was alive, he certainly hadn't been a paragon of good decision-making. And *his* bad decisions were so bad that they'd killed him. Leaving her alone. And her life had gone to shit since he'd died.

On the day of her father's funeral, she'd floated along on a cloud of cortisol and coping mechanisms, cracking jokes: *At least now he doesn't have follow through on his promise to poison the president if he wins another term…* One or two nervous chuffs followed each dead-guy joke, and people thought to themselves, *She's crazy, but so strong; Michael would be proud.*

After the service, mourners had poured into the house, filling every room, every corner. Stella couldn't get away from them. Her bedroom had been designated the coatroom, so she couldn't even hide in there. Her body tingled with rage and anxiety, and she wanted to be alone, standing in the middle of a wide-open desert, miles from the nearest human. Instead, people she didn't give a shit about crowded around her, touching her, talking to her, asking her questions.

Everyone knew how close she and her father had been, so they all felt the need to tell her what a wonderful man Michael had been, how lucky she had been to have him as a father.

Finally, while she was talking to her great aunt Mildred, her brain cracked open, and she screamed in the middle of the living room: "Stop telling me how fucking lucky I am! If I was really fucking lucky, my father wouldn't have gone for a hike in a canyon during a goddamn flash flood!"

The house fell silent, black-clad bodies standing motionless. Stella stormed upstairs to her bedroom, flinging the piled coats into the hallway, slamming and locking the door behind her.

Now, trapped in a jungle at dusk, she felt shame when she thought of the funeral-day tantrum. It hadn't made her feel any better. It had made her mother, and probably some of the other mourners, feel considerably worse. And since that day, things had spiraled out of control.

So many of her life's actions filled her with regret. Today, though, she'd made the worst decision of her life: leaving her group.

And now, she'd have to spend the night in this desolate wilderness. She knew better than to walk any farther. In the dark, she would injure herself, or step on a snake and die a painful fucking death and nobody would ever find her body. It would decompose here, jaguars licking their lips at the smell of carrion.

And if she did make it through the night, she'd surely die of hunger or thirst before she found another goddamn human.

Lying on her side, she hugged her knees to her chest as darkness bloomed.

In the cooling air, a swarm of mosquitoes descended—or maybe it rose from the ground—and jockeyed for position on every patch of exposed skin. Cursing, she swatted at herself and smothered herself in a cloud of bug spray.

As she pulled on her yellow hoodie, invisible nocturnal creatures began to scrape through the undergrowth and swish through trees overhead. Something howled, making her jump. The jungle had finally come alive, but she couldn't see the creatures that she was hearing.

She closed her eyes and struggled to calm her breath.

Something swept across her cheek, and she screamed, waving at the air.

Desperate to see her surroundings, she pulled out her cell phone and turned on the flashlight, panning it in a circle in search of predators. Moths as big as an eyeball swarmed the light, and she inhaled one of them, spitting and coughing as she flicked off her phone.

To distract herself in the dark, she counted seconds, forcing her brain to steady itself in the numbers, knowing that each passing minute brought her closer to tomorrow.

Several hours before dawn, a light rain settled in. At first it was a welcome reprieve. The cool wash had a purifying quality. Baptismal, almost. But as her sweatshirt soaked through and the rain gathered strength, she began to shiver.

When she finally gave in to mental and physical exhaustion, lying limp on the sopping leaves, bugs wriggled into the crevices between her body and the ground. She hugged her thighs tighter into her chest, tucking them underneath the sweatshirt. The rain grew in volume, crashing erratically into branches and roots, loud and wild like panicking horses.

Again, she counted the seconds to keep herself awake: one, two, three, four... five thousand thirty-four, five thousand thirty-five...

Fingers blue from the cold, she shuddered so hard that she thought she might have a heart attack. The cold shoved away thoughts of predators and spiders and snakes.

Finally, the first grays of dawn started to lift away layers of darkness.

Just as she began to sink into the shredded relief that comes with first light, a pitter of footsteps whispered at her from the undergrowth. They were not the footsteps of a human. A beast was circling her.

This would be her end. The beast would eat her, she knew for certain.

JUNGLE

Day Two

STELLA WOKE WITH a shriek, slapping her cheek where a nickel-sized mosquito had speared her skin. Riddled with bites, she clawed at her legs, arms, and neck with bloody fingernails. The little shitheads had even drilled through her jeans. One had flown inside her sweatshirt and chomped on her abdomen.

Sitting tall, the dog stared at her from two body lengths away, alarmed by her shriek.

The dog. For a moment, she had forgotten about him. How had she allowed herself to fall asleep next to a mangy *wild dog*?

She scanned the forest. Nothing moved.

She was screwed.

Why hadn't she told her mother—or *anyone* other than Alé—that she was going on this hike? Would Alé notice that she hadn't returned?

Stella usually called her mother once a week (though her mom often didn't answer the phone), but they'd spoken just a few days ago, and she hadn't mentioned the hike. So her mother wouldn't expect another call any time soon. Stella wondered how long it would take her mother to notice if she never called again. Probably a few weeks, she guessed. She tried to remember the last time her mom had called *her,* rather than vice versa. Maybe before her dad died?

After his death, Stella had tried to bring her mother closer, but it seemed like closeness, to her mother, was a high cliff; and if she approached the edge, she'd be certain to lose her footing and fall to her death.

Still, every month, Stella invited her mom to come to her roller derby matches.

"We could go to dinner after the match," Stella told her a dozen times.

Her mother always gave her the same confusing look, a knot of sadness and disapproval and regret and hope. "Maybe," she would say.

During the match, Stella's eyes would scan the stands for her mother's wiry ponytail, her baggy cotton t-shirt.

Stella would hurtle around the track, her compact body elbowing past taller, stronger competitors. She would score points through force of will, feeling powerful, wondering if her mother was hiding in the stands, marveling at her daughter's strength.

In the days after each match, Stella would say to her mother, "I looked for you," and her mother would avoid her eyes, "I know, Stell. It's just... not my scene. Maybe next time."

Now, breathing in the stench of the stray dog, Stella bit her lip. She braced her hands on the ground and pushed up to a seated position, looking around. What predators stalked out there? Would the dog know if something dangerous was watching them?

The mutt's gaze confused her—he watched her with rapt attention—did he fear her? Or was he interested in her? He lowered his head to the ground and looked up at her, reminding her suddenly of her father's dog Torres. She looked away.

Her body ached. Gingerly, she unlaced her sneaker, pulling out a swollen ankle. It might be mildly sprained, but she could deal with that. Worse than the sprain, the burst blister on her heel glowed red and raw, throbbing. Still, she'd suffered worse injuries in derby.

Last year, a six-foot-tall blocker had elbowed her in the ribs, sent her flying through the air before she crashed down to the track with a thud. Without missing a beat, she'd leapt onto her skates and lapped the girl, scoring a point for her team. Later, when her wrist and ankle began to throb, she drove herself to the emergency room and discovered that she'd fractured her ulna and torn a ligament at the base of her leg. Four weeks later, she was back on the court.

Pain could be ignored. In the rainforest, pain was not her enemy. She knew that she *did* have enemies in this forest, but she couldn't see them, didn't know them, wouldn't know them until they were upon her.

The dog rose to his feet, startling Stella. He was so *close*. Sharing space with a feral animal seemed like a fairly obvious misstep on this fucked up journey. She couldn't allow her clarity to be muddled by a dirty dog. She didn't even like dogs. She'd never trusted them.

Admittedly, the only one she'd ever spent significant time with was her Dad's mutt, Torres, and she'd never understood why he loved that nasty thing. He'd found Torres in the desert as a puppy, all skin and bones and mange and fleas. Despite the objections of Stella and her mother, her father named the dog Torres and kept her in the basement, feeding her boiled chicken until she looked more or less like a house pet.

Stella could still see her mother standing at the bottom of the stairs, her usually-meek voice charging up the stairway, "Michael! Torres shat on the carpet again!"

Torres followed her dad everywhere, gawking up at him like her deity, her singular reason for being. He fawned over her, and Stella felt deeply jealous of his love for the animal. Until Torres had come along, Stella was the object of nearly *all* her father's affection (with a small portion reserved for her gin-swilling mother). Suddenly, she had to share that precious commodity with a damn dog.

Not to mention that Torres destroyed seven pairs of her shoes, one cell phone, and a new Alicia Keys poster still rolled up inside a cardboard sleeve.

Worse still, Torres had killed her father. At least that's how Stella had always seen it. Torres loved water—she was named after the Olympic swimmer, Dara Torres. Every weekend, her dad loaded the dog into "Moby Dick," his seventeen-foot-long white 1965 Pontiac Tempest, and they drove out dusty roads in search of swimming holes all over central Texas. As a rule, Stella was invited on these excursions, but she almost always declined.

Just over three years ago, her father had gone for a hike with Torres one summer afternoon, and their bodies had been found 25 miles from the trailhead, washed up on a riverbank after a flash flood. Nobody knew how the flood had overtaken them, but Stella imagined that Torres had been swept away by the rising river and her dad had jumped in to save her. She could see no other plausible explanation.

Now here she was, 24 hours lost in a rainforest with nobody to help her except a feral dog with fleas in his eyes.

The sun shone high in the sky, not quite straight overhead. It must be either just before noon or just after, Stella wasn't sure which. Seemed like it had to be just before noon. She couldn't have slept through the entire morning and into afternoon, given the bugs and the moldy stench of the dog and the decaying rat carcass.

Reaching into her pocket, Stella pulled out her cell phone.

Sitting erect, the dog tracked her movements.

She sighed. "I know I won't get a signal. But I have to try."

The dog contemplated the ground.

Stella held the phone up and pressed the power button, waiting for the swirl of neon letters.

It blinked on: no service. Battery: 13%. 11:12AM.

The dog stood and slinked to the dark edge of the forest, picking up the dead rodent, which had previously been lying just a few feet away from where Stella spent the night. When had he moved the carcass?

Sniffing the remains, the mutt looked up at her.

She shook her head, scrunching her nose. "I'm not gonna touch it. All yours."

He lifted the stiff corpse in its mouth and moved to lie next to the tree covered in thin white mushrooms. The dog braced the rodent under his feet and chewed into the belly, blood squelching onto his lips.

Stella's stomach lurched.

Torres used to bring dead animals to the house and leave them on the patio. Mice and squirrels mostly, but sometimes birds too. As a child, Stella had found this barbaric. She'd never accepted her dad's assertions that this was Torres's way of showing devotion and loyalty.

I don't need loyalty in the form of dead animals, she'd said.

You're killing a turkey right now, her dad said, pointing to the sandwich on her plate. *I brought you that dead turkey.*

That's different, she said.

Is it, Squirrel? Her dad shrugged and picked up her sandwich.

As he winked and took a bite, she whined, *Give it back!*

But she hadn't been mad. Her dad's wink always made her smile.

She would give anything to see him wink at her right now, to feel him sitting next to her on the carpet of leaves, telling her what to do. Because in truth she had no effing clue.

She scanned the jungle. It unfurled wide and lonely in every direction. Stella crammed down her fear and looked at the dog. If danger were nearby, the dog would sense it, right? He seemed perfectly relaxed, so she wouldn't let herself spin out, depleting her energy on unnecessary anxiety. If the dog started freaking out, *then* she would let herself freak out.

Overhead, a toucan chattered, its Froot Loop bill opening and closing with each squawk. Somewhere in this wilderness, another American was pointing at a toucan, delighted, pulling out her iPhone to take a photo.

Stella tugged the wet sock back onto her swollen ankle, moaning as she pulled on her shoe and cinched the shoelaces tight over the blister.

The dog crunched into the rodent's skull, cracking and slurping noises echoing through the copse. Her stomach lurched again.

Unzipping her daypack, she pulled out its contents. A map of Costa Rica. Two granola bars. Two week-old apples. A bottle of half-gone bug spray. A sheath for Alé's knife. Half a bag of potato chips. Two hair ties, one lip balm, a dirty napkin, an airplane bottle of vodka. The water bottle, containing less than a cup of liquid.

She should've filled her water bottle with rain last night. How had she not thought of that?

"Dammit," she whispered. She imagined herself turning her face upward, rainwater gushing into her open mouth.

Packing everything back in her bag, she figured she could survive with just this stuff for another day. More, if she could find water.

Her sweatshirt, still damp hours after the rain had stopped, clung to her skin. She assumed she was sweating underneath it, but she couldn't tell. The air hung so wet and hot, she found it hard to take a deep breath.

Pulling the sweatshirt off, she wrung it out into her mouth, but it didn't produce droplets.

Tossing it onto a nearby branch with one hand, she grabbed one of the apples and sank her teeth into it with a satisfied groan. The sound and smell of food drew the dog toward her.

She shook her head. "Go eat the dead thing. This is *mine*."

She looked up into the canopy, shielding her eyes from the dappled sun. How long ago had she last eaten? Breakfast yesterday, before the hike?

"Where *are* we?" she asked the mutt, who fixed her gaze as if he wanted to answer.

With one massive bite, she devoured a quarter of the apple, speaking to the dog as she chewed. "Can you show me where to go?"

The dog didn't move.

She swallowed half her bite and kept chewing. "Do you have a name?"

Tentatively, he approached until he was only a foot or two away and then turned away to face the forest. As if it were no big deal, he sat down next to Stella, his flank pressed against hers.

The touch felt both comforting and unsettling.

"Of course you don't have a name. You've obviously never seen the inside of a living room."

She shifted her shoulder and twisted her head so she could study the dog, and he craned his neck up and back to meet her eyes.

Gently shoving the animal aside, Stella teetered to her feet, gesturing around her and throwing the apple core at his feet. "I need you to show me where to go."

The dog grasped the apple core in his mouth and then stood, tail alert.

"Where do I go, dog?"

After wolfing down the apple core, he met her eyes again.

She stomped her good foot and yelled, "Show me where to GO, Dog!"

He cowered, tail disappearing between his legs. Lowering his belly to the ground, he slinked away.

"WAIT!" Stella didn't want the dog to leave her. She felt safer with him around. Unettled by this unfamiliar dependence upon an animal—a feral one, no less—she relaxed her posture, sitting cross-legged on the ground. Holding out a hand, she lowered her voice. "Please don't go."

The dog flopped onto the ground, exposing his belly.

Stella brushed a bug off her cheek, her fingers rasping over a film of grit.

In the midday heat, cicadas ramped up their songs until it sounded like each one was competing to scream louder than the others.

Leaning over the dog, Stella had an urge to stroke his wet, nasty belly. She reached out tentatively, then withdrew her hand. Who knew how many ticks and viruses scrabbled around in that fur? She couldn't touch the dog, for her own sake and his. She couldn't give him the idea that she was his new pack member. That wouldn't end well.

Her dad would know how she should talk to the dog. She wanted him to be there so badly she could almost see him, over there, in the flat space between the two trees. She imagined him pointing at her backpack, saying: *Look at the map, Squirrel.*

Nodding, she pulled the map out of her backpack again, unfolding it carefully, not daring to place it on the sodden earth.

The dog watched her manipulate the piece of paper.

She glanced at him. "I'll figure this out."

As if he trusted that Stella would, indeed, figure this out, he lay his head on the ground and closed his eyes.

On the map, the Osa Peninsula jutted southward into the sea from the west coast of Costa Rica. She was somewhere on that peninsula, which stretched about 15 miles across at its widest point. Yesterday, Alé had driven her a couple hours from Dominical—she wasn't sure how long, because she'd slept most of the journey, awakening only when the bumped through the rutted roads of a town. She thought maybe they'd driven through a town, presumably Puerto Jimenez, to get to the trailhead in Corcovado National Park. Unless her sense of direction was turned on its head, they must have driven along the coast road to the parking lot at Carate, and from there walked into the National Park. If that was right, she was probably just a little bit east of the coast.

West. Stella would head west. If she headed straight west, she'd hit the beach eventually.

She hadn't retained much from the camping trips with her dad, but she did know that the sun rose in the East and set in the West—any sixth-grader could tell you that much.

Yesterday, the clouds and canopy had obscured the sun for most of the day. But now it was partially visible through the branches, so she should be able to mark her path by placing the late morning shine just behind her. As she moved, she would realign her course whenever she caught glimpses of the sun.

If Stella could find the beach, she'd know which way was south and she could walk along the coast toward the parking lot at Carate. Maybe she'd even encounter some other tourists along the way. With luck, she might make it back to Puerto Jimenez later today.

The plan felt solid. Hope flickered in her gut.

Gaping up into the canopy, beads of sweat pooled on her forehead. Above the tree line, a cloudless sky promised no rain. Normally at this time of year it rained almost daily, so the rain would come again soon.

Drinking another small sip from her water bottle, she forced herself to tuck the remainder inside her daypack. Hunger gripped her nearly as strongly as thirst, but she would save her two granola bars for later. She couldn't imagine swallowing dry granola right now anyway, without a bottleful of water.

As she packed the map back in her pack and retrieved her sweatshirt from the nearby branch, she looked down at the dog. "You gonna follow me?"

He stood, ready to follow.

She squinted at him. "You need a name."

The animal held her eyes.

"Dog? Should I just call you Dog?" Knotting the sweatshirt arms around her waist, she shook her head. "Shit. No. That's not very nice, is it?"

She stooped, and his stink wafted over her. "Damn, you are nasty. What about Tick Magnet? Is that a good name?"

Something caught the dog's attention, and he snapped his head to the left, leering into the forest.

"No? Don't like that? Well you're too dirty for a cute name, so what do you suggest. Dirty? Should I call you Dirty?"

The dog swiveled back toward her, then slammed his butt on the ground and scratched an ear so vigorously that his whole body convulsed.

"Fine. Dirty it is. Let's go, Dirty."

She set off into the jungle with Dirty at her heels, walking away from the sun. She could only see ten or twenty feet into the thicket. Trees and bushes and vines seemed to sprout one from another, challenging every step. She moved *slow as molasses*, as her mother would say.

Was her mom worried about her right now? Could she *feel* that Stella was in trouble?

She longed for her mother, and the longing felt foreign, surprising. They hadn't been close in years. Not since she was a child, too small to remember the closeness. But she felt certain that there had been a time when her mother had held her in her arms, looked down on her infant features, full with love. Surely her mother had clasped her hand as they walked down the street, ready to throw herself between her daughter and danger.

When Stella got out of this jungle, she would call her mother, tell her she loved her.

"Ah!" Scrambling over a waist-high vine, she tripped on a branch and caught herself by grabbing the vine with her left hand, yowling.

A two-inch thorn protruded from her left palm. She grasped the backside of the pricker with the fingers on her other hand and yanked it out, gasping from the pain.

Low to the ground, Dirty crawled under the vine with canine elegance, tail down, fur shielding him from thorns. Turning back and approaching Stella, he sniffed the air around her for the scent of her blood.

Lying back on the ground to catch her breath, a loamy scent washed over her. Stella squinted up at the dog. He leaned in to sniff her nose.

His eyes seemed—what was it—kind? Could there be *kindness* in a dog's eyes?

"You're just a *dog*." She spoke softly, her tone not as strident as her words.

As she raised her head, something colorful caught her eye. Perched on a flat, wide leaf, a small green frog assessed her with outsized, round red eyes. Its body about the size of her thumb, azure stripes ran the length of its flanks, offset by a splay of orange tentacle-like toes. The animal's dewy skin flapped in and out with each miniature breath. Stella wanted to touch it, but didn't want to scare it away.

She pictured her dad squatting next to her, smiling. *Didn't think a frog could be so pretty, did you, Squirrel?*

"I didn't," she said out loud, her voice cracking, parched.

Dirty followed her line of sight and spotted the frog, zeroing in on it, ready to pounce.

Stella sat up. "No. Leave it."

With Dirty looming, the frog hopped under a banana leaf and disappeared. Dirty pounced after it, but missed his mark.

Stella's head ached. Dehydration tugged her joints apart like old lace, made her head feel swollen and heavy.

Bug bites pockmarked her skin, and in every moment where her mind wasn't occupied by thoughts of her own death, or calculations about how to get the hell out of the forest, she obsessed over the relentless itch of the swollen welts.

Taking one more sip from her water bottle, she summoned every scrap of resolve to avoid drinking the rest of the half-cup that remained.

For the millionth time, she surveyed her surroundings for a puddle, or maybe a leaf with some water pooled in it. This primeval hellhole felt drenched, like a towel thrown in a swimming pool. Last night it had rained like the world was ending. She felt like she could drown just breathing in the soppy air. But somehow there was nothing to drink.

She was tempted to lick the sweat that pooled in her armpits and the crook of her elbows and knees.

Next to her, Dirty took a break from panting to gnaw at a bald patch on his wrist. Stella wondered how he'd come to live in a rainforest, and whether he'd always been alone.

He'd glommed onto her quickly, as if he understood the benefits of pack life. As if he'd once had a pack of his own. But that was probably an instinctive thing for all dogs, right?

Torres used to whine pitifully whenever her dad left the house. Before heading to work, her father would hold Torres's face in his hands and say, "Don't worry, baby, I'm always coming back."

Stella would roll her eyes and say, "She's just a dog, Dad."

He'd wag a finger and wink at Stella. "See, that's the thing. She's *not* just a dog."

Now, she wondered if Torres had understood the meaning of her father's words. It certainly always seemed like Torres knew that he'd never abandon her, that he was always coming back. Except that now, neither of them was ever coming back.

"Stop it," she said to Dirty, disconcerted by how much he made her think of her father. She'd crossed paths with hundreds of dogs since her father's death, but this was the only one who made her feel like his death was still present, following her around like a heavy cloud.

The dog held her gaze.

"You know what you did."

He did not seem to know what he had done.

A mosquito fanged Stella's muddy forearm and she slapped it dead, breathing in and out, observing the contours of the bloody stain on her arm.

She pressed fingertips to her swollen eyelids and mumbled to Dirty, "Let's go."

Her muscles ached as she stood, and dizziness nearly sent her crashing back to the ground.

Tail raised, Dirty watched her teeter. When she steadied, he padded forward.

For hours, Stella stumbled along with Dirty deftly clambering nearby. Blisters seeped pus into her waterlogged sneakers, and she frequently bit down hard on her bottom lip, to avoid screaming from the pain.

On her arms, scrapes stung from her sweat, and on her legs, bruises swelled in grotesque purple patches. Mosquito welts pockmarked her face and neck. Something shrieked in the distance, and Stella gasped, clenching her hands in sudden fists.

She closed her eyes, took a deep breath in, and then let it out.

Nothing in the forest wants to hurt you, her father used to say when she was scared of the wilderness at night. *Everything out here is trying like hell to steer clear of humans. Being scared of the forest is just a waste of energy. It's like being scared of a bunny. Are you scared of a bunny?*

No, she would tell him.

"The forest is just a bunny," she said out loud to Dirty, looking up at the canopy, unable to smile at her own joke. Ignoring the anxious simmer in her stomach, she took another step forward, the dog following one step behind her.

Without turning her head, she said to him, "I wish you could *talk* to me. Distract me."

He said nothing.

"Okay, then I'll talk. But I will not use a goddamn baby voice." Every time her dad had used a baby voice with Torres, she'd blushed, humiliated for him.

Dirty panted and sniffed the ground as he strode confidently forward. Occasionally he paused to sniff a tree or leaf pile, and then lifted a leg to release a few drops of urine. Stella wondered how he could produce any pee at all. When was the last time the dog drank anything?

She wiped her brow, now crusty with dried mud, no longer sweating. "What do you want to know?"

She braced herself on a root, stepped over it, and Dirty followed. Pausing, she tried to ignore the pain wrenching so many corners of her body.

Yes, she needed to talk to the dog. To take her mind off the pain. And thirst. And the jungle.

"My shitty boyfriend? You want to hear about *him*?" She panted, her speech halted by frequent breaths. She paused for a moment, eyes glazing over, seeing Garrett's face, the dark hair falling backward as he tipped his head back to take a sip of beer.

Dirty looked up at her.

"Well, Garrett and I had talked about coming to Costa Rica together…" breath, "But he got a shitty banking job and got addicted to meth…"

She sneered down at Dirty, wiping a line of sweat from her upper lip. "I know. He even got me to try that shit a couple of times…" breath, "and then he overdosed…" breath… "And he went to rehab and missed my college graduation…" breath, "And then I dumped him…" breath, "And came here by myself."

Dirty looked up at her.

"Don't judge me." She whacked through a stand of knee-deep ferns. "I haven't done drugs… since he left for rehab… Which his parents paid for, by the way… Rich asshole."

The space between the trees widened a touch, allowing them to walk unfettered. The ease of motion flooded Stella's body with relief.

She stopped to watch Dirty move, lithe and grubby, tail raised gleefully as he sniffed forward.

Muddy sweat dripped from her upper lip into her mouth, and she tasted the salty dirt, wiping it away.

Dirty sniffed the base of a tree, looked up at her, and lowered his muzzle again to the ground, not breaking his elegant gangly stride as he turned his head back to make sure she was following.

Stella wiped sweat from her forehead with the collar of her t-shirt and pursed her lips at Dirty. "No, I haven't dated since Garret. There was a girl, Gigi, who was working on me."

Dirty slowed his pace to walk right beside her as the space around them opened up further.

Stella reached down and touched the top of his head with two fingers, noting the gritty texture of his fur. "She's on my roller derby team. She's cute, but she asked me out right after I broke up with Garrett. Tried to kiss me one day after practice, but I dodged it and played dumb, like I didn't know what she'd been trying to do. Then the next week she asked if I wanted to go watch sunset at some spot she likes to go to on Lake Travis. I ghosted her after that and things were really weird between us in practice."

Dirty glanced back at her and then sped up to walk directly in front of her.

Stella shook her head. "I know. I know. But, I didn't blow her off because she's a girl. I just wasn't ready to date anyone."

Dirty halted in his tracks, swiveling his head right to left. He'd heard something. Stella stopped, too, a chill crawling over her body. She strained to catch a wisp of whatever had alerted him. When Dirty relaxed, deciding that they faced no imminent threat, Stella moved forward.

"I am not going to fucking panic," she said out loud. Then, more quietly, "I am not going to panic."

She stepped around a series of ferns. "Okay, more talking. More talking. Why am I in this particular fucking forest? Great question."

Here, she could reach her arms out in any direction without touching a vine or tree. The earth stretched out almost bare, holding only a flat scatter of leaves. In this open copse, the jungle seemed less hostile. At a glance, almost idyllic. A place where some pioneer family might decide to build a cabin, start a new life.

Stella placed one foot easily in front of the other, moving more quickly in this terrain. The throb in her ankle drifted to the back of her consciousness.

"My dad always wanted to take me to Costa Rica to hike Corcovado," she said to the dog.

Cicadas sang so loudly that they drowned out her story, but she didn't raise her voice. "But obviously that didn't happen. So after college, I didn't know what I wanted to do. I'd planned go to grad school in psychology, but I don't know if I really ever want to do that. I don't really have a clue *what* I want to do. So I decided to take some time to figure my shit out. I waited tables for a couple months, and then came here to *live my dad's dream for him*, or some stupid thing like that. Which obviously was a terrible idea."

She shook her head, guilty for voicing aloud the blame that she placed on her father's shoulders.

As Dirty squatted to poop, he locked eyes with her.

She almost looked away, uncomfortable from the bizarre intimacy of looking in a creature's eyes while he took a shit.

"And then Alé told me *not* to come here."

She glanced up. No sign of the sun through the matted branches. She hoped she was still heading west.

Struck by an overwhelming urge to sit, she lowered herself inelegantly to the leafy ground, grunting from the pain in her heel and her toes, which had also started to blister. Dirty contemplated her, then swiveled back in the direction they'd been heading, as if beseeching her to keep moving.

"I know I should've listened to Alé." She spoke slowly, racked with self-loathing. "He was always so nice to me."

Dirty sat down facing her, taking this opportunity to scratch some vermin on the side of his torso.

Stella shrugged. "I met him a couple weeks ago and he's been sort of trying to protect me because I did him a favor when I first got to Costa Rica."

Dirty stopped scratching, contemplated Stella again, and then continued scratching the same spot.

Stella's mind wandered back to her third day in Dominical, when she'd met Alé. It felt worlds away, rather than 100 miles north.

Picking up a browning leaf nearly as long as her arm, she tore the drying flesh from the stem. "I was sitting at the bar one day, and I overheard a dude telling some mechanic that he didn't have 30,000 Colón to fix his taxi. I didn't understand much of the conversation because it was in Spanish, but I picked up something about someone dying—I found out later that his wife had died earlier that year, and his daughter died a few years before. Alé has had such shit luck in his life, and that day when he was talking to the mechanic, he sounded so sad and miserable. I have some money my Dad left me, and that dude was seriously hard up, and my dad would've wanted me to help him. Plus, 30,000 colón is like 50 bucks. It's not even all that much. So I went over to the mechanic and gave him the money. I thought Alé was gonna start crying. He wouldn't stop thanking me. It was kind of embarrassing."

Dirty shifted his scratching efforts to his ears, clawing at the inside of them like he was trying to dislodge a spider.

Stella looked at her hands, nails cracked and bleeding. "And then a couple nights later, I got hammered at Rum Bar."

The pinky finger on her left hand was crimson red and swollen. When had she hurt her finger?

"There was a girl who wanted me to do body shots off her neck, so…" She shrugged.

Dirty stopped scratching, took a deep breath like a diver coming up for air, and listened politely.

Stella pulled the last remnants of leaf flesh away from the stem, and held the stem up to look at it, twirling it in the half-light. "Anyway I passed out on the beach and woke up in the middle of the night, no clue where I was. The dude with the taxi, Alé, was sitting next to me on the sand. Freaked me out at first. But he just looked at me and said with barely any accent, 'I will take you home.'"

Stella paused her story to listen to the cicadas, wondering how many thousands, or millions, of them would be within eyesight if they weren't hidden. She wished she could be an insect, dumb and functional. Sometimes the jungle terrified her, and sometimes it seemed endlessly dull and mundane. Always, the endless nature of it felt suffocating.

Calming her breath, she reached across her chest and scratched at a mosquito bite on the back of her shoulder, forcing herself to keep talking so she wouldn't spiral into an uncontrolled panic. "I said to him, 'How long have you been sitting there?' And he said, 'A little while,' and I was like, 'That's creepy,' and he said, 'I don't like girls to get hurt. I had a daughter.' I asked him what happened to his daughter but he wouldn't say. Not at that point, anyway. He was cagey at first, but he didn't really seem creepy. He's probably my dad's age. He has a dad vibe about him, not a creep vibe."

Still listening, Dirty rested his head on his paws.

Stella twirled the naked leaf stem between her hands, squinting into the spaces between the trees, scoping for the movements of large animals or snakes. Suddenly chilled, goose bumps rose on her skin, and she cradled her arms around her chest, letting out a long breath before she continued talking. "After that, we started having breakfast together on the beach. I went there every day with a smoothie before my surf lessons, and he showed up with some ugly meat pastry. He spoke amazing English, but I helped him with some vocabulary words, and he helped me with my Spanish."

She dropped the stem on the ground. "Anyway."

Standing, she gasped as her feet reacquired the brunt of her weight.

Stepping tentatively, the searing blisters allowed her no more than one step every couple of seconds. She refused to let herself consider the full scope of her current nightmare. Instead, she obsessed over thoughts of water, visualizing herself diving into rivers and standing beneath crystal clear waterfalls, open mouth catching the flow. She imagined herself holding a clean drinking glass, filling it from the faucet in her mother's home, gulping down cheek-puffing mouthfuls.

As sunset approached, she collapsed, terrified and defeated. Her head and body ached.

"Shit," she said to Dirty, her voice barely audible.

He lay on the ground next to her, looking up with eyes that suggested sadness, as if he sensed that they were in trouble. Stella pulled out a granola bar and unwrapped it. Dirty watched her, licking his lips, but not encroaching.

Stella shook her head. "Sorry, Dirty. Go kill another rat?"

The dog looked away, pressed his flank into hers.

Lifting the granola bar to her mouth, she placed it between upper and lower teeth. Her parched gums wouldn't let her bite into the dry wafer, but she knew she had to eat. She couldn't just let herself wither away.

Taking a tiny sip from her water bottle—just a few drops—she mixed the liquid in her mouth with a small bite from the bar. Barely moistened, the granola was hard to swallow, but she forced herself to do it. And then do it again. With each bite, she took another sip, until the water and granola were both gone, with neither her hunger nor thirst lessened.

Light dwindling, she cried, softly at first, and then choking on heaving sobs. Again, she longed for her mother. For the comforting presence of someone who would go to great lengths to end her pain, despite their differences, despite their history. Her mother would do that for her if she could. Wouldn't she?

The only relationship she could remember with her mother was a contentious one. She'd never understood why her father loved this somber, quiet woman, but she was his "moon and stars," as he frequently told her. When her mother sat in a chair in the backyard staring blankly, her wiry hair reaching in every direction as if desperately searching for answers, he would kiss his wife on the cheek and proclaim to Stella, "Look at your mother! Pretty as a peach in June."

Late one night in 9th grade, Stella padded barefoot downstairs to get a snack from the kitchen. Through the moonlit living room, Stella had a clear view into the kitchen, illuminated by a wan bulb above the sink. Her parents clutched each other in a silent dance, her mother's head resting on his shoulder, face tucked into his neck. He cupped the back of her head with his hand, his eyes closed, mouth relaxed into a smile meant for nobody. They moved side to side in a slow synchronized rhythm, arms pulling each other as close as possible, as if they feared that they might be ripped apart.

Hidden, Stella had watched them, struck by the honest urgency of their embrace. Until then, she'd wondered whether her mother truly cared for her father. This image of them dancing in the kitchen ricocheted through her mind for years, raising ever more questions about who her mother was, why she was the way she was.

She wondered what had turned her mother from a functional, engaged human into a gin-sipping shadow. Sure, her mom's parents had been less than ideal. So were everyone else's. Had the normal pressures of life sucked out her mother's joy, pounding her with the stress of a mundane job, a child's needs, a lackluster marriage, and then a dead husband?

Lying back onto the uneven forest floor, a lump rose in Stella's throat as she imagined her mother lightly touching her forehead.

Dirty stood and leaned in to lick her face. Flinching, she pulled away just in time to dodge his tongue, and then cursed herself for rejecting the tenderness.

"I'm sorry, Dirty." Her voice quavered. She stretched toward him, presented her cheek to him. "Do it again?"

He watched her, not understanding, wanting to understand.

As twilight deepened, the mosquito swarm burgeoned, buzzing like a horde of bees. Stella sprayed herself with mosquito repellant and noted that her bottle was down to the last swish. Dirty twitched and snapped, attempting to murder the vermin mid-air.

Stella scooted closer to the dog. "I'm scared."

Facing away from her, watching the forest, he pressed his body into hers. Raising a leg, he scratched convulsively at an ear, shaking Stella's body. The agitation felt comforting.

She knew she couldn't walk farther tonight, with sunset approaching and her feet throbbing. She would have to spend another night in this goddamn jungle. For the first time, she allowed herself to wonder whether she might never find her way out.

Pulling on her sweatshirt, she clutched her knees to her chest underneath the still-damp fabric. Lying next to Dirty with her head on her pack, she braced herself against his back. His fetid odor wafted over her and she turned her head to the side for a fresher breath of air. But unlike yesterday, his stink didn't turn her stomach.

Reaching an arm around his torso, she pulled her knees out of her sweatshirt so she could scoot him closer, maximizing their body contact. Her hand almost grazed the wound on his hind leg where maggots squirmed, and she stopped herself from retching, sliding her hand higher onto his belly. Fleas were probably hopping from his skin to hers, but she wanted to feel him, feel his chest rising and falling as the minutes and hours unfolded. His breaths reminded Stella that she was alive, made her feel hopeful that she would see the morning.

A mosquito stung her cheek and she brushed it away with an indolent hand. Angling her head toward the ground, she tucked it between her backpack and the curve of Dirty's spine. His fur rasped on her cheek like a carpet tossed in the ocean and left out to dry.

Frogs screeched in high-pitch croaks so loud that Stella couldn't hear herself breathe. How were there *frogs* nearby, but no water?

Half-asleep, Dirty pressed his body closer to hers and lifted a front paw off the ground. Was he trying to tell her something? Unsure what to do, Stella took the paw in her hand, and he relaxed.

Dirty snored next to her, paw in her hand. She considered waking him so he could help her listen for danger, but she didn't want to risk the possibility that he might reposition himself farther from her, so she let him sleep.

Minutes passed, or hours, and a chill flowed through Stella's body, starting with her feet and hands and head, and seeping into her core.

Something whooped in the darkness, and Dirty awoke sharply. He raised his head, but seemed unperturbed. The dog knew more about this rainforest than she did. If he didn't sense danger, maybe there was no danger. Maybe she could close her eyes for just a minute. Just one short minute…

As her mind floated past the terrain of consciousness, she pictured her father, tossing a stick out into a river, Torres jumping into the water after it. She whispered to herself to wake up—she didn't need to watch this dream unfold again.

Startling awake, she tried to scream, but her voice was trapped beneath a heavy weight.

Was that a branch breaking? A night predator? Was the man with the machete nearby?

She flailed her arms in the darkness, searching for Dirty. He was gone. Dirty was *gone*.

"Dirty?" she whispered. "Dirty?"

Nothing. No sounds other than the ceaseless vibrato of frogs and insects.

Her chest tightened and she breathed harder and faster. She still lay on her side, afraid to move.

Despair welled inside her, pressing on veins and arteries, shoving her organs into unnatural configurations.

A series of howls broke the stillness.

This was it. This would be the moment of her death.

She couldn't bear this jungle for one more moment. She wanted a jaguar to come get her. She hoped it was swift. She wasn't *built* for this. Her dad could have survived out here. Not her.

Footsteps approached quickly, and Stella hyperventilated, unable to see what was approaching, certain that she would have a heart attack.

Something wet slapped her in the face and she gave a dry, feeble shriek.

A smell wafted over her. Mold, and rotten flesh.

Dirty. It was Dirty.

She reached out in the black and sank her fingers into his wet rough fur, collapsing into him.

"Thank you," she wept, pressing her face into his mangy neck. "Thank you. Thank you. Please don't leave me."

He licked her face and lay next to her, placing his head on top of her head, almost suffocating her. His rancid fur covered half her nose, so she had to open her mouth to breathe, but she stayed as still as possible so he wouldn't move.

Snuggling his body against hers, he inhaled deeply, releasing his breath all at once in a satisfied sigh.

At some point in the night, he shifted his head off hers but stayed beside her. Every few minutes, she reached out to touch him, to make sure he was still there.

JUNGLE

Day Three

STELLA MUST'VE FALLEN asleep. She awoke at dawn to find both her eyelids nearly swollen shut from mosquito bites. Dirty chewed on another rodent carcass a few feet away.

Monkeys whooped overhead, shaking branches, sending the odd leaf in a lazy cascade down to Earth.

When Stella reached up to touch her eyelids, Dirty stopped eating and watched her. Fresh blood stained his mouth and snout, and splattered the ground.

Her body ached like she'd been hit by a truck, her feet worst of all. Lifting one foot from the ground, she almost cried out. She wanted to look at the blisters on her heels and toes, but the thought of pulling off her shoes and socks nauseated her.

Cramps waved through her stomach, and she clutched her knees to her chest until the worst of them passed.

Phlegmatic, she pulled the apple from her backpack. She couldn't imagine eating, as thirsty as she was, but maybe her body would let her eat the fruit since it was partly made of water?

Peeling away the apple's rough, dry skin with her knife, she threw the bits of peel to Dirty, who scarfed them down. Stella licked the exposed flesh of the fruit: slightly rotten, and overly sweet. Taking a small bite, she let the pulp roll around on her tongue and moisten her lips, groaning from the sweetness.

Quickly, the pulp's moisture seeped into the driest crevices of her mouth and became a wad of cement. She closed her eyes, forcing herself to swallow, nearly choking as the cement scraped down her esophagus. Still, hunger drove her to take another bite, and another, until she'd choked down half the apple, unable to tolerate another bite without water.

"Dammit," she said to Dirty.

The dog ripped a leg off his rodent, swallowing it whole.

She wished she could eat a rat's leg. She would squeeze out all the blood with her teeth, and it would quench her thirst and soothe her scraped esophagus. Blood would dribble down her chin.

Chewing the inside of her cheek, she glanced up at the monkeys bellowing in the canopy just as something long and skinny fell from above and nearly hit her head, *whapping* onto the ground beside her.

"Shit!" she yelped, scrambling backward.

Dirty jumped up with a bark, ready to fend off whatever intruder had crashed into their midst.

When Stella caught her breath, she leaned forward to look at the thing that had crashed down from above. Some kind of a bean pod – dark green and about a foot long. In the treetops, a dark brown monkey snapped a similar pod in two, fiddling with one of the pieces and then putting it to his mouth, presumably eating it.

Stella reached for the pod, her muddy fingers exploring the leathery skin. She snapped it in two like the monkey had done. Inside, a white feathery substance encased a line of seeds, each the size of an eyeball. The feathery guts smelled sweet and her stomach growled. She popped one of the seeds out of the pod and licked it—it tasted as sweet as it smelled. A little like vanilla. At first, the white pulp felt unpleasantly dry and fuzzy on her tongue, but when it came in contact with her scant saliva it melted into a slippery slime. Pinching the seed between two fingers, she scraped off a bit of flesh with her teeth, but immediately spit it onto the ground and flung the rest of the seed down after it. She couldn't eat the damn thing without water.

Dirty approached cautiously and sniffed the seed on the ground, looking up at her and back down at the seed.

"Go for it."

She bit her lip so she wouldn't cry. She was sick of crying.

Dirty picked the seed up in his mouth, spitting it out as quickly as she had, shaking his head like a kid who'd licked a lemon.

Stella smiled for the first time in two days. "Not as good as dead rat?"

Dirty approached her, turned to face the other direction, and pressed his back into hers, panting, licking the sore on his flank.

Picking up the bean pod, she stowed it in her pack with the half-apple and the last granola bar, thinking that maybe later she'd be able to eat a bit more if she could just find some *water*.

How the hell did people find water in the rainforest? Wasn't it supposed to be pooling in leaves and dripping off vines? Wasn't that the entire *point* of a rainforest?

Regardless, she should know how to find water in the freaking woods. She'd watched her father light fires using nothing but sticks and stones. He'd built shelters out of branches. He knew which berries were edible, and which were poisonous. He'd tried to teach her these things—he'd probably even tried to teach her how to find water in a forest—but she'd always declined to participate, burying her head in a book (no technology allowed on the camping trips) while he did all the work.

Not that this rainforest bore much of a resemblance to the ones where she'd camped with her father. Not that she could necessarily find water in *this* forest using techniques she might've learned in *that* one. But still, she wished desperately that she'd paid more attention to him. That she'd thanked him for *trying* to teach her things. That she'd engaged with him, even a little, when they were out in the woods.

Letting her mind wander back through all those trips, there *had* been some good camping moments, even during the dark days of high school. One night during sophomore year spring break, her dad had built a raging fire with boughs that had fallen in a recent windstorm. The four-foot-tall flames felt primordial, invigorating them both. Her father handed her a mug of fire-heated vegetable soup and said, "So you had a shitty week? Want to talk about it?"

She was surprised by the question. Being 15 was generally a miserable torment, but she never spoke to anyone (aside from Maria) about all the layers of crap she had to withstand. How did he know that this week had been worse than any other?

She started to say, *What are you talking about,* but instead, said, "Fucking bitches at school."

She knew this would push his buttons. He didn't like profanity.

He narrowed his eyes, the blaze illuminating his chiseled, crooked chin from below. He looked strong, fearsome.

She waited for the castigation, the outrage.

Instead, he said, "I hate bitches."

She exploded laughing.

"I hate bitches too," she giggled.

He laughed with her, and then said, "You want to try my moonshine?"

She raised an eyebrow. "You serious?"

As far back as she could remember, her dad made his own whiskey. She knew there was a storage room where he brewed his own hooch, hidden from his alcoholic wife. He never brought the stuff home—never drank any liquor in the house at all—but Stella knew that he sometimes invited friends to brew and drink with him in his redneck speakeasy.

For years, she'd asked him to teach her the process, but he'd refused.

You're too young, he always told her.

I'm not a child, she always retorted.

On that night by the bonfire, he pulled from his backpack a silver flask that read, *Emergency Drinking Water.* Unscrewing it, he handed it to her.

She raised it to her lips, choking on a brash sip. "Jesus!" she said, coughing. "That is disgusting, Dad! You actually *like* that?"

He reached for the flask, grinning. "Yep."

"It's nasty." She wiped her mouth.

A cinder cracked out of the fire, landing on her father's shirt. He didn't flinch, and Stella marveled at his composure.

He brushed the cinder off his flannel. "You still want to learn how to make it?"

"Yeah." Warming at the prospect, she wished he would offer her another sip.

He screwed the cap back on the flask. "I'll teach you when we get home."

Thinking of her father now, as she gathered strength for another day in this unfathomable jungle, comforted her and undid her simultaneously.

She tried to run her fingers through her dark shoulder-length hair, but the tangled muddy mat didn't give.

She had to get moving.

Dirty sensed her motivation and stood, focused.

Propping up to a seated position, she stretched one arm, then the other, and shook out each leg in turn. It felt like someone had cut off all her toes and jammed a knife into the back of her heel.

"Aah!" She slammed her eyes closed, telling the pain to fuck off.

Dirty walked two steps toward her, leaned in, and licked her face.

"Thanks," she whimpered, relaxing into the cool wetness for the first time, a lump rising in her throat. She wanted to put her arms around the dog, sob into his chest, but she wouldn't allow herself that weakness.

Her joints felt leaden, rusted shut.

Inhaling, she caught a whiff of something familiar. Something fresh. She couldn't place it.

She searched for the sun overhead, not directly visible. One direction shone brighter than the other. That direction must be more or less east. She would head in the opposite direction, which theoretically would send her toward the coast.

Bracing both hands on the ground, she lifted onto her feet but her legs buckled from the pain, and she tumbled down in a heap.

"FUCK!"

Dirty licked her face again, his eyes beseeching.

She bit her lip and put her fists on the ground again, propping herself against the dog's back and hoisting her bulk. This time she wobbled up, raising her arms away from her body for balance, grunting through each breath, pushing the pain out with each grunt. As she breathed, her coordination stabilized and she turned to face west-ish.

How had Dirty survived out here by himself? How had he even *gotten* here, so far from civilization? His ribs protruded, sores covering his haunches and scars crisscrossing his face and ears. He must be in as much pain as she was. He must be as thirsty as she was.

She cupped his face with the palm of her hand. "We gotta get out of here *today*."

His eyes held hers, unwavering. He was with her. He would help her get through this.

Taking the first step of the day required a monumental effort. Still, somehow she took another. And then another. And she got into a rhythm: step over whatever obstacle lay in her path, pause for a breath in and out, one more step forward, pause again…

In a trance, she panted forward, barely aware of her surroundings.

Dirty, now walking a step ahead of her rather than behind, looked back every few seconds. Each time, she met his gaze, and once or twice managed a wan smile, wondering if he knew the difference between a smiling face and an expressionless one. Without glancing up at the sun to assess their direction, she followed the dog. She hadn't been able to guide them out of this morass, but maybe Dirty could do better.

Every once in a while Stella doubled over at the waist, grunting through another wave of stomach cramps. Each time, Dirty padded back to stand next to her, gawking as he attempted to ascertain what was going on, waiting for instruction.

Several hours into the day, as they clambered over a thick root system, Dirty stopped so suddenly in his tracks that Stella nearly tripped over him. Frozen, he glared at something on the ground and growled, low and slow. When Stella moved to the side to see what he had spotted, he snarled at her, baring his teeth. The gesture sent a chill up her spine and she backed away, heart pounding hard.

A hiss rose from the shadows, and something struck at Dirty, lightning-fast. Just as quickly, he dodged out of the way, barking wild.

A bulky snake slithered into a patch of dappled sun, its hollow, sand-colored eyes trained on Dirty. Brown and black triangles crisscrossed the length of its body.

Stella gasped. She'd never seen a snake so large. Even the rattlesnakes back in Texas didn't posture this aggressively.

She stammered, "Dirty, come here."

Dirty didn't move.

"Dirty, COME!" she commanded.

Still, the dog didn't move.

The standoff continued for five seconds, six, ten, neither animal giving ground. Then as swiftly as it had appeared, the snake vanished into the vegetation.

When it was gone, Stella fell to her knees, trying to catch her breath. She held her arms out toward the dog. "Come here, Dirty."

Unmoved, he stared at the ground where the snake had been for several more seconds before approaching her. She wrapped her arms around him, and he buried his head in her chest.

Drawing a deep breath, he made a sound as he exhaled, like a sigh or whimper. Stella wrapped her arms tighter around him, and he whimpered again, doing it now with every exhale. It didn't seem like an expression of sadness. It was more like *joy*, like he couldn't contain all his happiness.

Like Dirty, she whimpered, whispering into the top of his head, "I would've stepped on it if you hadn't been here. Thank you, Dirty. Thank you."

Adrenalized from the sudden shock of fear, she felt the need to pee for the first time that day. Looking around, she felt unnerved at the thought of squatting above this snaky terrain.

Dirty padded over to a nearby tree, sniffed something at the base of it, raised a leg and peed onto a fern.

If he could do it, she could do it.

Trembling, she fumbled to unbutton her jeans, then pulled them down and bent her knees a few inches, barely squatting. The pee wouldn't come. She knew it needed to, but it wouldn't. She'd barely drunk anything yesterday, so how could there be any pee in her anyway?

Bolting upright with her jeans around her knees, she exclaimed, "Water bottle!"

Dirty raised his head.

She should collect her pee and drink it! Right? Isn't that what people did in the wilderness? If her survival hinged upon it, she would definitely drink her own pee.

Retrieving her empty water bottle, she held it beneath her as she squatted, strained, and finally let out a stream of dark yellow urine. The release made her feel almost giddy. Though the stream flowed for only a few seconds, she felt like she'd discharged a river of toxins. Closing her eyes, she sighed, jerking them open only when Dirty licked her face.

She leaned her head in to nuzzle his.

After pulling up her jeans, she tentatively raised the bottle to her mouth. The smell of urine made her gag. She lowered the bottle, breathed in and out, and tried again. Again she gagged. She couldn't do it.

Screwing the bottle closed, she decided to save the pee for later. Surely she'd be able to drink it if she *really* needed to. If she were *dying*. Maybe, the fact that she couldn't drink it meant the straits weren't dire yet.

She looked down at the dog, touching the top of his head. "You go first. Don't step on any snakes."

As if he understood every word, Dirty set off. Stella shook her head, humbled by his intelligence.

He moved with purpose, as if he had a destination. Stella was putting all her trust in him, though in truth he could've just been wandering lost through the jungle, like her. Still, she wanted to trust him, needed to trust him, because her mental compass was broken.

Brain buzzing as she battled the constant urge to fall to the ground wailing from the pain in her feet, she tried to discern whether they were headed in a straight line. But the jungle didn't allow for straight lines, nor for rapid progress.

Each step made Stella's heart pound—was there a snake under that fern? A spider lurking in these vines? Her mind raced on overdrive, calculating risks, shoving away thoughts of hunger or thirst or pain, reminding herself to focus on her next step. Reminding herself that she was *strong*.

Her father had often told her that she was the strongest person he knew. For years, she'd desperately wanted to be as strong as her father told her she was, but secretly feared that she never could be.

She remembered the first time he told her that her strength would be her biggest asset.

He'd wheeled Moby Dick into the pick-up line at Stella's middle school just as she confronted a group of popular girls picking on a skinny, black-haired girl.

The popular girls were laughing and pointing at the girl. A tall blonde wearing designer jeans and an Abercrombie sweatshirt said to the others, "You should've seen her in P.E. She *literally* can't *jump*! Like, when she tries to long jump, she falls down *every single time*."

Another blonde, practically indistinguishable from the first, said, "No way! Everybody knows how to jump. Jump for us, Maria!"

The skinny black-haired girl faced the group, chin up, hands on her hips. "I can *jump*."

One of the blondes held her arms out wide. "Prove it!"

"Yeah prove it," the other blonde intoned, and a group of similar-looking brunettes behind them nodded in symphonic support.

One of the blondes drew a line in the dirt with the tip of her snow-white sneaker and then dusted off the bottom of the shoe. "Start here and see how far you can jump."

As the skinny girl flipped them off, Stella marched up behind the group, pushing through the crowd and linking her elbow around the skinny girl's. "Go stick your boobs in a beehive!" she yelled at them.

The girls fell silent, dumbstruck.

"Excuse me?" said one of the blondes.

"You heard me, go stick your boobs in a beehive." Stella stood only four-foot eleven, but she spoke like she thought she was the tallest girl in the yard.

Maria squeezed her elbow around Stella's and raised her chin even farther.

Gape-jawed, one of the blondes smacked her gum. "I'm going to tell Principal Nadler you said that!"

"Fine," jeered Stella. "Then I'll tell him you that you're a racist, and you were bullying this girl because she's from Mexico."

"Ecuador," the girl whispered into Stella's ear.

"Ecuador," proclaimed Stella.

One of the blondes pointed at the skinny girl. "That is ridiculous. I'm *not* racist. Do you even *know* that girl?"

"Of course I do." Stella put her free hand on her hip, raising her chin up in the air to mimic the skinny girl's powerful posture. They were like a tiny gang. "Her father owns the rodeo."

There was no truth in either statement—she had never met the girl before, and the girl's father most certainly didn't own the rodeo.

One of the blondes turned her back to Stella and marched back toward the school building. "Let's go, bitches."

Stella turned the skinny girl around and quickly shuttled her toward the line of cars waiting to pick up traumatized middle-schoolers from the bloodbath. "I'm Stella."

"I'm Maria," said the girl, wide-eyed and grinning.

Stella glanced at her sideways, not wanting to stare, envious of the girl's wild, curly black hair. "What grade are you in?"

"Eighth," Maria said, acting unfazed by the scene that had just unfolded. "I started school early so I'm only twelve but I'll be thirteen this summer. My family just moved here from the other side of the city."

Maria's skin was smooth and tan, and Stella wished she had such beautiful skin.

She stood up straighter. "I'm in eighth too. Don't worry about those girls. They're horrible. They call each other *bitches* because that's what they are. If you say smart mean things to them they don't know what to say and they shut up."

Arms still linked, they stepped off the curb as the girl said, "Is there really a rodeo in Austin?"

Stella waved her free arm. "I don't know. Do you want to come over for dinner?"

Maria stopped in the middle of the street, unlinked her arm from Stella's, leaned over so her head was upside down, gathered her hair in her hands, and whipped her head back up, pulling a hair band off her wrist and looping it twice around the ponytail. The set of actions took no more than five seconds.

She took Stella's arm again. "I have to call my mom on my cell phone, but, yeah."

Impressed by Maria's ponytail technique, by the fact that she had a cell phone, Stella felt a surge of excitement. She had a new friend with a *cell phone.*

When they reached the car, her father beamed at her, winking.

"This is Maria," Stella said to him, unlocking the front door. "She's coming over for dinner."

"Hello, Maria. It's nice to meet you." Stella's father rearranged his bags in the back seat to make room for Maria, looking her in the eye before he turned back to his daughter. "Mark my words, when y'all are out in the real world, those girls won't amount to peanuts, and y'all will be running things. You have strength they'll never know, and that strength'll be your best asset. I'd put money on it."

Stella felt giddy whenever her father complimented her. With each word of praise from him her adolescent confidence had grown, and it kept growing until he died, when it evaporated like dew.

Now, with the light fading on her third day in the jungle, her spirit crashed to an all-time low.

She felt like she'd walked no more than a mile from where she and Dirty had spent the previous night. Her legs ached. Her stomach cramped.

Stepping over a thick vine, she grabbed a thin tree for balance and her toe caught on the creeper. She plunged down on the side of her foot, ankle wrenched into an unnatural bend.

Crying out, her wasted legs collapsed beneath her, and she lay back on a soft bed of moss. Or maybe it was a web of fungi. She didn't know, didn't care. It was soft and she was tired.

Her ankle throbbed. Her heels and toes throbbed. Her head throbbed. Her mosquito bites itched. Every one of her organs was cramping.

Water. Nothing interested her but water.

Above her, a tree swayed unnaturally, and Stella squinted at it. A hundred feet in the air, a small gray-brown monkey jumped from one branch to the next. Another appeared next to the first, and they squabbled about something, wrestling. From the ground, Stella could barely hear their angry squeaks. Two trees away, a mother monkey and baby pulled leaves, or something else, off a branch. As Stella's focus settled into the scene, she realized that there must be twenty of them up there, eating or playing or whatever they were doing. Had monkey families played and squabbled above her all day, unnoticed? Had they been watching her lurch through the jungle, befuddled by her inelegant movements, her unfamiliar grunts?

Her ankle—something was seriously wrong with her ankle. This time, she felt certain that she had sprained it. But what could she do about it? Nothing.

The early evening mosquito swarm gathered, settling on and around Stella and Dirty. He jumped and twitched, murdering as many as he could. Stella pulled on her sweatshirt and dusted herself with the last of her bug spray. Throwing the empty bottle on the ground, she stared at it, trying to figure out if she felt guilty for discarding plastic in a fragile rainforest. No, her body was too tired and painful for her to give a shit.

She wondered if Alé was driving his taxi around Dominical at that moment, shuttling an American tourist back to Dominical after a day at Manuel Antonio National Park. Had he noticed that she hadn't returned from her day hike? Would he tell someone?

Dirty stood above her, uncertain whether he was supposed to lie down, or coax his human to stand up.

Eyes glazed, Stella broke the silence. "Alé's daughter died when she was six years old. Cancer or something."

Peering into the treetops, chewing on the inside of her cheek, her mind wandered from Dominical to Texas, to her mom. What was she doing right now? Sitting at the front desk for the vacuum cleaner company, answering phone calls in her standard tone—half-annoyed but polite? Was she sucking on a paper cut after a day of filing? Was she thinking about Stella? *Did* she think about Stella? When she sat by herself at the table in the backyard, sipping her glass and wiping the sweat from her clavicle with a tissue, was she thinking about her daughter? Was she wishing that they could be closer? Or did she see Stella as an impediment to her consuming desire to wallow full-time in her mind's misery?

The soft bed of moss or fungus felt like a feather bed. If Stella never got up from this mossy bed, it wouldn't be a terrible place to spend the rest of her life. Dirty could bring her rat carcasses and she could drink the rain that would surely come.

Low light sifted through the canopy, bathing the forest in a dewy softness.

A pitter-patter rose all around them like a soft rain. Stella sat up. Holding out her arms, she felt no droplets.

Dirty, too, swiveled his head in search of the sound's source, and then let out a low growl.

Twenty feet away, a line of ants several inches across marched across the carpet of dead leaves. Within seconds, the army broadened into a massive swath, spilling over the landscape to their right, coating the ground as far as Stella could see. Millions of tiny feet hissed through the jungle.

"Jesus!" Stella leapt up, screaming from the pain in her ankle and feet.

Dirty bayed.

"Let's go, Dirty!" Stella grabbed him by the scruff and dragged him away from the writhing mass, grunting in pain with every step, stumbling over the difficult terrain, ants sprouting around her. Ants carpeted everything within a few inches of the ground—roots, bushes, leaves, branches. The forest hummed, squirming.

Dirty didn't know what to do. He yelped, yanking up a paw and gnawing at it as he ran. Stella struggled to drag him on his other three legs. The dog twitched and bounded left and right, unable to escape the fray.

Stella released him to limp over a series of tree roots, then grabbed his scruff again, forcing him to follow. They both panted hard.

Her vision blurred, black splotches obscuring the way forward. She rubbed her eyes, but the black spots didn't go away. Blinking, she floundered.

"Oww!" Something stung her sore ankle. Hopping on one leg, she jerked up her jeans, noting that the sprained ankle was swollen like a balloon. She wiped an ant away with her sweatshirt sleeve. Several other ants clambered on her shoe, and she brushed those off as well, grabbing Dirty's scruff again and dragging him forward.

The swarm tapered as they stumbled, still fluttering through the jungle just behind them.

When they'd skirted fifty feet past the swarm's edge, Stella and Dirty stood on a still patch of dirt. Through the black spots in her vision, Stella saw the edge of the swarm trembling in and out like an eddy, dissolving slowly into the forest.

As she gingerly lowered herself to the ground, she and Dirty stared at each other, horror-struck. Her ankle howled at her, bringing tears to her eyes.

"What the fuck?" She rubbed her face.

Dirty flopped to the earth and chewed at bites on his paws and legs and belly.

Exhaustion descended over Stella like an iron blanket. She hiked up the bottom of her jeans to examine her ant bites—only three, thankfully. The swellings ached like bee stings, but they blended in with all the other aches gripping her broken body.

The blurring in her vision grew, and fatigue tugged her eyes closed. What was happening to her? Was she dying?

She wanted her dad to walk out of the jungle and explain all of this to her. She'd never wanted anything more in her life. He knew how to make everything okay. He knew how to put everything in the world in its right place.

She wanted to be eight years old again, riding to gymnastics with him in Moby Dick. Grinding through traffic on the way to the gym—that's when he answered all of her biggest questions about the world and all its mystery.

For twenty minutes every Tuesday, Stella had her father all to herself. Inside Moby Dick, there were no distractions, no interruptions.

Each week, she presented a big, poignant question for them to discuss on the drive, like, "What is rain?"

Her father's answers bridged reality and fantasy. The trick for Stella was divining the difference.

"Rain," he said, "Is just clouds that fall out of the sky."

"Daaaaad!" Stella shoved his shoulder, and he made a dramatic show of focusing on the road to avoid swerving.

"No, really!" He grinned at her side-eyed and then wiped away his grin with an austere nod. "Rain is nothin' but a bunch of water droplets that used to hang out in the ocean. Then one day they get their panties in a twitch 'cause they're sick and tired of being in one place, so they start jittering back and forth until they jump way up out of the ocean, high up in the sky."

Sunlight streamed through the driver's side window, catching his ring of balding brown hair. His crooked chin jutted strong under his ears—*the bigger the chin, the stronger the man,* he liked to say.

He continued his explanation of rain: "Those rain droplets hang out up in the clouds for a while, tuckered out from the jump. And then they get bored again—there's absolutely nothing to do way up in the sky. Nothing goes up there but the occasional bird or two. So the water molecules decide they were better off down in the ocean where they could hang out with fish and watch people water ski and all that. A few of the molecules get together and wrap their arms around each other and hang on for dear life until they form a big fat water droplet, and then they fall out of the sky and land on your head and they break apart again into all the different little molecules and sink into your scalp and stay there for about a decade before they get tired and wanna do something else, but it takes a while for them to get bored 'cause the inside

LAURA THOMAS

of your noggin is more fun than a sack full of kittens, so why would they want to leave?" He gave a precise, quick nod. "And that's rain."

Stella's tinkling laughter filled the car. "Dad! Is that true?"

"True as steel, Squirrel." He put a hand on her head, grabbing her ponytail and giving it a gentle tug.

She loved her father's stories about the world. He saw everything through a whimsical lens, and when she was near him, she caught the whimsy. They laughed constantly and easily.

It had been years since she'd laughed so easily. Maybe, she thought, she hadn't laughed easily since he'd died.

Now, lying on the rainforest floor, she forced her eyes open, but they refused to stay, so she closed them again. Dirty lay a few inches away, licking his ant bites. She reached out to touch him. Everything hurt. She was so tired.

Within moments, she fell asleep.

Her father was there, again, standing at the edge of a river. Clouds amassed overhead as he threw a stick into the river, and Torres leapt after it. He smiled, and then something wet slapped his cheek. He wiped it away and looked up, squinting at the first raindrops as they fell from a fat, heavy cloud. Another drop splattered his face, and another, and another...

Stella twitched in her sleep, opening her eyes. Standing over her, Dirty's tongue whacked wet against her cheek. Beyond him, a navy sky clung to the edges of the trees.

Her body pressed numb and heavy into the ground. She could barely feel any part of herself aside from her feet, whose pain didn't relent even in sleep. She no longer feared the dangers of nighttime. This must be the steady state of creatures that live in the jungle: they become so exhausted by survival that they can no longer engage in the luxury of fear.

Dirty whined at her.

70

NOT JUST A DOG

Looking into his eyes, she felt no emotion.

He licked her face, whined more loudly, turned to peer at something in the jungle.

"I can't," she told him.

She didn't care whether a giant swarm of ants or a starving jaguar or a venomous snake skulked in the dark. She needed to lie there for a while. She needed to sleep.

Dirty's whining mounted. Just before she closed her eyes, he yowled and ran into the dark.

JUNGLE

Night Three

DIRTY WAS GONE. If she'd had more energy, she would've panicked.

She thought of her dad, holding Torres's face: "Daddy's always coming back."

Dirty would come back too. He wasn't abandoning her.

Her mind drifted back toward sleep, but a noise lugged her back to the waking world. She tried to ignore it, but it had a heavy pull.

Was something dripping? Or slurping? Could she possibly hear *slurping*?

She bolted upright. She could see almost nothing in the shrouded understory.

It *was* slurping. Something was drinking water. *Close by.*

Unable to stand on her swollen ankle and rickety legs. Through the darkness, Stella across the earth, crossing the swath where ants had swarmed not long before. The dirt here grew soft and deep, a blessing for her knees and hands.

She followed the sound of slurping for a few seconds until it stopped.

Blurry spots still obscured her vision. She didn't know where to go.

Dirty appeared between two trees, stopped to glance at her, turned, and returned to wherever he'd come from.

She crawled after him, emerging into a small clearing, open enough to let in the faintest spray of moonlight. A thin, muddy rivulet, only a few inches across and lined with moldy leaves, bisected the clearing.

Stella sighed. "Oh, Dirty."

Collapsing at the edge of the rivulet, she plunged her face into it, gulping, gagging. The thick water tasted of murk and waste. She spit it out, dirt pooling in the corners of her mouth. Lowering her face again to the water, she skimmed her lips across the top layer and took a slower sip, gagging again. By the third attempt, she stopped gagging, scooping her cupped hands into the water, swallowing large, sating gulps.

When she'd drunk so much that she gagged again, throwing up gritty sludge, she raised herself and sat back. Could she feel the water seeping into her parched places? Was it healing her already? She couldn't tell. At least her stomach wasn't quite so empty. She would drink more later.

Next to her, Dirty lowered his head to the stream, licking up several more sips with his dexterous, sinewy tongue.

Stella sank into fetal position and curled her knees into her chest. Before the dog stopped drinking, Stella sank toward the edges of sleep.

The dream came to her again, the one she'd been dancing around for years. This time, though, it played out farther:

Her father was hiking down a canyon. He smiled as Torres trots up ahead. Clouds billowed overhead and light raindrops began to fall. Picking up a stick, her father threw it into the river for Torres to fetch. Torres leapt after it, paddling hard, grasping the stick with her tongue, swimming back to shore, dropping the prize at her master's feet. The light raindrops became heavy raindrops, and her father looked at the sky, concerned. He said to Torres, *We better head back, T.* They started trekking up the canyon, rain thundering down around them. Torres slipped on the slick rocks, tumbling into the rising river. The dog swam toward shore in the mounting current. She placed her front paws on a boulder, using all her strength to hold onto it. Rain pounded her father's balding head, soaked his clothes and sneakers. He grasped a bush with one hand, placing a foot into the river, reaching his free hand toward Torres to grab her collar. The current strengthened, and

Torres began to lose her grip. Straining his hand farther out into the flow, her father slipped on the slick rocks, tumbling into the river. They thrashed in the waves, flailing their arms toward the boulders and bushes that lined the edges of the river, but neither could latch onto anything. Together, they floated, thrashing, gasping for air, toward the place 25 miles downstream where they would wash up on a rocky bank, lifeless.

A clap of thunder yanked Stella awake.

Thunder!

Dirty lay next to her, spooned inside her like an infant. Stella felt the dog raise his head at the thunder, though she couldn't see him in the tarry night.

Tears pooled in the corner of her eyes. Was she crying? She didn't know why. Had she been dreaming?

Lightning illuminated the forest, striking eerie shadows around branches and bushes. Then another clap of thunder, another lightning flash, and another clap of thunder. A fat droplet fell on the leaves above them, and then a few droplets made their way to the ground in wide splats.

Stella lay still as a drop landed on her skin. She reached out to hug Dirty.

Rain.

The globules cleaned fingerprint-sized patches on her face and she turned onto her back, opening her mouth, one or two drops landing on her tongue. As the sprinkle turned into a downpour, she ran her hand over her matted hair, willing the water to soak it through. Her sweatshirt dampened and a chill settled over her. She pulled Dirty in tighter and he let her hold him as if he'd lived his whole life on a living room couch, snuggling with his owner while she watched her shows.

They huddled together under the pelting rain until Stella yanked herself to her knees. "Fuck! I gotta catch it!"

It had taken her *several minutes* to remember that she needed to collect the goddamn rain.

Her hands grappled with the backpack, pulling out the water bottle and dumping out her pee. She held the bottle out in front of her to catch droplets, dismayed at how few found the bottle. It would take hours for the container to fill at this rate. Her weakened arms couldn't hold the bottle upright for long enough.

Ankle and feet screaming, she crawled through the storm toward a tree where a series of large leaves funneled rain into a trickle. She held the bottle beneath the trickle until it held a full sip, and gulped it down, repeating this several times. Her arms trembled. She needed to lie back down. Below the trickle, Stella braced the bottle between two roots knobbing up from the earth. Shoring it up on one side with her backpack, she braced it on the other with a pile of dirt and leaves.

Cold racked her body, and she dropped to the ground as Dirty skulked over to her, his wet coat plastered against his emaciated frame. Lying in fetal position, she opened her arms to him and he nestled into her armpit, shielding his face from the rain. She put an arm around him, burying her face in his fur.

Like this, they weathered the storm until it abated and then stopped altogether, Stella shivering and Dirty unmoved.

Though she'd never before experienced as much misery and fear as in the last three days, the warmth of Dirty filled her with something like happiness, or maybe gratitude.

She closed her eyes, trembling violently until the cold fell away, and her mind dragged her again toward torpor.

She must have fallen asleep, because a pungent smell roused her. She opened her eyes and looked around for Dirty.

"Dirty?" she croaked, pounding with fear.

Streams of moonlight sliced through the canopy, illuminating his silhouette a few feet away.

He panted, his breath rotten and hot.

On the soil between Stella and the mutt lay a dead fish, seven or eight inches long. Dirty rested his head on the ground near the carcass and peered up at her.

She sat up, sighing, sitting in a hunch. Her stomach roiled, wrecked from days of hunger and thirst and cramping.

She'd eaten sushi dozens of times. She liked raw fish, right? This wasn't so different, right?

Fish. Her cheeks flushed hot. Dirty had brought her a fish. Where had he gotten it? Were they near the ocean?

She held her breath and listened, straining for the crash of waves. Frogs and cicadas and other insects still screamed their night songs. No chance of hearing anything over the critters' ruckus. Still, maybe. Maybe…

She turned back to the fish. Was she hungry? She wasn't sure. All she could feel was pain, in every corner of her body.

She'd been starving for three days, but now the thought of eating nauseated her. Still, she knew she needed to eat. Grabbing the fish in one hand, the slimy skin nearly slipped through her fingers.

Dirty watched her.

She grabbed the fish in both hands, turning it over, examining it from all sides. Could she rip through the skin with her teeth? The knife! She reached into her drenched, muddy pack and pulled out the pocketknife.

Flipping the blade open, she sank its tip into the fish's eyeball and jerked to pry open the skeleton. But it didn't give way, and all she did was mutilate the eyehole.

Opening a fish couldn't be that hard. She'd seen it on the fishing shows her dad used to watch. Turning the carcass on its back, she plunged the knife into its belly and wrenched downward, exposing pink wet flesh.

Raising the carcass to her mouth, she bit off a small chunk of meat and chewed it, the taste and texture not unpleasant. Her face tingled with pleasure and she dug her fingers knuckle-deep into the belly of the fish, ripping away chunks and wolfing them down, tossing bones and intestines in Dirty's direction. Her fingers shone in the moonlight, glossy from guts and blood.

Dirty watched her, intent, waiting for scraps.

Had he eaten a fish before he'd offered her this one? Or had he brought her the first one he caught, before feeding himself?

How would he catch a fish, anyway? Would he stand in shallow water and wait for one to swim by? She wanted to watch him hunt.

"Thank you, Dirty." She held the remains out to him, and he took a tentative step toward her. "It's okay. All yours."

He didn't approach farther, so she tossed the skeleton at his feet. Flopping down next to it, he crunched into the bones, devouring every scrap of meat and guts.

As Stella watched him eat, a *crack* emanated from the darkness. Something was nearby. Something *big*.

Growling, posturing low to the ground, Dirty slinked between Stella and the rustling sound.

In the shadows, piecemeal strands of moonlight illuminated the creature just enough to show its girth: large—a lot larger than Dirty, who probably weighed thirty pounds soaking wet.

Dirty's low growl evaporated into the insect songs, and Stella wished he would bark, scare the thing away. He stood at attention, ready to pounce.

Separating Stella and Dirty from the creature, the muddy rivulet still ran dark and slow. Maybe the animal was seeking out the water source. Should they move away and give it room to drink?

Stella resisted the urge to cower behind Dirty's skinny frame.

Dirty snarled as the hulking animal—big as a jaguar—sauntered into the clearing.

This was no jaguar. The slow-loping mammal swished toward them, a dark puffball with a fluffy tail as long as its body. From its head, a grotesque snout protruded like a giant phallus, swinging from side to side as it walked, elegant in its ugliness.

Anteater? Was it an anteater? Anteaters only ate ants, right? So this animal wouldn't hurt them?

Dirty unleashed a salvo of falsetto yelps, jumping from side to side, not charging, but making his position clear.

The anteater observed him calmly and then slowly, unperturbed, sauntered back into the black.

Stella shook her head, wondering how few people had ever seen such a creature.

Probably, even fewer people would believe that a feral dog she'd known for two days had placed himself between her and danger *more than once.*

She felt deeply privileged, and deeply despondent. This was the worst time in her life, and also one of the most beautiful.

On her knees, she leaned awkwardly toward Dirty, ignoring the pain in her ankle and feet, and held his face in her hands. "Thank you, Dirty. Thank you for helping me. I see how you're protecting me. I'm sorry I was mean to you when I met you."

She'd never understood why people fawned over their domesticated animals, professing "love" and "friendship"—things she had previously understood as exclusively human—until she was lost in the jungle with one.

She once asked her father why he cared about Torres so much, and he told her, "It's rare for anyone to be loved like that dog loves me. No matter how grumpy I am, or what I say to her when I'm in a bad mood, she'll still live and die for me. And she's always trying to find ways to show me how much she loves me. When someone loves you that much, you gotta be grateful for that gift and love them back."

At the time, she'd shrugged her shoulders, saying, "She's just a dog," jealous that he seemed to think an animal could love him more than she herself did. Which, in retrospect, was not at all what he was saying.

Still holding Dirty's head in her hands, she felt like she could see a piece of her father in the animal's eyes.

She pulled her hands away from his face and stared at her dry, scabby knuckles, and the scratches and welts maiming her fingers. Her worn hands look middle-aged.

A pang thrashed her stomach, and she cradled her abdomen. Feeling like she might vomit, she took deep breaths until the nausea passed.

With the crescent light, frogs stopped screeching, insects paused their chatter. As the racket eased, something caught her attention. A sound, so faint that it almost didn't exist. She inclined her head, straining to hear it.

Waves. She heard waves.

JUNGLE

Dawn, Day Four

WHINING, DIRTY LICKED her face and glanced into the undergrowth, toward the faint whoosh of ocean.

She nuzzled his cheek. "You did it, Dirty."

Maybe there would be people on the beach. Maybe, at that moment, search teams were scouring the dunes, their flashlights punching holes in the red simmer of dawn.

The ocean's nearness infused Stella with enough energy to pull her backpack onto her shoulders. She braced her knuckles on the ground, giving herself a moment to gather strength before mustering a stand. As her feet and ankle took the brunt of her weight, she cried out. It felt like a hammer was bashing the side of her ankle, hornets stinging her heel and toes.

She cursed and then took a step, punching the hornets' nest, swinging the hammer. Fingers tingling and weak, she plucked up her still-open water bottle, only half full from the rain. Taking a sip and moaning at the freshness, she screwed on the top and kept moving.

With each stride, she chuffed, "UFF," funneling her pain into the chuffs. When she could, she grabbed tree trunks, propping her weight to favor the sprained ankle.

She wanted to stop, to raise her foot and let it rest, but she knew that if she stopped moving, she might not be able to start again.

Dirty walked in step with her, slowing his gait to match hers, using the extra time to sniff a pile of shit or a glistening leaf.

The soil gave way to sand, and dawn to day, clear blue light pouring through the canopy. Straight ahead on the horizon, a clarion sky beckoned through the tree line. They had almost reached the jungle's edge.

Pausing, panting, she put a hand on Dirty's head, and he looked up at her.

She pitched one excruciating foot in front of the next.

Here, trees grew straight out of the sand. Bracing on a fig tree, Stella stifled a sob. Two more trees lay ahead, and past that, a swath of tawny beach framed by an ocean so turquoise that the color seemed impossible.

The air smelled salt-fresh, sun shining hard above the horizon, not a wisp of cloud.

Stella collapsed to her hands and knees, dizzy, limbs tingling. The dizziness escalated and her body shook, convulsing. She spewed a stream of vomit, all fish parts and muddy water.

Wiping her mouth, she doubled over and puked up more muddy water until her stomach was empty but still thrashing.

Fatigue drew down her body.

Dirty stood over her, whining.

She dry heaved again two times, three, four.

She had to get to the beach. It couldn't be more than twenty feet away. There would be people on the beach. This would all be over if she could just get to the beach.

Dirty whined, sniffing her vomit and the air around her body.

Closing her eyes, she pictured her mother on the beach, yelling for her, desperate to find her.

On hands and knees, she scooted her left knee forward, then her right hand, right knee, left hand. Soft sand cushioned each shuffle.

Dirty stayed in step, his gaze wide and focused.

Left knee, right hand, right knee, left hand…

Dirty licked her cheek and she leaned her face into him.

Bracing against a tree trunk, she took a breath, dry-heaved. Left knee, right hand, right knee, left hand.

Emerging past the last tree, she pressed her forehead to the ground, grateful and miserable.

She looked up, squinting, searching for people. At the shoreline, a triangle-shaped sand bar twenty feet across fanned out into the surf, the peculiar peninsula splitting an otherwise unbroken stretch of beach. The coast curved slightly so that Stella was only able to see a couple hundred yards down the beach to her left, and maybe a quarter-mile to the right.

She took in the vast expanse of camel-colored sand, and the impossible turquoise water, and the soft crash of waves over coral.

Nobody was there.

Lacking the strength to cry, she curled into fetal position. Dirty folded his body around her, resting his head on her neck, whimpering.

If she died here, it would be a good death, in the sunshine, with her friend nestled on her neck. She sank into a stupor, hypnotized by the waves and the wind.

A sound roused her; a sound that didn't belong in this expanse. Something mechanical. Maybe a beep? Was that a cell phone?

Dirty raised his head. He heard it too.

Clenching her teeth through a wave of nausea, she reached into her jeans pocket with her eyes closed, fingers fumbling for her cell phone. Was it ringing?

Holding the phone in front of her, she tried to focus on the screen. Did it say anything? Blurry black spots again clouded her vision, and she couldn't see clearly. Swiping a finger across the screen, she held the phone to her ear.

"Hello?" Her voice passed out of her in a listless whisper. *Hello?*

"Mom?"

I love you, baby.

"Mom, is that you?"

Stella, I love you, you know that, right?

"Yes. I love you too, Mom."

I'm looking for you, baby.

"Thank you. Come find me."

I will, baby.

"I'm on the beach. Mom, where are you?"

Waves swished, and gulls squawked overhead.

"Mom?"

Dirty licked her face.

Stella looked at the phone, black spots clearing enough for her to see the screen. It was black and cold, the battery long dead.

Had she imagined the conversation? And the mechanical sound? Dirty had heard something too, right?

She wailed, cursing hoarse into the azure sky, into the rhythmic music of the waves.

The pain in her feet mounted, maddening. Still lying on her side, she reached toward her left shoe, yanking on the laces awkwardly, tying them in a tighter knot. She fumbled with the knot, but couldn't loosen it.

Dirty reached out a paw to touch her shoulder.

"Fuck," she slurred, reaching for her right shoe, tugging the muddy laces. As they gave way, pain raged through her bulging ankle. She cursed and moaned, her trembling fingers pulling off the shoe and then the soggy sock.

Her ankle had swelled to double its normal size, bruised black and purple. A moist crimson splotch, maroon around the edges, covered her heel. Skin peeled off in pus-covered patches. Every toe shone slippery red, infected, skin sliding off at the knuckles.

Seeing the damage to her feet worsened the pain, and she wished she hadn't taken off her sneaker. There was no way she'd be able to put it back on.

Nausea gripped her, and she leaned over to retch on the sand.

Her stomach churned and cramped. She hadn't pooped in three days, but suddenly she was going to explode.

Feeling like she weighed a thousand pounds, she raised herself to her knees, exposing her blistered toes to the sand. Unbuttoning her jeans, she squatted on her stronger foot, balancing the opposite thigh on a tree root. As she grunted, her body purged itself violently, as if death itself were passing out of her.

Dirty stood two feet away, waiting for any sign that he might help.

"Sorry, Dirty," she whispered, pitching forward, away from the stinking pile. "You bet on the wrong horse."

He leaned in to lick her face.

Pulling her jeans most of the way up, she licked her parched lips and ran her tongue over her teeth. Why did her teeth feel so strange? Sand. They were covered in sand. Her tongue too, coated in sand. How did that happen? When did that happen? She spit out what she could and ran her dirty finger through her mouth, scraping out more.

The smell of feces made her want to throw up again. She had to get away from it. Laboriously, she pulled her pants up over her hips, cringing at the thought of soiling them from lack of toilet paper, and crawled a few feet along the tree line, away from the smell.

Pulling the water bottle from her pack, she took a tiny sip, swishing it in her mouth to gather up the rest of the sand, spitting it out.

She took another small swig, unable to gulp what her body needed, unsure whether anything would stay in her stomach.

Closing her eyes, she longed for the relief of sleep. Her body felt like it was rotting from the inside out. She'd never experienced sickness this intense, this debilitating, this close to death.

In college, she'd had mononucleosis, confined to her dorm room for two miserable weeks. This felt worse than that. In middle school, she'd spent two nights in the hospital with the flu. This felt far worse than that.

She'd nearly overdosed one night with Garrett, head in the toilet vomiting for hours. Only that night felt comparable to this. But this time, she'd have to weather the affliction without medical intervention, alone. Or, almost alone.

Dirty lay on the sand next to her, pressing his face next to hers. She reached out to sink her fingers into his fur.

Closing her eyes, she spoke to her father, "Daddy, I don't feel good."

Hi, Squirrel. Her father's voice swam through her head. He sounded clear as day, close to her ear. Was she dreaming? Probably. The dream felt nice. She didn't open her eyes.

His warm hand alighted on her shoulder, firm, gentle.

"I need help, Daddy." Tears welled.

I know, baby. His voice—so familiar, slightly pinched but confident— settled over Stella like a blanket.

He spoke again: The dog will protect you. I sent him to you.

She cried, soothed by weight of his hand on her shoulder.

"I know, Daddy." Closing her eyelids tighter, she said, "I saw you in his eyes."

She waited for him to answer.

Seagulls cawed.

She opened her eyes. Dirty's chin rested on her shoulder. Her gaze flicked up toward the shimmering blue sky and back down toward the dog.

She felt a bottomless well of regret. For three years, she'd been angry with her father for being reckless enough to go for a hike under a flash-flood sky, and her mother for being weak enough to drift away from her on a cloud of sadness. Now she'd made a choice more reckless than her father's, more selfish than her mother's.

She could've tried to break through her mother's armor of sadness, but she always felt like her mother should be the one to reach out. Now she wished she'd swallowed her pride, reached across the divide. Maybe they would've had more good moments together. Maybe they could've learned to laugh together. She could count on one hand the number of times she remembered *smiling* with her mother.

The day her mom dropped her off at her freshman dorm—that had been a good day. Fourteen months after that day, her father would be dead, and she'd be forced to move back into her family's house, unable to afford the university's room and board. But on her first day at college, the future loomed glossy and big. Stella tingled, giddy in the driver's seat as she and her mother bumped through a car wash.

With soapy spray all around them, Stella sang along with the radio.

"*She told me, don't worrrrrrry about it,*" she crooned, barely on pitch.

Her mother grinned, shaking her head.

Stella beat the steering wheel as she sang. "*She told me you'll never be in love [beat], oh [beat], oh [beat], woo!*"

Raising her fists, Stella wailed, "*I can't feel my face when I'm with you!*"

Hardly moving, with a shy smile, her mother sang quietly, "*But I love it. Yeah, I love it.*"

Laughing, without missing a beat, Stella warbled: "*I can't feel my face when I'm with you!*"

Her mother replied, *"But I love it. Yeah, I love it."*

The car wash ended, and they smiled all the way to the dorm, where her father eyed them suspiciously as they exited the car.

"What have y'all been up to?" he asked, amused by their lightheartedness.

"Good car wash," Stella said, winking at him.

At the door to her dorm room, her mother hugged her, and Stella closed her eyes, and they lingered, saying nothing.

Now, lying next to a skinny dog at the edge of a remote jungle, Stella fell asleep thinking of her mother, awakening only when her body once again convulsed with desperate need to poop and puke.

She squatted on a root again, moaning as her body clenched and contracted, pressing out every remaining drop of moisture.

The water from the muddy rivulet had sickened her, she assumed. She'd been so grateful to find it that she hadn't considered whether it could harm her.

Tentatively, she took a sip of the rainwater in her bottle, vomiting it back up immediately.

Again, a faint mechanical sound drew her gaze, and Dirty's, upward. Was the sound real?

Dirty's eyes flitted across the sky. If he heard the thing, surely she wasn't imagining it.

Could it be a really big bird? A pelican?

She scanned the horizon, the line of trees above her, saw nothing. The rhythmic thrumming amplified until she became certain… It had to be a helicopter.

Clumsily grabbing a tree trunk, Stella pulled up onto the foot still laced into its boot.

Face skyward, still as a grasshopper, she waited, waited, waited…

And then the helicopter burst around a bend at the end of the beach, soaring toward them.

Raising her arms, she waved, attempting to scream. Her cracked voice drifted into the waves.

The helicopter swooped toward her, as if the pilot knew exactly where she was, and then it was overhead, and she waved more vigorously, and Dirty barked and jumped, and then… the copter passed by, buzzing down the beach, not even slowing.

"God DAMMIT," whispered Stella, dropping to her hands and knees, exhausted. Her ankle screamed, the pain shooting through her entire body.

Dirty stood over her, sniffed the back of her neck.

She looked sideways up at him. "They were looking for me, right?"

The dog flopped down on the sand.

"Why didn't they see us?" She studied her surroundings. She and Dirty were perched at the edge of the tree line. Her clothes, muddy and muted, wouldn't stand out against the stand of trees. Nor would Dirty's mottled fur. The people in the helicopter didn't stand a chance of seeing her from that altitude, especially if they weren't specifically looking for her.

She beat a fist into the sand. "Fuck."

Still on hands and knees, she touched her forehead to Dirty's. "We gotta move out onto the beach."

Picking up her backpack, water bottle, shoe and sock, she crawled ten yards onto the sand, to the edge of the high-water mark. Dirty padded onto the oblong peninsula of sand jutting out into the ocean.

She rinsed her muddy yellow sweatshirt in the surf, waves carrying away whirling runnels of mud until the color started peeking through.

Squinting to minimize the harsh light on her pounding head, she cursed herself for forgetting to bring sunglasses on her goddamn day hike.

She spread her sweatshirt on the soft-sloping dune, yellow sleeves reaching wide in opposite directions. Not much brighter than the sand, the sweatshirt wouldn't provide a strong beacon, but it was better than nothing.

In the hard-packed beach, she punched her fingers several inches deep and drew her arm down to create a line. Sitting up, she assessed it—it was faint. There was no way that line would be seen from above.

She punched her fingers into the sand again, deeper, and scraped out the hard damp slush in handfuls, creating a deeper line. This one looked better. Maybe someone could see it from a helicopter. Maybe.

Dirty stood knee-deep in the ocean, waves grazing his belly as they rolled past him. He rocked with the motion of the water, staring at the horizon. This was his home.

Stella sketched out an "H" in the packed sand, as long as her body and nearly as wide. With that letter complete, she lay back, staring up at the harsh blue sky.

Dirty approached and lay next to her, facing the sea.

She would rest for a while before drawing the "E, L, P."

The helicopter would come back, right? Someone up there was looking for *her*? They wouldn't just take one pass over the beach and then give up? No, they wouldn't do that. They would come back.

The pounding sun pressed her into the sand, and she closed her eyes against the blinding force of it. Maybe this was the end, she thought, too exhausted to be disturbed by the possibility.

Reaching out her left arm, she draped it over Dirty's back and they listened to the sound of waves as she drifted toward a fitful sleep.

JUNGLE

Afternoon, Day Four

SOMETHING PRICKED STELLA'S skin through her jeans, rousing her from a heat-soaked dream.

Reaching into her pocket, she pulled out several broken pieces of a quarter-sized sand dollar. Her vision blurred as she slid her thumb over the smooth white surface of a fragment. It felt alien to her, this remnant of a long-dead animal from a world so different from the one she'd known for twenty-two years.

Stella had never spent much time at the ocean. Her mom didn't like sand or seawater, and the ocean was just far enough from Austin to keep her dad from taking her there for a weekend camping trip.

She'd gone to Corpus Christi with Garrett once, early in her senior year. They jumped in her old Honda Civic on a Friday morning, skipping their classes, grinning over burgers as they hurtled toward the sea. They told each other about their childhoods and hook-ups and vague career ambitions. Fresh out of college, Garrett was dabbling in finance, hating every moment of it, planning to make big money for a couple of years and then bail out of corporate America to travel the world.

At the beach in Corpus Christi, they'd rented surfboards, bobbing in the surf for two days. They tumbled awkwardly over the waves, laughing, and Stella quickly became more skilled than Garrett.

His dark brown mop of hair glinted in the salt spray, and he seemed so bright and alive that Stella wouldn't have believed it if someone told her he would launch headlong into his own destruction later that year.

On that weekend in Corpus Christi, her father's death had felt like less of a weight. She'd had the feeling that she could move past it with this man at her side. Sometimes she still missed *that* version of Garrett, the one that made her feel happy and confident. But that version of Garrett had disappeared in a puddle of methamphetamines.

Now, as the sun sapped away her last fumes of energy, Stella let all but one of the sand dollar fragments fall to the sand, running her index finger over the jagged broken edge of the last piece. She'd found the sand dollar last week as she walked the beach alone at sunset, jeans rolled up around her calves, waves licking her toes. She'd stopped walking to watch a group of surfers float on the still surface, unbothered by the lack of waves. At that moment, Stella hadn't known what she would do for dinner that night, or how long she would stay in Costa Rica, or where she'd find work when she got back to Texas. Looking down at her newly-callused "summer feet" as a wave washed over them, her eye had settled on a perfectly round white sand dollar, one of the smallest and roundest she'd ever seen. She'd tucked it in her pocket, hoping to rediscover it there sometime and remember that perfect moment.

Lying next to her, Dirty craned his neck to sniff the crumbled skeleton on the sand.

Stella turned her head to the side to look at him, and they gazed at each other. She'd never looked into anyone's eyes this long before—person or animal.

Cinching her eyes shut as another wave of nausea passed, Stella dropped the last sand dollar fragment and imagined her father standing over her on the beach, saying, *You look happy.* In her mind, she replied, *Dad, I'm half-dead and shitting my brains out.* Her dad smiled and said, *You'll be okay, Squirrel. He'll never leave you, you know.*

When Stella opened her eyes, Dirty still stared at her.

Shifting her body to lie on her side, she reached out to stroke his filthy head. "You won't leave me, will you, Dirty?"

He closed his eyes as she touched him.

The rising tide, cool and gentle, tickled Stella's toes. She lay still, counting the seconds between each wave.

Pelicans dove for fish just past the break.

Somewhere in the distance, the whirr of a helicopter purred over the jungle canopy, but didn't move closer. Stella couldn't see the copter, could barely hear it, but it was out there.

She willed it to come back toward them, visualized it touching down on the sand just over there, rescue workers pouring out onto the beach with bottles of water and food for Dirty.

The whirring faded.

She put a hand on Dirty's cheek. "You have to go find them, Dirty."

He stretched his face toward hers, resting it on the sand so that their noses nearly touched.

She raised her voice a touch: "Dirty, I want you to GO find them." Her eyes welled at the thought of watching him walk away from her, but she needed his help.

Dirty raised his head, seeming to understand that she was telling him to do something, but not understanding what it was.

He lowered his head back onto the sand, his nose wetting her cheek. He reached out a paw and touched her shoulder, and she took the paw in her hand. He let out a long, contented sigh.

She'd almost never felt this physically close to another being—not her parents, her boyfriends or girlfriends. Except Maria.

She and Maria used to be this close. Through high school, they rarely left each other's sides, spending weekends at each other's houses, sprawled shoulder to shoulder across their beds as they did homework, Stella tutoring Maria in grammar and Maria tutoring Stella in math.

By the time they graduated, the popular kids had stopped messing with them. Maria had honed a sarcastic wit that rivaled Stella's, but with a wilder edge. Nobody could out-insult them. The pretty girls kept their distance; boys and girls alike started flirting with them.

Only Stella's mother seemed not to understand the power and charm in her friendship with Maria. "You're so mean when you're together," she said to Stella one night, exasperated after picking her 17-year-old daughter up from the Principal's office.

"We are *not* mean," Stella retorted, dropping her black leather backpack on the kitchen table. "We defend ourselves from idiots."

Stella's mother took out a loaf of bread and slathered peanut butter on two slices, handing one to her daughter. "You told a girl to stick her head in her ass."

Stella folded the slice in half and took a bite, talking while she chewed, which made her mother roll her eyes. "Mom, what I was trying to tell you in Principal Nadler's office was that the bitch told me and Maria that we would both look better if we wore a little makeup."

Stella's mother sighed. "That's terrible. I'm sorry she said that, Stella. You're pretty girls, and nobody should..."

"Whatever," said Stella. "I'm not pretty and I don't give a shit. I gave up that dream a long time ago. Anyway, that girl goes, *Have you considered wearing a little makeup, you'd both look better if you put in a little effort*, and I said, *Have you considered sticking your head in your ass until you can think of something nice to say*?"

Stella's mom stifled a chuckle, then looked sadly out the window and said she had to go get groceries. She came back 30 minutes later with a bottle of gin and a bunch of bananas.

That was one of the few times Stella remembered making her mother laugh. Or, *almost* making her laugh. She'd made her father laugh a thousand times; a million, maybe. Her mother's sadness had always made her so inaccessible, like a different species sharing her living space.

Lying lost and withered on a beach in Costa Rica, she wanted to fold herself into her mother's sadness, feel her mother's melancholy arms around her. Together, they could mourn the world and its brutality.

Since her father's death, Stella had become obsessed with peering behind the curtain that shielded most people from the world's brutality. In college, one of the few subjects that interested her was psychology, which provided a telescope into the far reaches of the human soul. Her own soul felt mostly dead; she had allowed herself only a small range of emotions, aware even at the time that this was a coping mechanism designed to keep at bay the bottomless well of sadness and emptiness and anger that she felt toward her father for taking a hike during a goddamn flash flood.

Somehow, though, despite her own resistance to emotional expression, she was fascinated with the layered and complex and often tragic psyches of other people. As she ignored her own frailties, she studied those of others, learning how they moved through trauma, how they armored their weaknesses.

And as she pored over psychology textbooks, barely skating through college with an armful of B-minuses and Cs, she learned the lesson that so many college students take more seriously than any other: that an epic boozy night softens nearly every woe, but only for the duration of that epic night. Stella suffered greatly from the reality crash that came with hangovers, until her weekends became one long, epic night, in which she led her friends in raucous sing-alongs, and encouraged them to carry kegs into the forest so that they could keep drinking until dawn, or maybe until two-days-later dawn.

Probably, Stella would've ended up much like her own alcoholic mother if not for roller derby. In derby, she could dredge up that bottomless well of sadness and anger and bash her body around the court until the well's reserves seemed slightly less bottomless. After every match, Stella's body was bruised, but her mind felt a fraction less broken.

Now, her body and mind equally bruised, Stella scooted higher on the sand to escape the rising surf.

The hours ticked by in a lazy blur of swooping seagulls, crabs scuttling in and out of boreholes, Dirty's tongue licking cool on her cheek.

Her usually-pale skin stretched tight and hot over her face and arms, glowing red. Blisters cracked open her lips. Every once in a while, she turned on her side to dry-heave into the sand.

Late in the afternoon, Dirty wandered into the jungle, and she spoke softly to him as he walked away: "Come back soon."

She ran her hand through the sand, ring finger catching on something smooth and flat. Reaching under the exposed edge of the flat thing, she gently extricated a sand dollar and held it over her head. The edge of the disc jagged asymmetrically. Four small holes punctured the sand dollar near its edge, and one larger hole punched a dash just north of center. Straddling the dash, a perfect five-sided star was etched into the creamy surface. She shook her head, looking down at the fragments of the other sand dollar nestled into the sand, almost smiling at the coincidence of two sand dollars from different parts of Costa Rica colliding here on this brutal beach. How could such a thing of beauty exist in this harsh place? She tucked the small shell into her sagging bra where her small breast would cushion it, cool and scratchy on her skin.

Dirty returned sometime later with blood on his muzzle. Pausing to sniff her face, he wandered knee-deep into the ocean. A breeze lifted the edges of his short dark fur, and he opened his mouth, letting the breeze wash over his tongue, nose twitching.

As the sun dipped over the ocean, shadows sprouted from her propped-up knees, stretching toward the canopy behind her. Half-asleep,

Stella extended an arm toward the shadows, as if she might catch them and pull them over her like a blanket.

Dirty leapt to his feet, spraying sand on her face. Spitting, she opened her eyes to find the dog craning his face toward the sky.

"What is it, Dirty?" She reached out to touch him, ran her fingers along his fur, stubbled with sand.

The whirring sound rose again in volume. The helicopter was approaching.

She pushed to her feet, ankle buckling, forcing her to her knees. She squinted at the sky, unable to pinpoint the direction of the sound until it came bursting around a bend in the beach a couple hundred yards away, barreling toward them. Her eyes ached from the brightness of the sun.

She raised her arms, waving them frantically above her head. In front of her, the bottom of her "H" was melting into the waves. She'd never sketched the rest of the letters.

Barking wild, Dirty leapt repeatedly at the helicopter, like he might be able to pluck it from the air.

As it got closer, the chopper seemed to pick up speed, swooping down. It was going to land. They'd seen her. She threw her arms around Dirty, burying her face in his coarse fur.

Looking back up, Stella watched the helicopter swoosh directly overhead, her skin vibrating from the engine's thrum, hair lifting off her shoulders. She craned her neck as the aircraft soared past them. She expected it to start hovering lower, drift down onto the sand, but it flew high above the crashing tide until it rounded a bend in the coast and disappeared.

She shook her head, jaw hanging low, unsure what to say or think. What had happened? They'd seen her. Hadn't they? Could they have missed her? Were they flying too high?

She looked down at herself, covered in mud and sand. Could a flailing human blend in with the beach? Her heart crashed into her stomach.

Now out of her range of vision, she could still hear the helicopter's buzz. She strained to calculate its position. Was it receding? She didn't think so. If it were flying away from them, the sound would soon disappear. But there it was. The sound was not disappearing. Was it hovering?

She clenched Dirty's fur.

The dog stared in the direction of the vanished copter.

There, the engine slowed. Was it landing? Stella felt hopeful that it was landing. She rose to her feet again and lurched one step down the beach where it had disappeared.

Yowling, she fell to her knees, doubled over from exhaustion, and from the cramping in her stomach and the pain in her feet and ankles. She dry-heaved into the sand. She was going to shit herself.

Goddammit, she told herself. *Get the fuck up.*

She stood again, lurched two more steps down the beach before her ankle buckled and her bowels clenched furiously, forcing her to pull down her jeans and squat, swaying and dizzy.

She shook her head and beat a weak fist into the sand. "FUCK!"

Struggling to her knees to pull up her jeans, she fell back onto the sand and lay on her side, looking up at Dirty. She reached out to touch the right side of his face, and then the left, and looked him in the eyes. "Go get them, Dirty."

He licked her cheek, his tongue scraping off a layer of sand that clung to her skin.

Cupping his face again, she said more forcefully, "I need you to go GET them, Dirty."

He stared at her, frozen.

She cleared her throat, tears welling in her eyes. She could not let herself cry. As sternly as she could muster, she barked at him: "GO GET THEM, Dirty!"

He whined, looked down the beach, looked back at her, and lay down next to her.

Choking back a sob, she reached out to shove him away, forcing him to roll onto his side. "GO!," she yelled, her voice breaking.

He whined again, standing.

"GO, Dirty!" He leaned in to lick her face, but when he was an inch or two away, she yelled again, "GO!"

He looked toward the vanished helicopter, and back at Stella, and then ran down the beach.

As he loped away, she sobbed into the sand. For the first time in three days, she felt utterly alone.

Minutes passed. Or was it hours?

The copter's whirring disappeared, and now there was silence.

The waves stopped crashing; the sea was still. A sea bird alighted down the beach, pecking at the sand.

And then a dog barked.

Did she hear a dog's bark? Or had she conjured it, like her mother's call?

She began to lose hope, and then there it was again, a dog's bark, and voices, and the voices came closer, and closer, and then people were running down the beach, three or four of them, or maybe more, and she lay back on the sand, saved, and they were upon her, smiling, hugging her, saying things in heavily-accented English, like, "We so happy we found you," and "Your mother will be so happy. She is looking for you."

She recoiled from their touch, her body raw and fragile. Someone held a bottle of water to her mouth and she turned her face away, mumbling, "Sick.

Vomiting." People spoke in Spanish, and someone put an I.V. in her arm and loaded her onto a stretcher.

"The dog," she said to one of them, and the men ignored her, so she said it louder, "THE DOG!"

The men ignored her still and she flailed, dumping herself off the stretcher into the sand, yanking the I.V. from her arm. Wild, untethered, she looked around. Dirty wasn't there.

"WHERE IS THE DOG," she screamed, her voice broken but loud, overwrought.

She looked past the tight curtain of paramedics and saw Dirty behind one of them, struggling to make his way to her, tongue hanging out of his mouth, panting, straining.

One of the rescuers hissed at him, "Ccchhh," kicking him away. Another man yelled at the dog, "Vete, sal de aquí," and the men formed a barricade with their bodies so that Dirty couldn't get to her.

She crawled one step toward him before several hands yanked her backward, lifting her onto the stretcher, and she screamed, "Let me go!"

One of the men grimaced at Stella, wagged a finger at her and then at the dog, saying, "Dog diseased! Bad for you!"

She wailed at them, "Let him come to me!"

They shook their heads, kicked him away.

Dirty leapt at her, and a man grabbed him around the neck, holding him back.

Stella wept, pummeling anyone who neared her, and someone pulled out a syringe and stuck it in her arm, and everything went softy and blurry.

On the other side of the fray, a familiar form stood next to Dirty. Was that…? It was. Her father. He squatted, putting his hand on Dirty's back, and the dog calmed, stopped barking, stopped thrashing toward her. Her father winked at her, pulled the dog closer, gave her a sad smile.

He mouthed something—what was it? It looked like he had said, *I'll wait for you.* Is that what he had said?

She strained her hand toward him and yowled. "Dad!"

Through a whizzing morass of bodies, Dirty still held her eyes.

Fading into a tranquilized haze, Stella reached her free hand toward the dog. She tried to scream again, her voice slurred and fading: "He is *my dog*! You can't…"

And then she blacked out.

TEXAS
Day One

STELLA STARED AT the sand dollar on the bedside table: five cracked pieces reassembled into an asymmetrical circle. Someone had found it tucked into her bra in Costa Rica and preserved it for her. Worlds away, another unknown person had arranged it carefully next to her hospital bed in Texas. Maybe both of these people had seen the urchin as a talisman, a reminder of her good fortune, her miraculous survival. But for Stella, the sight of it conjured only horror and pain.

The horror rose like steam from her vivid memories of the jungle, still visceral and present.

And pain: her body ached with an existential sadness, a physical longing for Dirty. Only the agony of her father's death had hurt more than this.

She had awoken in Texas following a haze of helicopters and stretchers and hospitals and airplanes. During the six maddening days in Costa Rica post-rescue, she'd been sedated every time she'd tried to speak, to frantically tell paramedics and doctors and nurses and her mother that they had to go back, they had to find Dirty, she wouldn't leave Costa Rica without him.

Now Dirty was thousands of miles away, and Stella was in Austin, and she felt dead inside. She wanted to close her eyes and fall asleep for a month or a year or forever.

Physically, she'd improved tremendously. The doctors had debrided her blisters several times, and pumped her full of pain medications and antibiotics and anxiety pills and god knows what else. She was no longer nauseated, and ointments had been slathered repeatedly on her sunburns and scrapes.

Earlier that day, she'd grimaced through two hours of physical therapy, starting with ankle circles, then gritting her teeth as the therapist forced her to bend up her knees as she lay in bed, and put pressure on her feet, lifting her lower half off the mattress. Tomorrow, the physical therapist said, they would try to walk with a walker.

Stella's feet and ankle still throbbed, but less so than they had a few days ago when the pain meds still slow-dripped into her arm through an I.V. to control her full-body aches and thrashing pains. The ankle sprain and blisters were healing, the doctors told her, but it would be a few more weeks before she could walk without pain.

Scabby mosquito bites, some infected, splattered her arms and neck like chicken pox. She'd been given tubes of antibiotic ointment and itch cream; she and her mother had spent much of the last hour dabbing every bite.

Despite it all, despite the trauma and pain, all she wanted was to get up out of the bed and run on bandaged feet out of the hospital, straight to the airport, onto the first flight back to Costa Rica, back to Dirty.

But she didn't have the strength. She didn't have a fraction of the strength that would require. Her body had survived four days in the jungle, but now it was done.

She'd slept for most of the last week and had spoken little since awakening that morning.

Compassionate doctors and nurses had subjected her fuzzy brain to a barrage of questions. She responded with shrugs (Doctor: How many times did you vomit when you were in the jungle?" Stella: *Shrug*.), and monosyllables (Doctor: "Did you handle any wild animals?" Stella: "Hmh?" Doctor: "I heard you were with a stray dog. Did you touch him?" Stella, with tears in her eyes: "Yeah."). Most questions, she answered with "No" or "Yes" (Doctor: "Was there any blood in your urine or feces?" Stella: "No." Doctor: "Did you drink any dirty water"? Stella: Nodding, closing her eyes, "Yeah.").

These were not the questions that interested her.

Was Dirty okay? Was he alone? Had he returned to the jungle? Was he sad that she had disappeared? What was he doing *right now*? Was he waiting for her on the beach?

These were the questions that needed to be answered. These questions paralyzed her.

She pictured him standing knee-deep in the surf, breeze flicking through his mottled fur, dark brown eyes trained on the sky, waiting for her to return in the giant mechanical bird.

After the initial slew of medical questions, the debriefing commenced. Everyone on the hospital staff was eager to tell her what they'd heard about her rescue, her *miraculous* rescue; she was *so lucky* to be alive.

She learned that Dirty had approached the rescuers barking and leaping and one of them understood that Dirty was trying to communicate with them. He followed the dog, who galloped down the beach, looking back every few paces to make sure the man was still behind him. When the paramedic caught sight of Stella, he called to his colleagues, and they ran to her, and they saved her, and they left the nasty dog standing alone on the beach.

They left him. On the beach. Alone.

Stella's mother had held her hand through the doctors' questions and nurses' stories. When they were alone, her mother repeated over and that she loved Stella, that she'd been scared she would lose her, she had thought she'd never see her daughter again.

Stella couldn't remember her mother ever expressing so much emotion, so much love for her. Just seven days ago, wasting away on the beach, Stella had craved her mother's voice and touch, but now, those things exhausted her as much as everything else.

This morning, in the face of her mother's expression of love, which she had yearned for her whole life, she'd told her mom she loved her, but she was tired, she needed to sleep. She'd closed her eyes, willing the medications to take her back into the dream-space where she lay with Dirty on a soggy jungle floor.

Eventually, her mother had excused herself to let Stella rest. And Stella lay awake, wondering whether her memories were real. Had Dirty stood between her and a venomous snake? Had he scared off an anteater, and led her to water, and then to the beach? Had he lain with her on the sand, his face on her face, filling her with the naïve hope of an animal, willing her to get better?

She wouldn't have survived the jungle without Dirty. This seemed clear. Now, back in the sterile wilds of civilization, she still wasn't sure how to survive without him. He was the only being who understood what she'd been through. Only Dirty could comfort her now, and she crumbled inside wondering whether he longed for her comfort as well.

She stared out the hospital window into the constant growl of the highway. Dust floated in shapeless swirls through an oblong patch of light. All of it seemed like an affront. How could that highway, and that dust, and the pressed bed linens around her waist, exist in the same world as Dirty and the anteater and the impossibly turquoise water?

The door to the hospital room swung open and Stella's mother emerged under the fluorescent bulb holding two cans of Coca-Cola, her brown hair frizzed and messy, eyes drained, deep worried furrows etched into her forehead. Her waifish frame drowned in jeans a size too large and a blousy maroon t-shirt with some kind of stain on it. She looked older than her 47 years, and Stella felt the surprising urge to hug her, to clutch her mother's neck and cry.

In the corner, a silver balloon broke its tether and sailed up to the ceiling, flipping backward so Stella could no longer see its rainbow-colored imperative to *Get Well Soon!*

Sighing, Stella's mother shuffled across the room. With a wan smile, she sat in the chair by the bed and turned to look at the table crammed with flower bouquets and propped-up greeting cards.

Stella knew by the way her mother avoided looking directly at her that she must look terrifying.

She had avoided mirrors for six days. Everyone who saw her sighed with downturned eyebrows, and said things like, "Oh, honey."

Stella's mother stuck a straw in one of the Coke cans and held it up to her daughter's lips. Taking a sip, Stella moaned at the satisfying sweetness.

"Feeling any better?" Her mother looked desperate, lost for what to say, how to act.

Stella nodded, her voice raw, "A little."

Her mother waited for her to say something else. Anything else.

The *Get Well Soon!* balloon settled in the back of the room, pressing its face into a corner.

Stella closed her eyes and whispered, "I saw Dad out there."

Her mother let out a long slow breath.

Stella cleared her throat and opened her eyes. "He said he sent Dirty to me. The dog."

Stella reached up to place a cold hand on her neck. Her trachea—was that the name of the body part she breathed through?—ached, as if she'd been hard-coughing for days. Had she been coughing?

Her mother rubbed her eyes. Stella couldn't remember when she'd last seen her mother with no makeup on.

Something beeped down the hall, and they both turned toward the door.

"Stella…" Wiping a line of sweat under her eyes, her mother spoke in a broken whisper. "I know you wanted them to bring the dog, but they couldn't." She looked around the room as if searching for someone who could lift this explanation off her shoulders. "They... They couldn't put a wild animal in the helicopter. You were almost dead. They had to focus on *you*."

Stella turned toward the window. "I'm tired."

"I..." Putting down the Coke, her mother took her hand. "I love you, Stell."

Her mom's thin fingers felt soft, the structure of them both foreign and familiar. Their hands were so mismatched; Stella's was smaller, more thick-fingered. Bloody scratches, dried maroon and purple, crisscrossed her hand and arms. Several of the knuckles on her right hand were swollen, aching when she moved. She had no memory of injuring them.

At the end of her mother's pale fingers, her yellowing nails looked overlong. They needed a trim. On the back of her hand, a vein snaked its way through skin that was just starting to sag. Her mother's fingers twitched, tugging Stella toward memories from many years ago. How long had it been since they'd held hands?

She squeezed her mom's fingers. "I love you too, Mom."

With her free hand, Stella's mother pinched the skin on her opposite elbow. When she opened her mouth, she paused and then said, "I'm... sorry I haven't been a good," her voice broke, and she swallowed, "mother."

Stella closed her eyes. For years she had longed for this apology, had imagined this conversation, exactly what her mother would say. She'd imagined how she would ask her mother why she was always so sad, and her mother would open up to her and tell her all the things that had hurt her, and they would hug and feel closer than ever. But now her mother's sincere apology felt sad and heavy, adding darkness to a moment already so dark that Stella could hardly imagine a way through it.

"It's okay, mom." She wanted to be alone, wanted to pull her hand back, but instead ran a finger along her mother's thumb. "I know how hard it was for you, losing Dad."

Her mother sighed, attempting a smile. "It was harder than I…" Her voice trailed off.

Stella drew her mother's arm closer. "Do you think there's some way I could, maybe, get Dirty? The dog? Get him back here?"

Looking down at her lap, her mother licked her lips and took a deep breath.

Stella lifted her mom's hand an inch off the bed, squeezed harder. "Mom?"

Her mother gently extracted her hand and stood, smoothing her t-shirt in three downward strokes, adjusting it on each side to make sure it hung symmetrically. "Let's talk about it later. I'll go find us some food."

Turning toward a bouquet of lilies, her mom fiddled with a long white petal, bending it down and out. She spoke to the flower, "Stell, some reporters wanted to interview you for the local TV news, and I didn't know what to…"

"No," Stella said, lying back, closing her eyes. The thought of doing an interview enraged her. She would not brush her hair and put on makeup and recount her harrowing tale for a bunch of reporters who just wanted to use her trauma to make themselves slightly more D-list famous. "No reporters," she said, "I just want to sleep."

TEXAS

Day Two

STELLA JERKED UP in bed with a gasp, realizing that she'd been dreaming, and Dirty was not standing over her in the sand, licking her cheek.

It made no sense, this nostalgia for the worst moment in her life. Nobody would understand it. Maybe it was some symptom of the PTSD that doctors kept talking to her about. Her mother found her nostalgia troubling at best. At worst, Stella's wistfulness for her near-death experience might signify some sort of mania or psychosis.

Slumped into the uncomfortable armchair, her mother opened her eyes. She gripped the chair's wooden arms, sweat dripping down her long forehead and neck despite the chill in the room. "You okay, Stell?"

Stella wiped her face, pulling the blanket up to her armpits. "I want to do that TV interview. Today."

Her mother straightened her posture and fiddled with her naked ear lobes. "Are you sure? You're okay with cameras?"

Stella nodded. "Yes. I want to do it. Do you know who to call?" "I do." Standing, her mother pulled a clump of business cards from the back pocket of her oversized jeans and rifled through her frayed navy purse. "I'll go call the reporter. Will you be okay for a few minutes alone?"

As Stella's mother fished a phone out of her bag, their eyes met, and they both quickly looked away.

"Yeah." Stella sank back on her pillow. "Thanks."

Her mother slipped out the door, and Stella looked around the room. Should she check herself in a mirror? Did she want to know what she looked like? She rarely looked in mirrors anyway—since she was a tween she'd called them "confidence murderers."

She knew she looked rough. Since she was going to be on camera, she was curious just *how* rough. Lifting her arms into the cold hospital air, she assessed her scabs and bruises. If she did a TV interview, she'd have to wear a long-sleeved shirt.

She ran her fingers through her hair, trying to remember whether it had been washed since she got back to Texas.

Should she wear makeup for the interview? Should she have her mother go home to pick up her roller derby makeup bag? Or would makeup just draw attention to her morbid face?

Maybe the interview was a mistake.

No, she had to do this.

Swinging her feet over the side of the bed, she placed her stronger foot onto the cold hospital floor, grunting. Pain shot through the blisters on her toes and radiated through her body.

Balancing a hand on an I.V. pole, she tentatively shifted herself into the wheelchair by her bed. She breathed hard as she wheeled herself across the room and pushed open the bathroom door. Reaching up with one hand, she yanked down the towel that had been hung over the mirror at her request, and drew in a sharp breath.

Her face still swelled red, making her look puffy despite her drawn, hungry cheeks. Bloated eyelids gave her already-small eyes a squinty appearance. Raw lips nearly disappeared into her sunburned face, skin peeling in patches. Mosquito scabs had dried into irregular bumps and dents. Her hair appeared to have been brushed and washed, though it hung stiffly from so many hours flattened against a pillow.

Putting on makeup would only make her look more like a monster. She'd have to do this interview au naturel. People would pity her, and there was little that made her more uncomfortable than pity.

Reaching into her toiletry bag, she pulled out a hair band. As she raised her hands above her head to pull her hair back, pain shot through her right shoulder and bicep. Why was her arm so sore?

She twisted her dark hair into a pony tail. Slight improvement; not much.

Slathering Vaseline on her lips and aloe moisturizer on her face, she closed her eyes, relieved by the cool wetness.

Outside the bathroom, the door to the hospital room opened and closed and her mother called out, "Stell, what are you doing?"

Jogging into the bathroom, her mother tried not to wince when she saw her daughter looking in the mirror.

"Your hair looks nice like that," her mother said flatly, grabbing the handles on the wheelchair. She rolled her daughter across the room and helped her back into the bed.

Exhausted, Stella lay back. She wouldn't look in the mirror again until she got home from the hospital. She forced a smile. "Could you please put the towel back over the mirror, Mom?"

"Of course." With a sigh, Stella's mother pulled the sheet and blanket up over Stella's legs. "Do you want me to put on the television?"

"Sure."

As her mom leaned over to tuck in her daughter's blanket, the shirt fell away from her chest, and Stella saw her mother's clavicle and ribs, protruding pitifully from her torso. Too skinny, like Dirty.

Stella took another sip of her Coke and pretended to watch television while her mind scrolled through every moment she'd had with Dirty. She tried to conjure the smell of him, the feel of him. She wanted to sear the memories into her brain before their edges blurred from time and distance.

Late in the afternoon, as Stella was recovering from another physical therapy session—slightly less excruciating than the day before—a tidy blonde reporter breezed into the room with a lipsticky smile and a green silk blouse that called attention to her piercing turquoise eyes. A shaggy cameraman followed the reporter around, going to great lengths to avoid looking directly at anyone.

"Stella, hi!" The reporter shook Stella's hand delicately, plum lips arching into a polished smile. She didn't flinch at Stella's wounds. "I'm so happy to meet you! I'm Theresa."

"Hi." Stella scrutinized the lines under Theresa's eyes. She must be in her late 30s, already Botoxed. She had the air of someone desperate to be perfect and charming, no matter whether her husband had called her fat last night, or her cat had just died, or her child had refused to eat breakfast.

Theresa moved the empty wheelchair away from the bed and pulled up a chair, gesticulating toward the cameraman. "Can you get both of us in the shot if I sit here? Do we look good?" She winked at Stella, as if she cared whether Stella looked good. As if Stella *could* look good.

Stella's mother leaned in to pull the blanket up a touch higher, covering the nipples that pressed through her daughter's long-sleeved t-shirt.

In a flurry of movement, studio lights were erected, making Stella squint, and then the cameraman was poised and ready, and Theresa presented all her teeth. "I'm here with Stella Raiman, who survived *four days* in the Costa Rican jungle by herself. Stella, thank you for sharing your story with us. We're all *so happy* that you survived."

She leaned in and touched Stella's arm. "Tell me, how did you get lost? Why did you leave your group? What was it like out there? And how are you feeling now? If you don't mind, please include the questions in your answers, like, *I left my group because… Does that make sense?*"

Stella struggled not to pull her arm away from Theresa's manicured fingers.

Steeling herself, she answered the questions succinctly, giving just enough details to keep a viewer engaged. She was feeling better, she said, aside from her feet and ankle. She left her group because she had twisted her ankle. Her guide told her to wait on the trail, and another guide was supposed to come and get her, but the other guide never showed up, and a creepy-looking man with a machete appeared out of nowhere, and she wanted to get away from him, so she decided to hike back to the trailhead by herself.

She told Theresa how the jungle swallows people because everything looks the same, and she couldn't tell which direction she'd come from, and then it got dark, and she'd been terrified.

Theresa nodded, pouting, touching Stella's arm repeatedly and occasionally murmuring, "Mmmmh…"

Her plum lipstick glistened in the lights, and she tilted her sculpted eyebrows inward. "Were you afraid you weren't going to survive, that first night in the jungle?"

This was the moment. The reason for doing this interview. Stella resisted the urge to scratch a mosquito bite on her forearm. "Yeah, I was really scared. But then a stray dog found me. He protected me for three days. He saved my life."

Theresa's eyes went wide. "A dog? Like a wild dog? What do you mean, *he protected you?*"

Barely taking a breath, Stella spilled the story: She called the dog Dirty, and he stopped her from stepping on a huge snake, and he scared off some kind of anteater, and he brought her a fish when she was starving, and he guided her to water after two days drinking almost nothing, and he led her to the beach, and then it was Dirty who brought the rescuers to her, and then they *left him* on the beach, refused to bring him back, and all she wanted now was to find him, he wouldn't survive for very long out there, he was so skinny and had sores all over him, and he needed her, she needed him, they had survived together, and now she couldn't imagine her life without him, and she was hoping somebody could find him for her.

Tears washed down Stella's face. She was embarrassed to be crying *on television*, but this was her story. Her story was shitty and sad, and if anything could help her save Dirty, it was telling this shitty sad story.

Theresa dabbed at the corners of her eyes with her pinky. She asked Stella what Dirty looked like, and whether she'd touched the dog, and did he seem like a *pet* dog, and did he try to get on the helicopter?

Yes, Stella said, he acted like a pet dog, but no, he didn't seem to belong to anyone. And yes, he had tried to get on the helicopter, but the rescuers, who Stella was so grateful for, really, but they kicked Dirty, they treated him like a rat, not like a hero. Which is what he was.

Theresa cleared her throat, and it seemed like she was struggling to keep herself composed.

Stella wondered if Theresa had a dog, and wanted to ask, but this wasn't the time.

Sighing, Theresa took Stella's hand, and again Stella almost flinched. But the reporter's eyes were kind and compassionate.

"So what are you going to *do*? Are you going to *go back* to the jungle where you *nearly died*, to find him?" Her inflection on those last words made it clear how outrageous, how impossible, this notion sounded.

"No." Stella shook her head, desperate to scratch the mosquito bite. She wanted the interview to be over. "I don't think I can go back there. I just know I need to find him. I… I don't know how yet. Maybe I can hire someone to find him for me."

She was tired. Still, so tired.

Theresa must have noted Stella's fatigue. She released her hand and touched her lightly on the shoulder. "You're incredibly brave, and everyone is very glad you survived. Thank you for talking to us, and I hope you find the dog."

Theresa looked at the cameraman. "I think we have what we need."

Again, she touched Stella's hand. "Let us know if there's anything we can do to help. Take care of yourself."

Stella's chin trembled. "Thank you."

TEXAS

Day Three

STELLA'S HEART RACED as she dialed Alé's number.

His voice strained through the crackly connection: "Taxi Dominical…"

"Alé?" she said, suddenly conscious of her limited ability to speak Spanish. She couldn't possibly figure out how to say what she needed to say. "Es Stella."

"Oh, Stella! Mija!" His voice vibrated, harboring none of the fragility with which everyone else seemed to speak to her. He rattled off something in Spanish, and Stella couldn't make out any of it.

She responded in English. "Alé, I'm sorry if you were worried about me. You may have already heard, but I was lost in the jungle for four days. I met a dog in the jungle and I need to find somebody to go back and get him."

His voice dipped in and out. "Can you say that again? We have a very bad connection. What did you say?"

"Alé, I'm sorry. I will send a translated text, okay?"

"Si, mi amiga! That is a good idea. Send me a text."

Stella wished Alé were there with her, in Texas.

Google helped her translate a series of texts:

Alé, I've missed you. I'm sorry if you were worried about me. You may have already heard, but I was lost in the jungle for four days. You were right—I should have listened to you—I never should have left my guide. I was very, very stupid. You tried to warn me. Anyway, I survived and now I'm back home in Texas. The ordeal was incredibly shitty, but I survived because I met a dog who protected me. I named him Dirty. He saved my life, and when they rescued me, they wouldn't let him on the helicopter. I know this sounds crazy, but I need to find him. I will pay someone to find him. Whatever it takes, I will pay it. He'll probably be near where they picked me up, which I think was on the west coast of Corcovado. Do you know how I can find out where they rescued me? Do you know anyone who could help me find him? Dirty is about thirty pounds, I think. He has brown fur with dark spots on it. He looks a little like this dog that I found on the Internet, except that Dirty is much skinnier, and his ears flop forward at the edges:

Staring at the photo, she catalogued the ways in which Dirty was different: in addition to Dirty's floppy ears, his fur was a little longer and a little darker, and the white patch under his chest was bigger. Could this photo possibly lead anyone to him? There couldn't be more than one stray dog who looked like this on the west coast of Corcovado, could there?

Surely, with enough resources, Dirty could be found. She still had almost four thousand dollars left from her dad's "death money," although the idea of spending it nagged at her. Her mother had spent a small fortune looking for her—she wouldn't say how much—and Stella felt like she should use her inheritance to pay her mother back.

But her mother wouldn't allow it. "That's *your* money."

That didn't feel right to Stella. "But you used *your* money to find me."

Her mother had touched her daughter's cheek. "Stella, I haven't been a good mother to you, and there's nothing I can do about that. Let me do this one thing for you. Your father left me some money too, and this is how I want to spend it. We won't discuss this again."

Stella laid her phone on the bedside table and examined her arms and legs. The mosquito bites and scratches looked better than yesterday. The bruises on her knuckles were fading to a sickening palette of browns and yellows.

Today, for the first time, she'd eaten a full meal: chicken and potatoes and broccoli with some kind of disgusting cheese sauce on it. The doctors said her kidneys and liver were mostly back to normal.

Only her feet and ankle still racked her with pain, even when she used crutches. The doctors said she'd have to use the crutches and wear soft slippers and an ankle brace for a couple weeks.

Her phone buzzed with a translated text from Alé:

Thank God you're safe! I know some people who might be able to help. I will talk to them.

Her face flushed. Alé would figure out how to find Dirty. He used to work as a guide in Corcovado—he knew the area as well as anyone in Costa Rica. Maybe he could talk to the local authorities out there and find out the exact coordinates where she was rescued. And Dirty would be waiting there for her, she felt certain. Or mostly certain.

She closed her eyes, picturing him there, standing just under the tree line, his black eyes looking out onto the camel-colored sand.

Waiting for another text, Stella clutched her phone, checking the screen every two minutes.

TEXAS

Day Four

"IDIOTS." STELLA SCROLLED through the comments beneath her news story on the station's website.

"*I knew Stella in high school.*" said *LaceyManillo<3*, "*She has lost a ton of weight, she looks fit and strong, I'm not surprised she survived! We love you, Stella!*"

"Lacey Manillo is a bitch." She glanced at her mother, who was also scrolling through comments on her phone.

Her mother peered up over her reading glasses. "But most of the comments are supportive, right? "

Someone knocked at the door, and her mother looked up quizzically, as if uncertain what to do.

Stella shrugged and called out: "Come in."

A thick, mousy girl cracked the door, poking her peach-colored glasses through the opening, thin brown hair tumbling into her face so she had to reach up a hand awkwardly and brush it away. She looked terrified.

"I'm Kelsey?" she said, as if asking a question. "From Austin Pets Alive? I'm doing hospital visits and we saw you on the news, and thought you might want a visit from one of our therapy dogs? The nurse said it would be okay…"

Stella looked around the room, confused. A dog? Here? Was that legal? She took in a sharp breath, forced herself not to cry. Did she *want* to see a dog that wasn't Dirty?

Kelsey paused, and then started to retreat. "If you don't want to see her, I can…"

Blood rushed to Stella's face and she put down her phone, grabbing the bed's side-pole. She swung her feet over the edge of the bed. "No, it's okay… You can bring the dog in."

She looked back to see her mother clutching her chair's arms, eyes wide, as if Stella had invited a firing squad into the room.

Kelsey pushed the door open and a tan and white pit bull pushed past her, wagging a stubby tail. The dog's bright blue eyes were framed by a tan patch on the left side of her face, and a white patch on the right.

At the sight of the dog, Stella dropped to the floor, grunting from the pain in her feet and ankle. Sitting on the cold tile, she held out her arms.

The dog rushed toward her, red leash flopping behind. Stella wrapped her arms around the dog, burying her head in the animal's neck.

Kelsey's voice squeaked down quietly over them. "That's Coffee. She's a girl."

Coffee didn't smell like Dirty, and her fur was shorter, a different texture, much softer. But something in the heft of her, the shape and feel, felt familiar. As Stella hugged Coffee, her tail wagged so forcefully that she nearly knocked both of them to the ground.

Stella smiled, and her throat swelled. She breathed hard so that she wouldn't cry.

Kelsey reached for the leash, started to pull Coffee off of her. "Sorry, she's is really energetic."

The dog jumped up and put both front paws on Stella's shoulders.

She smiled up at Kelsey. "Don't be sorry. I like it."

"She's three. Years old," squeaked Kelsey. "She's been at the shelter for almost two years and we don't understand why she hasn't been adopted. She's so sweet and smart, and she's everybody's favorite, and we even trained her as a therapy dog. She loves it."

Stella locked eyes with the dog. "Hi, Coffee."

Her mother approached from behind and squatted next to Stella, putting a hand awkwardly on the dog's head, and then quickly retracting it. "Hello, Coffee," she said.

Stella reached out and rested a hand on her mother's knee. As she scratched behind Coffee's ears, the dog pressed her body into Stella's, still wagging.

Taking a step backward, Kelsey said, "Me and my coworkers, we're all so sad that they didn't let Dirty come back with you. We, um, wish we could help."

Stella's hands stopped moving along Coffee's back. "Yeah, me too."

Kelsey stooped and placed one hand on Coffee's head. With the other, she nudged her glasses higher on the bridge of her nose. "Are you going to, like, hire someone to find her?" She tucked her hair behind her ears.

Stella braced her hands on the cold floor and pushed herself up on one painful foot, balancing her backside on the bed.

"I'm trying," whispered Stella.

Coffee's body bobbed around Stella's knees. She stuck her head under Stella's hand, reminding her not to stop petting.

Stella sat back on the bed, one hand tickling the top of Coffee's head, and looked into Kelsey's spectacled eyes. "I know it sounds crazy since I knew him for three days, but I can't imagine living without him. I have this feeling that he needs me."

Kelsey spoke so quietly that Stella could barely hear her. "That doesn't sound crazy. Everyone at APA gets it. I hope you find him."

"Thank you." With one hand, Stella wiped her eyes while the other moved back and forth on Coffee's head. For over a week, nobody other than Theresa had really *heard* her, or understood how important it was for her to find this feral creature who had saved her life, who was at that moment struggling to survive. But this mousy girl, seemingly terrified of speaking to another human being—she understood it easily.

She pulled Kelsey in for a hug, and the girl reached around to pat two tense hands on Stella's back.

Bending over, Stella kissed Coffee's head and neck, closing her eyes as she pressed her face into the dog's fur.

Kelsey picked up Coffee's leash; Stella didn't want to let the dog go.

"People at APA want to meet you, and hear more about Dirty, if you wanted to, like, come by." Kelsey wrapped the leash around her fist twice, then three times, as if she was afraid Coffee might bolt away from her and tear down the hospital hallway.

"Come by where?" Wincing, Stella raised her right foot off the floor and rested it on the bed.

Unsure where she wanted to go, Coffee tugged left and right, jerking Kelsey like an unruly kite. "The shelter? Austin Pets Alive? It's on Cesar Chavez, downtown. If you want."

Stella nodded. "I'd like that."

With a string of apologies, Kelsey announced that she had to get Coffee back to the shelter.

Stella looked into the dog's eyes, searching for reminders of Dirty, and gave her one more scratch behind the ears. "Bye, Coffee. Thank you for bringing her, Kelsey."

Stella waved them out the door. When the room went quiet, she sat for a beat in silence and then turned to her mother. "Do you not want me to get him back?"

Her mother let out a tired sigh. "Stella, it's not that I don't *want* you to get him back. It's just…" She looked out the window. "I don't want you to get hurt. If they can't find him, it'll break your heart, and you don't need that right now. And, I know you—if nobody down there can find him, you'll go back to find him yourself. You'll go back to that place that almost took your life."

Her mother dabbed her eyes with her fingertips. "I can't *lose* you, Stella. I can't lose *both* of you."

"This isn't *about* you, Mom." Stella clenched the edges of her pillow.

Down the hall, someone yelled something, and footsteps slapped down the hallway, and several voices raised in a chaotic mash. A hospital door opened and slammed shut, and the voices disappeared.

Her mother stared limply at the floor.

Stella scooted a few inches away from her. "Dirty is the first *good* thing that's happened to me since Dad died."

Her mom took an unsteady breath and shook her head, still looking at the floor. "I should've been there for you."

The wheels of a gurney squeaked past the room, and a nurse barked something about an operating room.

Stella took her mother's hand. "What *happened* to you, Mom? You were so sad, even before Dad died. I don't remember you ever *not* being sad."

Her mother stared vacantly at the balloon hiding in the corner. "A lot of things have happened to me in my life, Stell. A child shouldn't know all her mother's troubles. A child just needs to know a mother loves her, and I'm afraid I didn't give you that when you needed it. But I did, you know. I always loved you. I still love you."

"I know, Mom." Stella's feet were cold, despite the bandages. Still sitting on the edge of the bed, she reached behind her and pulled the blanket off the mattress, wrapping it around her shoulders.

"I tried." Clearing her throat, Stella's mother reached over awkwardly to help her daughter drape the blanket around herself. "I tried to tell you I loved you. It was hard for me to say things out loud, so I left you notes in your lunchbox and things like that. Do you remember that?"

Stella squinted at her, confused. "In sixth grade? *Those* notes in my lunchbox? Those were from Dad. It was his handwriting."

Her mother nodded, avoiding her eyes. "Yes, well, you responded to him better at that age. At every age, really. So I would tell him what to write and he would write the notes."

Stella's jaw dropped, and she wondered whether it would've made a difference if she'd known her mother was writing those notes.

"And Dad just *did* it? He didn't think it was weird to be writing the notes for you? And taking the credit?"

Her mother's voice trembled, and she looked down at her hands. "Your dad thought the notes were a good idea, and I made him promise not to tell you they were from me. I thought if you knew, you would…" She twisted the skin on her knuckles. "Now I wish I'd written them myself."

"Me too." Stella lay back on her bed, needing more physical space between herself and her mother. "I can't abandon Dirty, Mom. He needs me."

Her mother traced a circle in the floor tile with the toe of her sandal. "Do you really think *he* needs *you*? Or are you just projecting your own needs onto him?"

Stella wiped her face softly, letting her fingers trace the scabby scrapes and scars. "You should've seen him, Mom. He was so skinny, I don't know how he lived as long as he did. He won't live for much longer. I can't leave him like that."

Her mother looked up, the dark circles under her eyes catching a shadow. "He's just a dog, Stella."

Stella grunted and shook her head. "He's *not*, though. Or, if he is *just* a dog, then dogs are a lot more valuable than people give them credit for."

Fiddling with her fingernails, her mother mumbled, "I didn't even think you liked dogs."

"I didn't." Stella shrugged, anger bubbling up inside her. She wanted the conversation to be over. "Dad tried to get me on the dog train, but I didn't listen to him. I wish I could meet Torres now. It would be so different…" Her voice trailed off and she chewed the inside of her cheek. "I won't be happy without him, Mom."

The air conditioner kicked on overhead, and her mother looked at the ceiling, locating the vent. She stood and walked over to stand beneath it, letting the cold air blow down over her. "I'm going to go get a soda. Do you want one?" Stella didn't hear the question. She was thinking about her father, squatting next to Dirty as she was shoved onto the helicopter.

I'll wait for you.

Her mother still stood below the air conditioner, waiting for her daughter's to answer the soda question.

Stella contemplated a brown stain on the ceiling, next to the vent. "Dad really did send him to me."

"Stella…" Her mom shook her head.

Stella closed her eyes. "You don't have to believe me, but I am 100% sure that I'm right."

TEXAS

Day Five

SUN SIFTED THROUGH the thin curtain hanging in Stella's childhood bedroom, glowing around the silhouette of the red cherry tree patterned into the fabric. In seventh grade, she had begged her parents to buy that curtain along with the matching comforter and pillows. She'd promised that if she could have them, she'd wear skirts to church for the rest of the year. Now, she couldn't imagine why she'd cared so much about curtains and bed linens. In the end, she'd worn skirts to church for three weeks and then reverted back to jeans, and then stopped going to church altogether.

Posters of Jay-Z and Coldplay, curled at the edges, clung unenthusiastically to the walls. The air still smelled vaguely of patchouli, a reminder of her regrettable hippie phase.

This room, it felt so familiar, comforting in its anachronistic awkwardness. She had outgrown the room, but she couldn't imagine going anywhere else. Not right now.

She wasn't interested in finding a job, or going to her favorite restaurants, or reconnecting with people. Several friends had stopped by in the past few days, but she'd asked her mother to tell them that she wasn't ready for visitors.

She had even turned away her roller derby teammates, her rough-edged pack of soulmates. They'd texted every day asking to visit, but she'd told them she'd be ready for visitors "soon, but not yet," because she looked like a bucket of shit in a tornado, and she wasn't good company anyway, because all she wanted to talk about was Dirty, all she could think about was Dirty, and nobody wanted to talk endlessly about a dog they'd never met, with a girl who was broken in body and soul.

She wanted to allow her teammates back into her life, she really did, but she couldn't be her old self around them. They were all so badass and cool. Complicated and troubled like all other human beings, sure. But their motto was strength and their synergy was palpable. This was why she'd craved their company from the moment she'd met them. But now, in her broken state, she felt like the friendship she could offer them would be inadequate. Right now, she couldn't muster even a hint of *badass* or *cool* or *"Derby Strong."*

Stella held her arms up in the milky light, examining the mosquito scars. Most of the scabs had healed and fallen away, the redness softening to pink, itching gone completely.

She stretched her sore limbs and swung her feet over the side of the bed, sliding her socked feet into fuzzy red slippers and tucking a crutch under her right armpit. On bandaged feet, she crutched through the house to the back yard, sitting in a squeaky rusted chair. Beneath the live oak tree, dappled light shifted over the scrubby ground.

Stella closed her eyes sunward, breathing in the hot summer air.

Her mother emerged from the kitchen carrying a sandwich—smoked turkey with Swiss and brown mustard—and a bottle of Stella's favorite beer, Shiner Bock.

"Thanks," Stella said, surprised that her mom knew what her favorite beer was. "You gonna have a beer with me?"

"I don't like beer, Stella, you know that." Joining her at the table, her mother smoothed down her t-shirt, sucking in her slim, middle-aged belly.

Stella flipped off the cap of the beer. "You gonna have a Tom Collins?"

At 4PM every day during Stella's childhood, her mother would wander into the backyard to sit at the wrought iron table, thumb and forefinger gripping a sweaty rocks glass. Usually she sat alone, checking her phone until her husband arrived home, which sometimes didn't happen until late at night. After those late nights, her parents often didn't speak for a day or two. On the days Stella's father got home early from work, he would join his wife in the backyard while she drank her Tom Collins, saying little, occasionally reaching over to take her hand.

"I… no, I don't think so." Her mother waved two fingers through the air as if gently shooing a fly.

They sat quietly, and Stella pictured herself on that beach, shitting herself on the last day in Costa Rica. She nudged her thoughts toward Dirty. Nothing else comforted her but Dirty. Dirty. Dirty. She couldn't stop thinking about him. Her gut punched at her, telling her that he was not okay. The thought pulled like gravity.

Car wheels squealed around a corner at the end of the block, and Stella grabbed her crutch, pushing up from the table. "Maria's here."

As she crutched around the side of the house, a convertible Jeep screamed into the driveway.

Maria threw open the door while she was shifting the gear into *park* and plunked her left foot onto the pavement before the vehicle stopped moving. Without closing the car door, she tore across the lawn and threw her arms around Stella, nearly knocking her backward.

"I'm so sorry I couldn't come sooner!" Maria huffed in Stella's ear, too loudly. "They told me they would fire me if I left before that presentation yesterday, and this job was just so hard for me to get and I…"

"Ri-ri, stop." Stella tugged her friend closer. "You called me six hundred times in the hospital. And now you're here."

Maria pulled back, clutching Stella's shoulders so she could give her an up-and-down look. "Where is the rest of you, Stell? Did you leave it in the jungle? You're too skinny! We need to get you some French fries, right now. Do you want to go to HopDoddy's?"

Stella laughed, wondering when she'd last done so. Maria made everything feel more manageable.

"That sounds amazing, but I'm not hungry, and I'm pretty tired. Soon?" Stella kissed her friend's cheek, raising an eyebrow at her friend's outfit. "And, um, since when can you afford Rag and Bone jeans? Are you a rich person now? And if so, what's in it for me?"

"Listen," said Maria, kicking her car door closed and looping her elbow through Stella's. "If I'm going to work sixteen hours a day at this stupid finance job so I can make some serious cash, the least I can get out of it is some nice jeans, no?"

As they hobbled toward the house, the sun shone on Maria's slick black ponytail, and Stella leaned into her friend's shoulder. "Love you, Ri."

Inside, Maria shuttled her friend to a stool at the kitchen island. "Sit down, girl. You gotta eat. Did Marsha buy any groceries before you got home from the hospital?"

Stella raised her eyebrows. "Ri, not only did she buy groceries, I haven't seen her drink a Tom Collins since I got back to Texas." Maria pursed her lips. "We'll see if that holds."

Opening the refrigerator, she gawked at the milk and cheese and watermelon and bread. She opened the crisper. "*Lettuce*? Marsha bought *lettuce*? Dios mío, this is a month of miracles."

She pulled out a block of cheese, peeling back the wrapper and slicing a heaping pile onto a salad plate, which she plopped onto the laminate countertop. "Eat, woman. You look like you're on a hunger strike."

Stella reached over to pinch Maria's bony butt. "You're one to talk."

"Eat," Maria commanded, pointing at the cheese. "Anyway, you know I would trade my goddamn Crohn's Disease for your juicy ass. You probably only survived out there because your body lived off of that juicy ass for four days. Now you gotta build it back up in case you get lost again. You might not be so lucky next time."

"I missed you," said Stella, picking the corner off a piece of cheese.

Maria pulled two Shiner Bocks from the refrigerator and handed one to Stella "Even when you were out there getting eaten by lions and shit?"

Giggling, Stella nearly spit out the cheese. "Especially when I was getting eaten by lions and shit."

"Listen." Maria pulled up a stool and sat down next to Stella, opening her beer and drilling in with her black eyes. "I gotta tell you something. This is serious, okay?"

Pulling on a serious expression, Stella put down her beer and took her friend's hand. "Tell me something serious." Maria licked her teeth. "You gotta find a way to get that dog back here."

Blood rushed to Stella's cheeks. "Ri, I'm trying. I asked my friend to help me hire someone to go find him, but so far I haven't..."

Squeezing Stella's knuckles so hard she winced, Maria said, "No, listen, I'm serious. You have got to get that dog. My grandma Maritza had a dream about him, and you would not believe what she said about that dream. She wants me to bring you to see her so she can tell you about it."

Stella shivered. "Whoa. Yes, please. Maritza's one of the few people I could tolerate right now."

When Stella had met Maritza in middle school, the tiny old lady looked a hundred years old. Ten years later, she still looked a hundred years old, but she was as fiery as her Chihuahua, and just as hard to argue with.

And Maritza talked to dead people. Not in a fraudulent, desperate way. She legitimately believed that she could have full-fledged conversations with dead people. They spoke to her using their human voices and vocabularies, and they gave her very specific comments and instructions to pass along to living loved ones. Like when dead old Dolores said to "tell that bitch Juliana that I know she's sleeping with my husband, and I regret that I ever called her my best friend." Nobody had known about Juliana and Carl until Dolores busted them from the other side. After Maritza passed along the message, Juliana broke up with Carl and never spoke to him again.

Stella took a sip of beer, closing her eyes as it slid down her throat. "Does she still have that crazy dog?"

"Yeah." Maria shoved a piece of cheese in her mouth. "Wow, Marsha bought you good cheese. Yeah, that dog is nineteen years old, can you believe it? Still acts like he's going to murder any man who gets close to her. Still likes all the ladies."

Grabbing her crutch, Stella stood gingerly. "Let's go see Maritza. I want to hear what she has to say about Dirty."

"Now?" Maria plunked her beer on the counter and bubbles fizzed up to the lip, nearly spilling over. "I thought you were tired."

"Yeah now." Stella crutched toward the door. "I'm never too tired for Maritza."

Maria stormed across the room, pulling her keys from her pocket. "Okay girl, let's go. You're not gonna believe this shit."

On the way to Maritza's house, Maria yammered about a guy she'd gone on a date with. He was now obsessed with her, and she had tried to ghost him, but he wouldn't leave her alone. He had stood outside her apartment building for *two hours* waiting to run into her, and then he'd told her he wanted to *hang up his hat for her.*

Laying into her horn, Maria flipped off a black Escalade as it careened into her lane and almost clipped her bumper. She stuck her head out the car window and yelled, "That ugly car is a waste of money!" Tucking her head back in the car, she turned up the fan and pointed one of the vents on her face, wiping away the mascara under her eyes with one finger. "What does that even mean, *hang up his hat for me?*"

"I think it means he wanted to marry you." Stella gathered her thick mass of hair above her head, draped it over the headrest and wiped sweat from the back of her neck.

"Fuck that." Maria sped past the Escalade at 80 miles an hour, honking again.

Stella tilted her seat back and rolled down the window, letting the Texas wind whip strands of hair around her face.

As they pulled up in front of Maritza's house, a volley of dog yelps cascaded out of the house's open windows.

Stella leaned on Maria's arm and crutched up the walkway to the sound of Lupe's canine hysteria. "That little rat" used to annoy her, but now she couldn't wait to see him.

Before Stella had finished hobbling up the stoop, the front door burst open. Maritza's black Converse sneakers—a gift from Maria that never left her feet—peeked out underneath her long yellow skirt. Her white hair was piled neatly in a bun on Maritza's tiny head. With one arm, she cradled Lupe underneath her floral cardigan, flinging her other arm wide. "Bienvenidos, mijas!"

"Hi, Maritza." Stella crutched onto the top step and leaned in for a hug, overcome by an urge to cry. The old lady had always disarmed Stella in a way that no other person could.

Maritza made everyone feel like she could hold a piece of their sadness for them. Or maybe she would take that sadness and release it into whatever dimension she traveled when she talked to dead people.

Under the woo-woo bluster, Maritza's heart was big. When she'd finally made it to America eight years ago, she told Maria's abusive parents that if they laid another hand on Maria, she would go straight to the police and expose their decade-long telephone scam company. Maria moved in with her grandmother, and rarely spoke to her parents thereafter.

As Stella's fuzzy slippers followed Maritza into the house, she was hit with its familiar smells of chicken and tomatoes and incense.

Maritza babbled in Spanish and pointed at the plastic-covered couch, where Stella understood she was supposed to sit. Moments later, a bowl of tomato-soaked chicken and rice appeared in her hands, and Maritza chattered in Spanish and motioned to the chicken, sitting across from the girls in a plastic-covered armchair. Lupe burrowed in beside her and she kept one hand on him, gesticulating with the other.

Stella moaned. "This is delicious, Maritza. Thank you."

Unsmiling, Maritza pointed at the bowl. Stella was not supposed to talk until she had finished eating.

"You better eat your pollo guisado, girl." Maria smirked and licked her lips, peering at Stella through her thick black bangs. "I told you you were too skinny."

While Maria and Maritza watched her scarf down the stew, Stella let her eyes wander to the crucifix over the door, and the altar in the corner where a tall candle burned in a glass holder emblazoned with a colorful drawing of a patron saint and the word *"Salud."* At the foot of the candle, a small bowl held a few coins and some rosary beads and the stalk of a plant that looked like wheat. Dozens of familiar photographs of Maria—including one of Maria and Stella together at their high school graduation—adorned the walls and mantle and side tables.

Light pressed through the white lace curtains, providing the room's only illumination.

As Stella swallowed her last bite, Maria turned to her grandmother, "Abuela, cuéntale sobre el perro."

Maritza took a dramatic breath and scooted her chair knee-to-knee with Stella. Lupe looked up at his master—irritated that she had jostled the chair and awakened him from his nap—and then rested his head on Maritza's thigh, closing his eyes.

With her cold, veiny fingers, Maritza leaned in and took Stella's hand, delivering a solemn speech that Maria translated:

My darling girl, I am so happy that you are safe. Maria told me about the dog, and she said that you saw your father with him on the beach. I have tried to contact your father many, many times since he died, but he has never spoken to me until yesterday.

Stella shivered, holding her breath, and the old lady continued:

He told me that he sent you the dog, and you know that he did, but people are telling you it is not true. He said to trust your heart. He sent you the dog to protect you in the jungle since he could not be there himself. He said to tell you not to forget how much he loves you, and not to forget how much the dog will always love you."

Stella exhaled, doubling over in her seat, overwhelmed by the closeness of her father, the clarity of his message. She held her face until her hands ran wet from tears.

Maria rubbed her back. "See, I told you. You gotta get that dog."

Lying back on the couch, Stella opened her mouth to speak and then closed it again. The room spun as Maria gently lifted Stella's sore feet into her lap.

Maritza stood, looking down over them. Enunciating through her thick accent, she put a hand on Stella's head. "I am happy you are home, niña. You are welcome in my house."

Maria pulled a blanket from the back of the couch and draped it over Stella. "Do you want to stay the night with us? I gotta go back to Houston tomorrow. On a *Sunday*, for chrissake. This fucking job."

Stella closed her eyes. "Yeah. I'll stay. Thanks Ri."

"Love you, Stell."

"Love you, too, Ri."

TEXAS

Day Six

STELLA LAY BACK in a mess of sweat-soaked sheets. Late afternoon light pressed through the drawn curtain.

Since she'd gotten home from Maritza's house that morning, she hadn't left her bed. Picking up her phone, she read Alé's text for the third time:

I have asked so many people about finding your dog, mija. I am very sorry to tell you this, but everyone agrees that it will be impossible to find the dog. The part of Corcovado where you were rescued is very remote, and the dog probably will not be in the same place, and how would anyone know if they found the right dog? There are many stray dogs that match your description near Corcovado, and everyone is afraid that they would pick up the wrong dog. They might even pick up someone's pet dog. I would go into the jungle to look for him myself, but I do not feel confident that I would know whether I found the right dog. There are some people who would take your money and say that they tried to find the dog, but I know that they would not deliver the dog to you. I am very sorry, my friend.

Carrying a Shiner Bock, her mother appeared in the doorway. "Want a beer?"

Her mom's features were drawn, a thick layer of makeup straining to cover the black circles under her eyes. For the first time in a few days, her frizzy hair was brushed and pulled back in a ponytail. She put the beer down on the bedside table and drew open the curtain.

"No thanks." Fighting back tears, Stella patted the empty space next to her on the bed. "I gotta go to P.T., and then I'm going somewhere after that. But you can join me here for a few minutes. If you want."

Her mother slid out of her petite flip-flops and pulled the sheet taut before sitting on top of it and lying back on a pillow.

Stella rested her head on her mother's shoulder, inhaling the familiar sweet smell of her shampoo. "Mom, I… I don't think I've seen you with a drink since I got back home?"

Her mother crossed her arms, pinching the skin on one of her elbows. "I haven't had a drink since you disappeared."

Stella turned onto her side and placed a hand awkwardly on her mother's clammy arm, still a bit uncomfortable with these new expressions of physical intimacy. "I'm proud of you. That must be really hard."

"Thanks." Stella's mom massaged her own temples with her thumb and forefinger.

The closeness of their bodies made Stella ache for Dirty, for the ease of being near him. She closed her eyes, remembering his feral, sea-weathered smell, and the feel of his coarse fur under her fingers, the bony arch of his back as she reached around him for comfort.

The hopelessness in Alé's message made Stella's body feel like it would shatter into pieces. She wanted to disappear, to fall asleep for a long, long time. She grabbed a corner of the bed sheet, twisting it between her thumb and forefinger.

An ambulance whizzed by outside, siren blaring, and both women turned to look out the window.

Stella's mother put a hand on her daughter's hand and clutched it tightly, her fingernails pressing into Stella's skin. "I'm sorry for what you went through, Stella. Nobody should ever have to endure those things. I can't imagine how scared you must have been."

"Thanks. I…" Stella cleared her throat, desperate not to cry, and wiped sweat from her forehead and upper lip. "I know you've dealt with some hard things in your life, too. And you don't want to talk about it. But whatever happened to you, I'm really sorry you went through it."

Her mother sniffed and wiped her nose. "I'm sorry you know that much. I never wanted to put my difficulties on your shoulders, but I guess it's impossible for a mother not to. It hurts me to know that I might've made your life harder, or maybe just less happy, than it needed to be."

Outside the window, the mailman strode up the sidewalk, rifling through his bag. Across the street, a dog barked and strained on his leash.

Stella and her mother listened to the metal postbox by the door clink open and shut, and they watched the mailman disappear toward the neighbor's house.

"In college…" Stella's mother wiped mascara from beneath her eyes. "Someone… hurt me, and…" She sniffed again and paused. "…and your dad made me feel safe. He made me feel like I was going to be okay. I think… I think maybe I would've died without him."

Stella's mother reached over to touch her daughter's head, patting the thick brown hair so unlike her own. "I shouldn't have told you that. That's not for a daughter to know."

Stella fiddled with the thin gold bracelet on her mother's arm, remembering when her father gave it to her at Christmas ten or eleven years ago. She thought of all the times she'd rolled her eyes at her mother for being morose and withdrawn. If she'd known, as a child, of her mother's trauma, would she have been more empathetic? Or is a child incapable of understanding that trauma can change a person so deeply that anything good, even love, seems impossible and overwhelming?

"Oh, Mom." She lay rigid, uncertain what physical contact was appropriate. "I'm sorry that happened to you. You've been through so much shit."

Her mother wiped her nose again. "Yeah. I have. But at least I had you."

Stella's eyes drifted to the glow-in-the-dark star stickers above her bed. "I didn't make your life any easier."

Her mother fiddled with her fingernails. "Oh, you did, Stella. You did. You'll never know."

She cleared her throat. "Thanks, Mom."

Sitting up straighter, her mother smoothed her t-shirt over the waistband of her jeans. "Where are you going after physical therapy?"

Mirroring her mom, Stella straightened her posture against the headrest, and they sat side-by-side, straight-backed, staring vacantly. "Austin Pets Alive. The shelter. Where Kelsey works. The girl who came to the hospital with Coffee."

Her mother took in a deep breath and let it out. "Oh yes, I remember, that's good. Maybe you'll find a dog there you want to adopt."

"Maybe." Stella bit her lip, sitting up and swinging her feet off the bed. She leaned on her crutch and slid into her red slippers. "I gotta go."

Hopping out of bed, Stella's mom scuttled over to stand in front of her. "Do you need me to drive you? Are you sure you should be going out alone?" She pointed at Stella's slippers. "Your feet…"

"I'll be fine, Mom. I'm going to Uber. My left foot's a lot better, and I can put some weight on the right one now." She placed her right foot flat on the floor, lifted the crutch from the ground and took two steps, gritting her teeth so she wouldn't wince. "See?"

Her mom nodded, shoving her hands into her pockets. "Okay. Be careful. I love you."

Balancing on her crutch, Stella gave her mom an awkward side-hug. "I love you, too."

AFTER PHYSICAL THERAPY, as she Ubered to the shelter, Stella rolled down the window and inhaled the familiar mix of car fumes and river air. She pulled white sunglasses down over her eyes and hair blew around her face in confused tangles, her eyelashes trembling beneath the dark lenses. The blast reminded her that she was lucky to be alive. Wallowing in the loss of Dirty did a disservice to all the people who came together to save her.

Stella's eyes whizzed over the city outside the window: carefully-curated displays of midcentury modern furniture, and Whole Foods signs promoting expensive lemons and asparagus, and toned women rushing somewhere in Lululemon leggings.

These things, these people confused her. Some part of her wanted to *be* one of those Lululemon women, focused on getting to an exercise class or brunch with friends. But they seemed like they lived on a different planet from her. What would she talk about if she sat down at brunch with a rich housewife wearing designer leggings?

Just outside the shelter, the driver dropped her off. As she crutched toward the black building with its colorful red and green "Austin Pets Alive!" emblazoned over the doorway, she tested her right ankle with some pressure. The physical therapy, irritating as it was, had transformed her in the past week. Her ankle still hurt, but it was a lot stronger than it had been just a few days ago. Maybe tomorrow she'd try walking without the crutch.

Sidling toward her from the opposite side of the parking lot, three young hipsters whispered to each other, and one of them pointed at Stella. Their eyes went wide and they hurried across the lot, dodging a cyclist.

Twirling a poofy keychain around her finger, one of the trio—a nose-ringed girl wearing a belly shirt and no bra—said, "Hey, are you that girl who got lost? In the jungle? For like a week? And is it true that you got bit by a poisonous snake and some dog sucked the poison out of you?"

Stella blinked. Could she pretend that she was *not* the "jungle girl," as people were calling her? Would they know she was lying? If she said yes, would they trap her there with the same stupid questions as everyone else? Maybe. But they didn't seem like assholes. She couldn't just blow them off. It made her feel uncomfortable to think about blowing off people who weren't assholes.

Stella's gaze skipped from one hipster to the next to the next, searching for some affinity with them. Finding none, she said, "Yeah, that's me. But I didn't get bit by a snake."

The belly shirt girl tumbled into her, wrapping her in a vertiginous hug, kicking Stella's left slipper. Stella stifled a yelp.

"Can we take a selfie with you?" the girl bubbled.

Stella shrugged. "Okay."

A guy with a thin scraggly beard leaned in and mumbled, "I'm adopting a dog from here. I hope you can go get that dog that saved you."

Stella bit her lip. "Thanks."

The bearded hipster put an arm around Stella's shoulders while belly shirt and the other guy crowded in close, snapping a photo.

"Thanks! Good luck!" they sang in tandem.

As they walked away, Stella felt disoriented, like she'd watched the interaction happen to someone else.

The sidewalk burned hot under her slippers, and she wondered if she should've put on a cleaner t-shirt.

Crutching into the stale air of the shelter four minutes past the arranged meeting time, the smell of dog piss and wet fur wafted over her. In the "lobby," a messy entryway crowded by an empty desk filled with mail and stacked boxes and bags of dog food, Stella picked up a pamphlet that read "Volunteering at APA!"

From behind her, a mousy voice squeaked through the distant bedlam of barking. "Hi, Stella. I'm happy you came."

Stella dropped the pamphlet back on the desk and turned to see Kelsey peeking out of her oversized glasses.

"Hi, Kelsey." Stella fought an urge to hug the girl. She felt like she might cry, so she cleared her throat and breathed in and out slowly.

Kelsey pushed her hair behind her ears and cracked her knuckles. "So, I can give you a tour in a little bit, if you want. But there are a few people who want to meet you, if that's okay. They're, um, waiting in the meeting room. But if you're not okay with that…"

Stella looked down at her outfit: the t-shirt she'd slept in last night, and filthy jeans, and *fuzzy slippers*. She held out her arms. "I look like shit."

Kelsey shook her head, eyebrows nervous, looking down at her own *Austin Pets Alive!* t-shirt. "Everyone dresses like that. Like, t-shirts and stuff. I promise. We get pooped on all day."

Stella wondered whether she could convince this odd girl to be her friend, to get a beer sometime. If she was old enough to go get a beer. "Okay, let's go meet a bunch of people covered in shit."

Kelsey opened her mouth as if she might feel the need to tell Stella that people wouldn't *actually* be covered in shit, but Stella smiled and stepped toward a long corridor stacked high with folded-up crates and donated chew toys and blankets.

Barking still crowded in on her from the outside the building. Did any of the dogs sound like Dirty? *That* one, the high-pitched one, *that one* reminded her of Dirty's bark.

Kelsey pointed toward the door behind them and mumbled: "Coffee's still here. You could see her later."

Stella pictured herself flinging a cage door open, Coffee bounding toward her over piss-soaked ground. "That'd be nice."

At the end of the hallway, Kelsey stopped in front of a door marked "4," her big light eyes pleading with Stella to be okay with what she was about to encounter.

They stepped into a conference room where twelve or fifteen members of the staff, ranging from teenagers to middle-agers, crowded around a long scuffed table. Kelsey had been right—most of them wore old "Austin Pets Alive" t-shirts and dirty jeans. A few actually looked like they might have shit on their clothes. Two of the older women and one older man carried themselves a bit more professionally, their t-shirts tucked into cleaner jeans.

Everyone smiled at Stella, and a few people waved awkwardly and mumbled, *hi*. She felt instantly at ease.

Kelsey presided over the room with surprising composure. "Okay, y'all, this is Stella."

After the crowd muttered various iterations of "Hi, Stella," Kelsey informed Stella that, if it was okay with her, people wanted to ask some questions.

Stella slumped into an empty chair and then straightened her posture self-consciously, running her hands over her hair to make sure her pony tail wasn't too messy.

She steeled herself for the same barrage of questions she'd been answering for almost two weeks.

A mop-headed boy in a brown t-shirt raised his hand, and Kelsey pointed at him: "Jacob."

Jacob fiddled with a pencil, hair half-covering his eyes. "Hey, Stella."

She tipped her head toward him. "Hi."

"Um, I'm really glad you're okay…" He fumbled the pencil, dropping it to the floor, leaning down to pick it up. "Um, and I'm just really impressed that you survived. And, um, I just wanted to know, do you think that Dirty had a family? Like, a human one? The way he decided to stay with you that whole time, do you think he was, like, a lost pet?"

Stella chewed on the inside of her cheek. The question made her uncomfortable.

"I don't think so," she said, self-consciously straightening her posture again. "We were so far from any place where people would live, like really *really* deep in the jungle, and Dirty had obviously been alone for a long time. He was really skinny, and he didn't look like anyone had ever fed him or taken care of him. He did act like he understood people, though, like he thought he *was* a person. But the stray dogs in Costa Rica, they're different from the ones here. Even on the beach in Dominical where I was staying, the stray dogs wanted to hang out with tourists. They sometimes followed me around. I think being with people is just normal to them, maybe."

Every eye in the room was locked on her. She looked up at the ceiling for a break from all the eyes, remembering the way Dirty stared at her in the murky light of that first dawn.

She cleared her throat, turning back to Jacob. "So, my gut says he's never lived with people. I just can't imagine a way for him to get out there unless he was born out there or dumped there on purpose. I think, and I mean I know this is crazy, but I kind of felt like he was *telling* me that he didn't have a family, and he wanted *me* to be his family." She joggled her head. "I know that's ridiculous. I know dogs don't *talk* to people."

A woman in a black t-shirt spoke up. "I don't think anyone in this room would call that ridiculous. We're all pretty convinced that dogs *do* talk to people."

Everyone nodded, and a few mumbled that dogs definitely talk to people all the time.

For an hour, people asked her questions about Dirty: how big was he, how long did it take for him to let her touch him, what did he eat, did she ever see him hunt, how did he protect her from the snake, was he bigger than the anteater, how did he show her where the water was, how did he find the rescuers.

These were the questions that mattered. These were the questions she had been waiting for someone to ask her.

When she told the group that she'd had to *yell* at Dirty to get him to go find the rescuers, that the last time she touched him was when she shoved him away and ordered him to go find help, her voice broke and she looked down at the table.

Several people in the room wiped tears from their eyes, and one young girl blew her nose.

A clean-cut twenty-something young man leaned forward in his seat. "What did Dirty do when they put you on the helicopter?"

She looked up at the ceiling again, and then back to the people in the room. Her voice still shook, and a tear fell down her cheek. "At first he was freaking out, jumping everywhere, barking, and they just kept *kicking* him."

The staff gasped, shook their heads.

Stella wiped her eyes quickly, shaking her head. "And then, as we were taking off, he stopped jumping and just stood there. And I saw my dad with him."

She shook her head, blushing. "I mean, my dad is dead. So obviously he wasn't really there. They had tranquilized me at that point. I was hysterical, so fucking mad and desperate to get to Dirty, but they wouldn't let me near him. And then I thought I saw my dead dad next to Dirty. The whole time I was out there, for all those days, my dad talked to me in my head, telling me he sent the dog to me. And then on that last day, he just stood there with him while they took me away."

The faces in the room drooped, weepy.

Kelsey, standing behind Stella, sniffed, chin quivering, and muttered, "You have to go get him."

Several others nodded.

Stella leaned forward on her elbows. "My friend down there who's a jungle guide tells me it'll be impossible for anyone find him. Nobody knows what he looks like, and nobody wants to grab some random dog off the beach just because he matches my description."

"*You* know what he looks like." Kelsey nudged her glasses higher. "You could go get him?"

Stella looked down at her feet and held up her arms. "Look at me. The doctors and my mom and my physical therapists and basically everyone who's, like, rational is telling me I'd be stupid to go down there again after everything I went through. Everything my body has been through. The only way to get Dirty would be to hike back *into that jungle*. Where I almost died. And risk getting lost again, and the snakes and all the other shit. And I can barely walk. It's like a death wish. I can't do that to my mom."

Jacob twiddled his pencil. "If my dog was lost, I'd do anything to find him. I wouldn't care if people said it was a death wish."

The clean-cut young man leaned forward. "Can you find a guide to take you out there, someone you trust, and take really good equipment, once you can walk a little better? It wouldn't be like last time, would it? I have some camping stuff you could borrow, like a water filter and some other stuff"

Stella's blood surged. These people understood her. Her dad would love these people. "I do know a good guide.

Silence gripped the room. Someone shuffled a foot uncomfortably under the table. A puppy—was it a puppy—cried somewhere nearby. Was there a puppy in this building?

The older woman in the back of the room stepped forward until she was just a few feet away from Stella. "Hi Stella, I'm Rainey, the Director of

Operations here." Rainey smiled, and the kind look in her eye made Stella think that the woman would be a good mother. "We're grateful you came. We don't want to make you feel like you should do something that could be harmful to you. But when you're feeling better, we'd love to have you come volunteer with us. You could walk or feed the dogs. Just let us know. We're here for you. We want to know what happens with Dirty, okay?"

"I…" Clearing her throat, again trying not to cry, Stella braced on her crutch and stood up, scrunching her nose. "Can I *hug* you? Is that weird?"

Rainey smiled and put her arms around Stella.

"Good luck," she said, pulling away and looking Stella in the eye. "I think you'll figure out how to find him."

Stella bit her lip to hide her trembling chin. "Thank you. All of you. For caring." Waving to the room, she followed Kelsey out the door.

She floated down the hallway, detached from her body, hearing Rainey's voice over and over in her head: *I think you'll figure out how to find him.*

Kelsey opened the door that led outside, and Stella floated after her into the blinding sunshine, and they walked through a chain link gate, down a narrow cement corridor, and into an open area. Makeshift kennels unfurled around a courtyard, dogs' faces peering out, begging for attention—some of them demanding attention by barking or howling or launching their bodies against the gates. Stella cringed as she realized that this was where these dogs would live for weeks and months and maybe even years, pooping on the floor of their kennels in between outings, as they waited for someone to care about them enough to take them home.

On the far end of the courtyard, ten or fifteen dogs romped in a big fenced-in yard. "Playgroup," Kelsey said, pointing at the yard. "All the dogs get to go to playgroup every day."

NOT JUST A DOG

Volunteers and staff members scurried around everywhere, shoveling shit, replacing water dishes, opening cages to take grateful leaping dogs on short leashed walks.

A few members of the public peered into the dim kennels, tilting their heads in consideration.

Stella froze. There was too much pain in this place. Too many unloved dogs. How could she justify the thought of flying to another country to help *one* dog, when there were a hundred *right here* in desperate, heart-rending need?

Her breathing quickened, and panic swelled in her throat.

She put a hand on Kelsey's arm and squeezed hard. "Maybe not today..."

Kelsey turned to her, eyebrows furrowing under her big glasses. "Of course. I'm so sorry, I..."

Stella bit her lip. "Don't be sorry. I want to come back. Just not today."

TEXAS

Day Eight

STELLA SAT IN the kitchen, peeling the crust off her sandwich. Gray sky stretched wide and gloomy outside the kitchen window. From a distance, she heard a car engine—maybe two car engines?—whir and rev outside the house. More reporters?

Stella turned back to her sandwich, but a murmur of voices again drew her attention toward the front door. Someone was outside.

She wasn't in the mood for reporters. This week, she'd told six of them that she wasn't doing any more interviews, but they were relentless. Bloggers and gossip magazines told and retold her story, embellishing it with fabricated details: together, Stella and Dirty had fought off a jaguar. She'd been bitten by a venomous fer-de-lance. She'd lost half her body weight, surviving by eating her own feces, and that of the dog.

The bloggers had dug up her hideous yearbook photos, plastering them at the top of their articles. They'd interviewed people purporting to be Stella's friends, most of whom she barely knew and didn't give a rat's ass about.

Luckily, the curtains were drawn so the reporters couldn't see her sitting at the kitchen table, barefoot and unkempt, slumped over the table in three-day-old pajamas stained with last night's pasta sauce.

Music—now Stella heard some kind of music. She rolled her eyes, grumbling, "Leave me alone."

Something about the music, though… She recognized it. She'd heard that tinny riff before…

She stood and walked gingerly into the living room as the music grew in volume. She *did* know this song. She had skated to it a hundred times in derby.

With two fingers, she lifted a corner of the curtain and peered outside. A smile broke out across her face, as a chorus of voices shouted:

Live fast, die young

Bad girls do it well

Live fast, die young

Bad girls do it well

Her entire roller derby team stood on the lawn. Nineteen scruffy girls, singing terribly at the top of their lungs. One of them—Gigi—held a boom box over her head, blasting the song by M.I.A.

Her teammates looked as sloppy as they sounded. Some of them had dirt smeared on their faces. Leaves and sticks stuck out of their unruly hair. They all wore stained pajama bottoms and slippers and matching bright red t-shirts that said, "I LOVE DIRTY."

Stella laughed, tears welling in her eyes. She threw the curtain wide, and slid open the window pane. Several of her teammates cheered when they saw her, raising their fists as they continued with the song.

Two neighbors across the street and one next door stepped out onto their stoops, smirking, frowning.

Stella crooned through the open window, surprised at how relieving it felt to hurl her voice into the world:

Live fast, die young

Bad girls do it well

Live fast, die young

Bad girls do it well

Stella's spirit swelled into the din of music. With each chorus, she sang louder, and her friends sang louder, until all semblance of singing dissolved into a full-throated shout. When the song finally ended, her teammates cheered and rushed into the house without waiting for an invitation.

Inside, they piled on Stella, mindful of her injuries, laughing and hugging her and kissing her cheek. Someone said, "Be careful of her feet!" Someone else handed her an "I LOVE DIRTY" shirt and she nearly fainted from the dizzying swirl of energy.

"Let her sit down," said the team captain, Beez.

The cacophony settled, and the girls sat on the sofa and chairs and carpet. Stella hadn't felt this many bodies close to her since before her life had flipped on its head. She'd changed so much in the last three weeks, and much of the world loomed foreign and unfriendly around her, but these girls still felt like family.

Settling next to Stella on the couch, Gigi crossed her legs and turned to face her friend. She wore black flannel pajamas patterned with a hundred colorful images of a unicorn riding on top of a spaceship. Her shiny red hair was pulled back into a ponytail clumped with fresh grass clippings and something that looked like dried mud. Her foot slid over an inch, touching Stella's thigh. "When you coming back to the rink? You look like you're ready to play."

A nervous laugh spread around the room.

"Funny." Stella scanned from one girl to the next, smiling at the leaves and trash in their hair. "Y'all look like shit."

They laughed, giddy, and Gigi shrugged. "You said we couldn't come visit because you looked like shit, so we figured we'd just shit it up with you. You look a lot better than we do, IMHO."

Stella blushed, tucking her hair behind her ears, running a hand over the slick white letters on her new t-shirt.

Slouching back in an armchair, Beez said, "So tell us about him."

Stella looked up at her. "Who?"

"You know who, Stell." Beez beamed at Stella like it was her birthday. "Dirty. Tell us everything about him."

Stella let out a deep breath, shaking her head. "Dammit, I missed y'all."

Murmurs rippled through the room: "We missed you too!"

She looked down at the red t-shirt in her hands. "His eyes are so human. I didn't know how *human* a dog could be. He came up to me in the middle of the night like he'd known me for years. Brought me a dead rat—a present, I guess—and then lay down next to me." Gigi whispered under her breath, nervously touching her hair to make sure the leaves were still there. "Awesome."

Stella told the girls that Dirty's fur felt rough when it dried out in the salty sun, and he liked her to hold his paw when he was sleeping. She told them that she'd tried to hire someone to go find him, but everyone in Costa Rica told her it would be impossible to find him.

Her teammates listened for over an hour. They didn't ask how she was feeling, or if her feet still hurt, or whether she was looking for a job, or whether she'd talked to Garret. They didn't mention the news story.

"I totally believe your dad was there with him. That shit is awesome." Yaz, a giant girl, and one of the best players in the league, gave her a nod from the back of the room. "So you gonna go get him?"

Stella looked at her slippers, shook her head. "I thought about it. Thought maybe I could hire a guide and go back with equipment, but the doctors and my mom say it would be really freaking stupid to go back there. I only just started walking without crutches *yesterday*. My body's still weak, and who knows if I could even find him. The jungle is so fucking *big*. It almost killed me."

"Bullshit," said Gigi. "That jungle never would've killed you. You're one of the strongest people I've ever known. Your healthy body is ten times stronger than most people. So even if you're not 100%, you're still stronger that 80% of Texas."

"Truth," said Yaz, with a shrug. "If you went back there, I wouldn't worry about you for one second. You survived four days in the jungle *by yourself*—or, with just Dirty. You could survive another four with a guide and a cell phone and a bunch of rad equipment."

Stella bit her lip, nodding. "But, my feet…"

Yaz smirked. "Take some Advil. Wear some band-aids."

Stella's stomach flew up into her throat, and started bawling. They were right. For the first time, she felt like maybe she could do it. She *could* go back and get him. The doctors and nurses had her best interests at heart, but they didn't *know* her. Even her mom didn't really know how strong she was. These girls *knew* her. She could fucking do it. Maybe.

Her friends stood and walked over, puting their hands on her back until she stopped crying and caught her breath.

Beez pulled something from her pocket. "I know you're tired, so we'll head out in a sec, but first, we have something for you. We know you gotta get Dirty back, and we want to help, so we set up a Kickstarter for you. We all pitched in and we sent it around to a few other people. Some of the people at that shelter that you visited yesterday even gave some money. It's not much, but maybe it'll help you get that rad equipment that you're gonna need."

Stella reached out to take the piece of paper from Beez. It was a check for $625.

"What…" She took a few breaths in and out, unable to speak, and then looked up at her friends, sobs rising again. Barely able to speak, she cried, "Thank you. I don't know what to say."

They stood and crowded around her again, each of them stooping to hug Stella where she sat on the couch. Yaz touched her shoulder and said, "You don't need to say anything. We can't wait to meet him."

With her check in one hand and t-shirt in the other, Stella lifted herself to her feet as her teammates walked toward the front door.

Gigi lingered behind the others and leaned in, speaking low, so nobody else could hear her. "I'm really glad you're okay. When you're ready to hang out, I'm here. I promise I won't hit on you this time."

Stella gave her a side-smirk. "Bummer."

With a bemused shake of the head, Gigi slipped out the door, and all of Stella's teammates turned back toward her one more time, waving. "We love you, Stella!"

She called after them. "Thank you. I love all of you. Thank you."

They ducked into their cars with a chorus of, "Come back to the rink soon!" and "Let us know when you want another serenade!"

Stella sat on the stoop and watched them drive away. The bellies of the gray clouds hung heavy, warning of rain. Twisting the red t-shirt in her hands, she wondered if the belly-heavy clouds stretched all the way to Costa Rica.

TEXAS

Day Nine

SITTING CROSS-LEGGED ON her bed, Stella stared at the headline on her laptop's browser.

> *Hurricane Geraldo bears down on Costa Rica.*
> *Expected to cross overland from Caribbean to*
> *Pacific tomorrow. Dozens of flights canceled.*

Dirty was out there somewhere cowering under a fern, shielding his face as winds toppled branches around him.

She scratched her right upper arm, then her left, leaving long red streaks.

None of the travel sites showed flights available to Costa Rica in the next two weeks.

Flopping onto her stomach, she beat her fists into the mattress.

Throughout the previous night, Stella had lain awake, haunted by the image of her father, squatting next to Dirty, looking her in the eye, smiling, nodding.

I'll wait for you.

He wanted her to go back.

She was supposed to go back.

She had to go back. She knew this now.

But she couldn't get there. Because of a fucking hurricane.

She could think of almost nothing else. Her sanity felt tenuous, like it was seeping out of her body, through her pores.

Pulling up the website for Austin Pets Alive, she clicked through dozens of pictures of dogs available for adoption. The thought of those dogs lying in their enclosures at night, longing for the warmth of another being, made her queasy. Probably, all of those dogs would stand in front of a snake to protect their person.

Now that she could walk without crutches, she was going to the shelter each day to take the calmer, older dogs to the play yards in the courtyard—her physical therapist said that walking was the best therapy for her feet at this point—and the visits had brought her as much joy as pain. It buoyed her to see the dogs' tails wag when she picked up their fraying leashes. She let them kiss her face and lean their bulky bodies into hers when they sat together underneath a tree, breathing the fresh air.

But none of those dogs was *him*. And he was the only dog she wanted.

She slammed her laptop shut and threw it onto the pillow.

Huffing into the kitchen, Stella reveled in the slight sting of each footfall on her healing blisters.

She flipped on the kitchen light and gasped, startled to see her mother sitting at the table, staring at an unopened bottle of gin. The ceiling light bulb glowed naked and bright, uncovered since its frosted glass shade broke over a year ago. The beige walls suddenly seemed so bleak, paint peeling along the baseboards. A framed crayon self-portrait, drawn by Stella at age five, gave the room its only color.

Stella's mother looked like she hadn't slept in days. Messy hair shot in every direction, and the flesh puffed under her eyes.

Stella took a cautious step toward the table. "Mom, are you okay?"

Raising her hollow eyes, Stella's mother seemed to look right through her. Her voice was flat, "I saw you looking at flights. You can't go back, Stella. You're still weak. You can't even walk. And there's a *hurricane*."

Stella lowered herself tentatively onto the chair next to her mother, like it might hold a land mine. "Mom, I love you, and I know this has been hard on you." She took her mother's hand. "But I have to live my life. And you need to live yours. You're so skinny. You're hardly eating."

Stella reached out and gently slid the bottle toward herself. "When are you going to go back to work, Mom? You're gonna get fired if you don't go back soon. Maybe you'd feel better if you were working."

Her mother pulled her hand away from Stella's and rested two sideways fists on the table, her voice rising slightly in volume. "Stella, how could you go down there in a hurricane? You nearly *died* less than three weeks ago. Don't you know what it would do to me if you went back in a *hurricane*? After what happened to your father? How could you do that to me?"

Stella opened her mouth, ready to hurl an angry retort, but her mother looked so tired, so empty. She stood, picking up the bottle of gin.

Her mother closed her eyes and tipped back her head. "I'm supposed to take care of you. I don't have any goddamn idea how to take care of you."

Stella unscrewed the bottle and dumped its contents into the sink, watching the clear liquid gurgle around the drain. "Mom, you've done a really good job taking care of me this week. I am so grateful for everything you've done—really really grateful. I know I'd be dead if you hadn't sent people to look for me in Costa Rica. I couldn't have gotten through this without you. But now I'm going to be okay. I've been okay for a long time on my own."

Stella wondered if she believed that she would be okay. Did she actually know *how* to be okay? Or would she end up like her mother, lost and sad? She had lost her desire to go to graduate school in psychology—she couldn't have gotten into graduate school anyway, with her mediocre college transcript. She couldn't remember if she'd really *wanted* to go to graduate school, or if this just seemed like an acceptable path, one that nobody would question.

She knew she should get a job, move out of her mother's house, create a real life for herself. She had just encouraged her mother to go back to work, but she didn't have the energy to get a job of her own. Right now, she didn't give much of a shit about anything, really. Except Dirty.

The last of the gin swirled down the drain and Stella turned to her mother. "I need you to take better care of yourself so I don't have to do it. Okay?"

Her mother slowly swiveled her vacant gaze toward the living room. "Garrett came by. He left you something."

Stella's body flashed cold. She gently placed the empty bottle on the counter and walked to the sofa, picking up the ragged black leather backpack that Garrett had dropped off. She used to love that backpack, carried it everywhere through all four years of college. Inside, she found an old toothbrush, Garret's Gwar t-shirt that she used to sleep in (despite her dislike for Gwar), a few scrunchies, and a small gift wrapped in shiny gold paper and ribbon. Tucked underneath the ribbon was a cream-colored card with *Stella* written in Garrett's handwriting.

Stella zipped the backpack closed, walked to the corner of the kitchen, stepped on the trash can's kick-opener, and dropped the bag into the bin.

Watching her daughter, Stella's mother almost smiled as she shook her head. "How did you get so strong? You're so much stronger than I am."

Stella leaned back against the counter. "Maybe you're stronger than you think. When I got back, you seemed stronger than you've been in years. I'm proud of you for not drinking, Mom. Please go back to work. And maybe you could start drawing again? You used to love to draw."

Nodding, Stella's mother pushed her chair back from the table, but didn't stand. "Maybe. I'm trying, Stell. I really am."

"I know, Mom." Stella picked up the gin bottle from the counter and threw it in the trash, on top of Garrett's bag. "I see you trying. You *are* different."

Outside the house, a neighbor called to his wife, something about the sprinklers.

Stella's cell phone rang in her pocket and she pulled it out, biting her lip when she saw the name on the display.

"Hello?" She slid open the kitchen door and stepped onto the cracked cement patio as a few light raindrops started to fall.

The voice on the other end barreled through bright and sweet: "Stella? It's Theresa Branson. The reporter?"

Stella turned down the earpiece volume. "Oh. Hi Theresa."

Indistinct voices buzzed in the background behind Theresa. "I just wanted to touch base and see how you're doing!"

Stella wondered if Theresa still wore plum-colored lipstick, if she looked just as polished sitting at her desk as during the interview.

"Thanks. I'm doing better." Stella held her left arm out past the awning, watching a raindrop settle on her skin and slide off the side of her wrist. "I'm trying to figure out how to get back to Costa Rica to get Dirty but I can't find any flights because of the hurricane. I guess they were canceled for a few days and then the ones that aren't canceled got all booked up."

Theresa's voice sang, "Ooh, let me check with our travel department! I might be able to help! Hold on a second, I'll be right back."

Crackly background music blasted into the receiver and Stella put the phone on the ground under the awning, clicking on the speakerphone. She couldn't breathe. Didn't want to breathe. Was this real? Could Theresa actually help? Was she actually going to go back to Costa Rica? Could she do it? Was she just kidding herself, thinking that she could handle it?

The music stopped, and Theresa's voice popped in, lower and slower than before, almost whispering. "You're right, Stella, it's hard to get a ticket right now. I'm so sorry, but the travel department can't find any available flights for this week. But if the hurricane lets up and more planes start flying again, they should be able to get a ticket right away. It might be a little expensive. Is that okay?"

Stella's stomach churned, anxious. "Of course. I'll pay whatever it takes. Thank you, Theresa."

Stella heard Theresa ticking away at her keyboard.

The reporter's voice trailed off, as if her focus had shifted to whatever email she was writing. "No problem. I gotta go, but I'll be in touch. Take care of yourself, okay?"

Stella tried to picture Theresa where she was sitting, couldn't quite get a visual. "I will. Oh by the way, I've been wondering, do you have a dog?"

Theresa let out a happy sigh. "I do. Benny. A greyhound. Six years old. She's a rescue."

"Nice." Stella would never have imagined Theresa to be a greyhound mother. "Thanks again. Bye, Theresa."

"Bye, Stella. We'll be in touch."

She lay back on the concrete, tucking the phone under her shirt, raindrops cooling her toes.

TEXAS

Day Twelve

THE STALE STORAGE room air still harbored a hint of the yeasty scent that had become so familiar to Stella when her father was alive. Staring at an unopened two-liter barrel in the corner, she sat amidst a jumble of chrome distillers, packets of yeast, and cheesecloth still crusted with corn mash.

She'd paid rent on the storage room for nearly a year, since her father's advance payments had run out, but this was the first time she'd set foot in the room since his death. She could feel him in every corner, and picture his strong, thick-fingered hands on every funnel and hose.

Every day for over two years, she'd thought about the last barrel of whiskey they made together, but she couldn't bear the thought of opening the spigot and drinking it away, sucking down this thing that she and her father had made together, this tangible vestige of him.

Picking up the barrel, she huffed across the room on healing feet and thumped it down on a folding table. As she ran her hand over the wooden contours of the planks, a splinter caught on her finger. She yanked up her arm, stifling a yelp, and pulled the sliver out with her fingernails.

Corcovado would be different this time. She would hire Alé to guide her. She still had almost three thousand dollars of her inheritance to spend on this trip, after buying her mom a new easel and pencils, and setting aside a thousand bucks for the plane ticket. If she could ever get a plane ticket.

Testing the barrel's bung to make sure it was still tight, she shook her head. She wouldn't let herself spiral into worst-case scenarios. She'd find a plane ticket, somehow. The hurricane had to end eventually, right? Dirty would be okay, right?

With three thousand dollars, she could outfit herself properly. Alé would know what equipment they needed, and where to buy it in Costa Rica. Somehow, he had managed to figure out the exact GPS coordinate where she was rescued, so he would know how to get there.

But anxiety scrubbed her gut. No, it was more than anxiety. She was terrified.

What if she got separated from Alé? What if he got injured on the trail and she had to find her way out again? What if *she* got injured on the trail? And worst of all, what if they *didn't find Dirty?* It had been almost *three weeks* since she left him on the beach. There was no way he's still be in the same spot, right? How could she possibly find him in that gigantic wilderness?

For several seconds, she stared at the spigot and then shuffled across the room, stooping down in a corner and rooting around until she found the tool that would remove the bung. Sticking it in her back pocket, she picked up the barrel and carried it out to her car, dropping it in the trunk with a *thwap*.

Her phone buzzed in her pocket, and she lifted it to her ear. "Hello?"

"Stella!" Theresa's voice assaulted the receiver so loudly that Stella flinched, moving the phone several inches away from her head. "It's Theresa! Good news - Our travel department can get you a ticket to Costa Rica. You'd leave in three days, on Friday. They say the weather's supposed to die down by Thursday. If we can't get you out on Friday, we should be able to get you out on Saturday. Does that timing work for you?"

"Wow." Taking a deep breath, Stella lowered herself to sit on the hot pavement next to her car. She swallowed hard. "Yes. I… I don't know how to thank you. I'll Venmo you the money. Just let me know how much it is. Thank you."

A muffled voice in the background said to Theresa, *It's time,* and she said, *I'll be there in two secs!,* and then she turned back to the mouthpiece. "Great! We are thrilled to help. We'll email you the ticket and an invoice. Let us know how it goes!"

The phone slipped from Stella's hand, and she scrambled to pick it up. "Thank you, Theresa. Bye."

"Bye, Stella."

Trembling, Stella pulled down the storage room's garage-style door, taking one more yeasty inhale. From her pocket, she retrieved the key her father had given her four years ago, and locked the door behind her.

As she drove home, sun blazed hot through the windshield. She rolled down her windows, letting the wind crash over her face, feeling stronger and more confident than she had in weeks. She was going to Costa Rica. It was going to happen. She wasn't going to let anyone else try to talk her out of it. Blood pulsed hot and fast through her veins.

Back home, she tucked the barrel deep in her closet where her mother wouldn't see it, and then walked out into the backyard, sitting nervously at the table.

Her mother would be home from work soon. They had barely spoken since Stella dumped the gin down the sink, but today Stella was going to make her mother understand why she needed to go back. She needed her mother to understand, to be okay with it. She couldn't bear this fracture between them. Not now. Not after everything they'd both been through.

The kitchen door slid open behind her, and she turned around to see Coffee, from Austin Pets Alive, bounding toward her. The dog jumped into her lap on the rickety chair, nearly knocking her over, licking her face with a slobbery tongue.

Stella laughed, wrapping her arms around the hefty dog. Her voice edged higher, approaching the *baby voice* range. "What are *you* doing here?"

In the doorway, her mother shrugged, holding up a leash.

Stella looked from Coffee to her mother, and back to Coffee, who was still plastering her face. "Did you… adopt her?"

"I…" Her mother nodded, shrugging, almost smiling. "Yeah."

"Did you do that for me?" Stella kissed the top of Coffee's head and nudged the dog off her lap. "I appreciate the gesture, but it's not about just needing *any* dog, Mom."

Coffee dashed off to pee on the perimeter of the crooked chain-link fence that her father had erected for Torres so many years ago.

"I know." Stella's mom sat down next to her, leaning back in the creaky chair. "I didn't adopt her for *you*…"

Coffee zig-zagged across the yard, creating a mental map of the smells.

Stella reached out and took her mother's hand. "She's beautiful, Mom."

Midday light shone hard through the branches of the live oak, speckling Stella's arms. With the collar of her t-shirt, she wiped away a line of sweat from her neck.

Coffee galloped over and stuck her muzzle under her mother's hand, begging for affection.

Stella reached out to pet the dog's head. "You sure you want to take care of a dog?"

"Yeah. You and your father can't *both* be wrong about dogs." Her mother shrugged again, with a nod, absently touching the dog with one hand. Tears welled in her eyes. "And she can be friends with Dirty when you get back."

"Oh, Mom." She bent down to kiss Coffee's head. "Yes she can."

Her mother stood. "I got you some things. They're in your bedroom." She turned to walk inside, murmuring over her shoulder, "Come inside, Coffee."

The dog trotted after her.

In the kitchen, her mother opened a bag of dog food and poured some kibble into a newly-purchased bowl, setting it on the floor. The dog plunged her face into the bowl like it was a puddle of water, spraying kibble in a wide circle.

As Stella walked toward her room, she noticed that her feet and ankle felt stronger. This amount of pain, she could handle. It wouldn't stop her from doing what she needed to do.

Stepping into her room, she inhaled sharply, and then held her breath. On her bed lay four bulky REI bags and a large camping backpack.

Tentatively, she approached the bags, not wanting to touch them, not wanting to disrupt this moment. Her mother hadn't bought her this many things since... ever? Not at Christmas, or birthdays, or... ever. And, REI? How did her mother even know what REI *was*? She looked up at the ceiling, wondering if her father was seeing this.

"Mom," she said. "You bought all these things? For me?" "I..." She hesitated. "Yes. I asked the saleswoman what you might need. She had seen the news story, so..."

Stella opened one of the bags, pulling out a box that read, *Satellite Communicator*. The box proclaimed that the device allowed the user to *stay connected off-grid*.

Stella gawked at her mother, wiping her eyes. "Mom. Thank you. I can't..."

Her mother shrugged and pointed at the box in her hand. "Supposedly you can use that to text even when you don't have normal cell phone reception."

In the kitchen, Coffee still crunched through her food.

"This is incredible, Mom." Stella reached into the bag again and pulled out a lightweight waterproof jacket, and some socks that were supposedly good for jungle trekking, and a new pair of hiking boots, and something called Moleskin, which you could put on blisters while hiking, and a water filter the size of a Coke can. At the bottom of the bag, Stella's hand alighted on a sturdy brown leash. Unable to speak, she ran the leash through her hands several times.

Turning around, she wrapped her arms around her mother's small frame. "Thank you, Mom. I… I really needed these things, but It's just… It's all so expensive. You must've spent a thousand bucks."

Her mother clutched her, speaking softly. "As I said, your dad left me some money. This is what he would want me to spend it on."

The sound of Coffee's tongue lapping up water floated into the bedroom.

Stella inhaled the familiar sweet scent of her mother's shampoo. "Thank you for everything. I know I haven't thanked you much in my life. For college, and braces, and keeping me alive when I was a kid, and everything else. I know I was a difficult kid. I'm sorry."

Stella's mother lowered them both to sit on the edge of the bed. Mascara ran down her flushed cheeks. "You have nothing to apologize for."

Stella linked her fingers through her mother's, and they sat in silence for a while until Stella said, "Why did dad go hiking that day, Mom? Didn't he know there was a flood warning?

Looking out the window, Stella's mother took a deep breath in, and out. "I don't know. I think so. I… I asked him not to go." She paused. "But you know, he was his own person."

Stella rested her head into her mother's shoulder. "I didn't know you asked him not to go."

Tucking her daughter's hair behind her ears, Stella's mother kissed the top of her head. "You are going to find him, and come back to me."

Stella nodded.

Her mother wiped away mascara with one finger, leaving a smudged trail. She sat up straighter, rolling her shoulders back and down. "You *will* come *back* to me. Do you understand?"

Stella nodded. "I do, Mom."

Gripping hard, Stella's mother dug brittle fingernails into her daughter's palms. "I will *not* lose you too, Stella."

Stella wanted to memorize the feeling of her mother gripping her this tightly. "I'll come back with Dirty. I promise."

Coffee loped into the room licking her lips. Without invitation, she jumped onto the bed.

Stella scooted across the bed and lay back with Coffee at her ankles. She patted the space next to her. Her mother crawled across the bed and propped herself on a pillow, sneaking an arm under Stella's shoulders. Coffee pressed herself into the space between them. Without another word, they all fell asleep.

COSTA RICA

Trip Two
Day One

STELLA STEPPED OUT of the airport terminal, hot wind lifting the edges of her hair. As she squinted into the grayness of the day, Alé barreled at her with a sweaty hug.

"Stella! You look good." His weatherworn face spread out in a toothy smile. He grasped her shoulders. "I see jungle strength in you."

His grip was strong and reassuring on her shoulders and she leaned in for a hug. "Hola, Alé. I don't know about jungle strength, but it's good to see you. Thanks for coming."

Raising a hand to shield her eyes, she peered into the sooty clouds. Rain clung to their bellies; it would fall soon.

Underneath the city stench of car fumes and garbage, Stella caught a whiff of loamy jungle. Or at least she thought she did. Hairs rose on her neck and arms.

Taking Stella's arm, Alé shuttled her toward his dented cab, yakking about how happy he was that she had survived, how brave she was to return so soon.

Stella dumped her bulky backpack in the trunk and stooped into the front seat of the cab, relieved to take pressure off of her feet and ankle. The car smelled like old leather and dirty shoes. She stared at fat clouds through the open window.

As Alé leapt into the driver's seat, he pointed to the back bench. A large camping backpack lay on its side.

"I am ready for our adventure. I have everything we will need."

"Already?" Stella blinked. "I thought you sold your equipment when you stopped being a guide? I thought we were going to have to buy some stuff?"

Alé cranked the car key, coaxing the engine awake. "When my daughter got sick, I sold my equipment to a friend. He will let me borrow the equipment for one week. We will have all the best gear so that we can be very safe in the jungle."

Stella flung her arms around him. "Thank you, Alé. Maybe after I pay you, you can buy back some of it…"

Behind them, the next cab in line honked, and they both jumped out of their seats.

"Oy!" Alé raised a fist outside his window and muscled his steering wheel to the left. "Okay then. Tomorrow, we will go to look for your dog. As long as the weather gets better."

On rain-slick asphalt, they sped away from the uproar of honking.

When they exited the airport grounds, tree limbs and leaves, ripped down in the storm, still littered the streets.

Cyclists hitched their bikes up onto the sidewalks to avoid hurricane debris, weaving a path among pedestrians and shopkeepers sweeping up leaves outside cement-walled stores. Utilitarian buildings, constructed with little attention toward aesthetics, rolled out away from the car in every direction. Before today, Stella had never wondered whether there were more beautiful neighborhoods somewhere in San Jose.

The car squealed through a turn as Alé lifted a hand from the steering wheel to point to the passenger foot well. "We will bring this with us."

Stella reached down between her feet and the seat to pick up a glossy package of vacuum-packed food. A series of phrases in Spanish framed a picture of a German shepherd on a bright yellow background.

"Freeze-dried dog food," Alé said, eyes wide. "This bag weighs only two pounds, but when we add water, it is food for a dog for two weeks. Incredible."

Leaning hard against the door as they wheeled around another turn, Stella stared at the German shepherd on the bag. "What if we don't find water?"

"I will find water." Alé pursed his lips. "Don't worry. The jungle does not know how to hide water from me. It is my home."

As he sped around a motorcycle, dodging oncoming traffic, he put a hand on her shoulder. "This time it will be different for you." She hugged the bag of food to her belly. "I hope so."

Humid air blasted in from the open window. A few rogue drops of rain fell from the sky, and she stuck out her arm to feel them slap her skin.

Alé swerved around a branch cast aside by the hurricane. Stella's eyes flitted from side to side as she took in a haze of auto repair shops and fruit vendors selling stacks of bananas and mangoes and pineapples and flip-flopped Costa Ricans walking to work.

Almost to herself, Stella murmured, "I brought a water filter. And a satellite phone."

"Excellent. It is good that we are both prepared." Yelling something in Spanish, Alé honked at a car trying to pass him and then flipped the car off, reminding Stella of Maria.

Alé lowered his voice and gave her a serious side-eye. "But do not tell anyone at your hostel that you have this equipment. Perhaps it is best for you not tell anyone you are going back to the jungle."

More raindrops fell, and Alé switched on the windshield wipers. "Bad people look for rich tourists who have equipment that they can steal. And other people, not so bad but so annoying, will try to convince you that you should pay them to be your guide. There are many bad guides. You have to be very careful about who to trust. I trust only myself, and I trust you. Remember this, okay?"

"Okay." Stella placed the bag of dog food back in the foot well and wrung her hands, rubbing her knuckles.

Her father would like Alé. She could imagine sitting down with both of them for a beer at Tortilla Flats in Dominical. They would clink glasses and laugh easily about small things. Her father would wink at her every once in a while to make sure she knew he was still with her.

"One more thing, Stella." Alé sighed hard, billowing his cheeks. "I will borrow a gun for us this time because..."

"No." she shook her head. "No guns."

Born and bred in Texas, Stella's father had defied generations of family history by refusing to have a gun in the house.

"My great-uncle Buddy shot himself in the foot once," her dad frequently told her. "He thought somebody was breaking into his house one night and ran down to the kitchen waving a pistol. When he turned on the lights and saw a pack of raccoons eating his Ritz crackers, it scared him so bad he shot his own damn foot. Didn't shoot a single raccoon. That's how much good a gun will do you."

Alé swerved through a traffic circle, rolling up his window. "But, mija, last week, American tourists in Corcovado were... how do you say... rob? robbing? A man with a knife took their wallets. This has happened many times this summer, so we must protect ourselves."

Stella could still visualize every feature of the man with the machete from last time, his green t-shirt fluttering. Had he robbed the American tourists?

She shook her head. "That sucks about the tourists getting robbed, but I don't like guns. I don't want us to bring a gun."

She rubbed her knuckles again. "If that's okay."

"Okay. It is your decision. You are paying for the trip." Alé glanced at her. "You are scared?"

"A little." Stella chewed her bottom lip.

Rain started pelting Stella's shoulder and neck, and she rolled up her window. "I've been dreaming about my dad—I think I told you he died three years ago? In my dreams, he keeps telling me to go get Dirty."

"This is important." Alé nodded, squinting as if trying to wring extra meaning from what she had said.

Stella leaned into the cool air from the air conditioning vent. "The day I was rescued, after they gave me some kind of drugs, I saw him there, on the beach, with Dirty."

The clouds overhead billowed like factory smoke, making Stella wonder if they would be able to leave tomorrow as planned. "I keep thinking that I should trust him, my dad. I keep thinking he wouldn't tell me to do anything too dangerous."

She wiped her forehead with the back of her hand. "I mean, I realize he's dead, and he's not actually telling me to do anything."

The city streets thinned, giving way to small wooden homes with tin roofs and blue walls and neatly-tended flowerboxes. And open-air discotecas where groups of men sat at plastic tables watching the cars go by as they drank cold Imperials. The people here looked happy; happier than back in Texas, where people rushed from place to place grumpy and anxious, pissed off that they didn't have enough time to paint their houses blue or tend flowerboxes.

Alé stared at the road, occasionally weaving around a downed branch or wind-swept trash bag. "My daughter comes in my dreams a lot. She used to come every night, but now she comes one or two times every week."

He rolled his window down to wave at a man standing in a yard, tinkering with the engine of a school bus in the rain. The one-room wooden house behind the school bus had a sculpture in the yard, a giant fish made of discarded auto parts.

"What are your dreams like? The ones with your daughter in them." Stella wiped her rain-moist hands on her jeans.

Rolling up his window, Alé took a sip from a water bottle nested in the console. "I don't remember, I just know that she was there, in my dreams."

As they whizzed past an abandoned gas station, the road started to climb into lush tree-covered hills.

Alé swallowed, staring straight ahead. "She liked dogs, my daughter. Did I tell you that? I was going to get her a dog when she was older, but then…"

Stella squinted between the trees, searching for familiar species of plants and animals. "Maybe she's happy that you're going to help me look for Dirty."

Stone-faced, Alé said, "Yes. She is."

Stella tried to picture Alé's daughter, carrying some of his softer features, her tiny body moving through the world with his bright kindness.

They rode in silence, winding through foggy rainforest. Everything outside the car window—the tropical trees, the humid air, the windy roads— reminded her that she had made it, she was back in this country that had nearly killed her, nearing the place where her life had changed inexorably for the worse and for the better.

An hour into their drive, when Stella got her first glimpse of ocean, she closed her eyes and put her hands on her knees, conjuring the feel of coarse fur under her fingers.

COSTA RICA

Trip Two
Day Two

STELLA SAT ON the beach in Dominical, soft rain tapping on the hood of her parka. The ocean simmered. With each new wave, storm junk washed up on shore: piles of seaweed, ratty palm branches, broken corals…

Despite the sloppy day, Stella felt relieved to be closer to Dirty. He was still 100 miles away, but that no longer seemed like an impossible distance.

She leaned back and propped herself on her fists, calmed by the palm trees leaning purposefully over the sand, and the smells of fish and ocean brine, and the vendors sheltering under large umbrellas as they sold sarongs and woven bracelets for cash.

She'd never felt this calm in Austin. She loved Austin because she'd grown up there, and because she admired the rogue aesthetic of her quirky city, where hundred-year-old live oak trees were valued as much as turquoise hair and queer rights. But her attachment for Austin arose from circumstance more than gut-level comfort.

Her attachment to Costa Rica—to this beach in particular—was born beyond herself. She felt like she'd always known this place.

True, Costa Rica had tried to kill her. But it had also awakened her. And now it seemed to be healing her.

The last remnants of pain in her joints and organs—which had faded to a mild annoyance before she left Texas—vanished completely after her arrival yesterday. As if the ocean air had expunged the dregs of her body's toxins.

She still felt an ache in her ankle when she walked longer distances, but it ached only as much as last year's ankle sprain from roller derby, and that sprain hadn't kept her off the court. She certainly wouldn't let a dull ache slow her now.

Clear in purpose, she couldn't think of anything but Dirty. Fear still clung to her like a sticky fog, but she shoved it down.

She could *feel* Dirty now. Her body knew he was close. She felt certain he was alive—although she knew that could be wishful thinking—but she couldn't shake the sense that he was in danger, or hurt. That he needed her.

And she struggled with the possibility that she might be concocting *his* need for *her*, his attachment to her, in order to soothe some kind of jungle PTSD, or fill a dead-daddy-sized void inside herself. Maybe he had already forgotten her…

She'd made so many assumptions about Dirty, about what *he* wanted and needed, but did she know him well enough to do that?

All day, her mind had charged through a thousand different reunions with Dirty: he would bound down the beach here in Dominical, and lunge into her arms. Or maybe he would muzzle his way into her hostel's dorm room while she was sleeping and crawl under the covers with her. Or maybe he would leap out from behind Tortilla Flats tonight during dinner, stinking of dumpster garbage.

She knew he couldn't possibly be in Dominical, 100 miles from where she'd left him, but still she looked for him everywhere.

A young woman slushed out of the surf, blushing at Stella as she skirted the water-line debris and toed up onto the soft sand.

Everyone here knew who Stella was. Everyone. Tourists, bracelet vendors, bartenders… Her story had become legend, exaggerated at every turn. Local news had run a story about her, similar to Theresa's, but replacing the in-person interview with photographs of Stella from the Internet: Stella holding up her diploma after high school graduation, Stella posing with her roller derby team after a tournament, Stella and her college friends reveling on a Saturday evening a couple years ago. She wondered how the reporters got these photos, whether it was legal to use them without her permission.

Locals and nomadic tourists in Costa Rica thirsted for details from her survival story. Though the questions of these people didn't differ substantially from those of back-home Texans, they irritated her less. These people seemed like part of her story, rather than voyeurs.

Still, she mostly wanted to be alone, to spend her minutes healing on the beach in the rain, checking the sky for signs of clearing, wondering what Dirty was doing at each moment.

This morning as the rain clouds gathered, Alé had told her they couldn't leave for Corcovado today. The rain—and resulting mud—would hinder their progress and raise the risks. They had to wait for a break in the weather.

"Two days of sunshine in the forecast, that is what we need," he had said as they sat on the sand by the tree line.

"I don't mind hiking in the rain," she'd said, drawing a series of circles in the sand with her finger. "I'm worried about him."

Last week, during the worst of the storm, ten-foot waves and thick fingers of lightning had pounded Corcovado National Park, downing trees, flooding roads and trails. Where would a dog hide while trees fell in a forest? There was no natural shelter: no caves, no open space aside from the wave-pounded beach.

Alé brushed a fly off his coffee mug. "Mija, it is better for you and for the dog if we wait for good weather. You do not want to be in danger again, do you?"

With the side of her palm, Stella wiped the sand circles flat and began redrawing them. "I don't know."

Alé patted her on the back and stood. "We will wait for good weather. Hopefully we can leave tomorrow. Now I will go visit my friend, who will give me herbal mosquito repellent. It is better than DEET!"

Lifting her chin toward him, she raised an eyebrow. "I'll stick with DEET. I've seen the gigantic fuckers out there."

Alé smiled down at her. "Okay, you can get all the bites while I sleep."

"Thank you for your help, Alé." She reached up to shake his hand, an oddly formal gesture that somehow felt appropriate.

"My pleasure! You helped me to repair my taxi one time, now I can help you." He held up a wad of cash. "Thank you for this payment. I promise that I will use it well."

Stooping to her eye level, his eyes narrowed. "And I must tell you something: I am excited for our journey. I wanted to become a guide again for a long time now. My daughter is gone for more than two years, and my wife is gone almost eleven months, and I thought that my life was over. You have made me live again, mija." He blinked. "So we can help each other."

Stella bit her lip, wiping the sand off her hands. "We can help each other."

COSTA RICA

Trip Two - Day Four
First Day Back In The Jungle

"WE MUST WALK eight miles along the coast to arrive at the rescue location."

Alé held up a GPS device so Stella could see it, threading his index finger along the digital route. Sun bore down on them, creating a glare so bright that they could barely see the screen.

Tucking the gadget into the back pocket of his jeans, Alé picked up the machete that he'd propped against the car. "Eight miles may sound like a small distance, but it is a difficult hike, even when we can walk on the beach. In some places the beach is covered with rocks, so in these places we will walk through jungle. And the path will be messy, because of trees and branches falling in the hurricane. Also, we will go slow, because your feet are not strong. Probably, we will arrive tomorrow morning at the place where you were rescued."

His voice trilled, dark eyebrows high and wide.

Stella nodded, hoping he couldn't sense her boiling fear.

She glanced toward the trailhead, where she could see thirty or forty feet into the jungle. The thick wad of trees, the biotic smells, the jumbled trail—all of it mirrored the wilderness that had nearly taken her life just a few weeks ago. Except that now, it was even more tangled, with hurricane-flung branches and leaves and trees crowding the understory, the flesh of newly-cracked trunks gaping moist and splintery.

Stella's joints stiffened, and suddenly she felt incapable of stepping into the canopy. But Dirty… Dirty was out there.

Something struck her shoulder, and she jumped, gasping.

With soft eyes, Alé yanked back his hand. "I am sorry to surprise you."

He lowered himself to sit on the parking lot, patting the dirt next to him. "Sit down with me."

Favoring her right leg—it felt pretty good, but she wanted to preserve its strength for the walk—she propped a hand on the bumper of the car and lowered herself to the ground.

Methodically, Alé pulled a few things from his backpack, laying them on the ground like duck eggs. "You had a difficult journey in the jungle and I know that you are afraid. But don't forget, this jungle is my home. Plus, there is no way we can get lost in the jungle because we have this Iridium satellite phone!"

He picked up a black gadget that looked like a walkie-talkie. "No matter how far we go into the jungle, this phone will always get a signal. Even if we go all the way to hell, this will still get a signal. Ha!"

He paused to let his joke sink in, and then handed her the phone. "So, it is not possible that we will get lost like you did the last time. Plus, you have the nice phone that your mother gave you, so today will be no different from going on a hike in Texas."

Stella turned the Iridium phone over in her hands, troubled by its lack of heft. It felt like a toy, probably weighing less than a pound.

Alé unzipped the top pocket of his pack and retrieved another gadget, neon green and a few inches across. "This is a locator beacon, just in case a jaguar eats my satellite phone *and* your satellite phone. This beacon sends out a GPS signal if we need rescue."

A pair of sea gulls whooshed over the clearing, reminding Stella that the ocean was near. The air hung wet and heavy despite the blueness of the sky, and she rolled up the short sleeves of her t-shirt, wishing she had worn a tank top. No, she told herself, short sleeves would keep away more bugs.

She pulled sunscreen and lip balm out of her pack, smearing them on her skin as Alé talked. Did she bring enough bug spray? Did she bring everything she needed?

Alé held the neon locator beacon in front of her so she had no choice but to look at it. She took it from him, turned it over in her hands, and gave it back.

Packing the locator beacon back in his pack, he pointed again to the satellite phone. "We will also send out GPS coordinates on this phone four or five times every day. Your mother will watch our GPS signals all day, with that application that you told her to download on her cell phone in Texas. Probably she will not stop looking at the application until we complete our mission! Right now, she probably sits with her coffee and her donut, waiting for us to send the next ping. Here, I will send her a ping."

He pressed a button with his forefinger. "She will receive it right away. Your mother is with us now."

Jamming his arm elbow-deep into the top pocket of his pack, he pulled out a bottle of pills. "These are iodine pills. When we find water, we put these pills into the water, and that will murder all the bacterias."

He smiled, as if he knew that the word *bacterias* wasn't quite right. "And even though the bacterias will all be dead, we will also put the water through the filter that your mother bought for you, and that will murder the dead bacterias again."

"And also." Unstrapping a sheath from the side of his pack, he slid out a hunting knife like the one Stella's dad used to take on camping trips. "You said no gun, so we brought no gun. But I have my machete to cut trees and vines, and I have this very scary knife."

He flipped open a compartment in the knife's handle. "In here, there are fishing hooks and a flint for lighting fires."

Alé placed a hand on each of Stella's shoulders and looked at her with kind eyes. "We are prepared. I will not let anything happen to you. Your father sent you to me, and you know that he will not let anything happen to you."

Gesturing around him with the knife, Alé's eyes widened. "We will have an adventure. Look at the beauty!"

Stella forced herself to smile. Four days—they would be in and out of the jungle in four days. Maybe three. As long as they could find Dirty. As long as he was still there. What if he wasn't at the beach when they got there?

Closing her eyes and tipping her head back to catch the sun, her mind flicked to the image of Dirty, sitting next to the dead rodent he'd killed for her, his beseeching eyes trained on her.

Leaning again on the bumper, Stella stood and hooked both thumbs under her backpack straps. She gave Alé a small nod. "Let's go have an adventure."

Checking his compass and GPS device, Alé jumped to his feet, hoisted his pack onto his shoulders, and skipped, whistling, onto an overgrown path no more than twenty inches across.

Stella tested her ankle—it felt fine. Eight miles would be no problem. She must have covered twice that distance last time, walking in circles with almost no food or water. She stepped forward, plunging into the canopy.

Within seconds, her breathing became erratic, and her body flushed cold. Desperate to run back to the car, she forced herself to put one foot in front of the next.

Towering trees careened toward her from all sides. Tree limbs and broken vines—hurricane victims—blocked the path.

Alé stooped to lug downed limbs off the path and his machete whacked back and forth through gnarled vines, alerting all the creatures to their presence.

With each inhale, Stella's brain reeled from the hot tang of ocean salt and dank vegetation. Sweat seeped into her cotton shirt, soaking her armpits, clavicle, and back.

She choked back panic as they moved slowly into the jungle; much more slowly than she had hoped. A low-level ache in her ankle reminded her that she was still healing, she had to be gentle with her body. She felt decades older than her 22 years, panting hard.

Her foot caught on a vine, and she flinched, screaming, "Snake!"

Alé turned back to her, and she bit her lip to hide the tremble in her chin. At her foot, a still-tethered vine sprang back toward its source. "Sorry. False alarm. Not a snake."

Dirty, she said to herself with each footfall. *Dirty. Dirty. Dirty.*

She catalogued a mental list of things that felt different this time: her feet, tucked into expensive hiking boots and water-wicking socks. Her ankle, supported by a medical brace. Heels and toes wrapped in moleskin to prevent blisters. Sunglasses perched on her head to ward off eyestrain and headaches. Full-sized camping backpack, a waterproof parka, a compass and a satellite phone and a liter of water and five days of granola and dried fruit and peanut butter and five freeze-dried meals. Not to mention the water purifiers and iodine tablets.

Most importantly, this time she was following a guide she trusted. He seemed confident that they would find Dirty, and that they would be back in Dominical in four days, five at the most.

Still, shit could go down. Phones could break. Jaguars could appear. Hurricanes could slam through. Dirty could be dead.

The last thought sent chills across her body. She shook out each of her arms and legs, in turn.

Alé turned over his shoulder, looking at Stella expectantly. He had asked her a question, but she hadn't heard him over the bedlam in her head.

She panted, "What?"

As she looked up at him, shifting focus away from her feet, she tripped over a branch and tumbled to the ground. The canopy spun above her. She thought she might puke.

Alé knelt by her. "Are you okay? Are you hurt? Is your ankle okay?"

Stella shook her head. "I don't know."

"I think you are just hot and, how do you Americans say it, stressed out." He pulled a water bottle from his pouch and unscrewed the top. "Drink this. It is time to breathe."

She sat back, taking deep breaths, scanning her body for pain—she'd caught herself on her good ankle, thankfully. She was fine.

He squinted to his left, scrutinizing something, and held up a finger. "Wait here one moment. I want to look for something."

Crouching off the trail and into the canopy, he sifted through piles of scrubby debris with his machete, lifting several large brown leaves to peer beneath them. His footsteps made almost no sound.

Grateful for the stillness of the moment, Stella closed her eyes and concentrated on the sounds beyond Alé: somewhere far away, a bird cawed. A gentle breeze fluttered through the leafy treetops.

"They are here!" Alé's voice jittered. "I want to show you something incredible."

She lifted herself to a seated position and opened her eyes.

Alé was pointing at something on the ground with his machete. Crawling a few steps into the canopy, as she focused on a small colorful rock beneath the point of his knife, she saw that it wasn't actually a rock – it was a frog the size of a child's thumb. Mostly black, with two orange stripes outlining the top of its torso. Glistening forest-green legs shone just brighter than the tree leaves nearby.

Slowly, Alé bent close to the animal and Stella tensed, anticipating that it would hop away. But it sat still, light glinting off its glossy eye globes.

Alé spoke quietly, still looking at the frog, as if he were speaking directly to it. "This is a Gulfodulce poison dart frog. It only lives right here, in this part of Costa Rica. Nowhere else in the world. Its skin has poison in it, and so many predators do not want to eat it. This small animal has found a way to stay alive in this big jungle."

Stella leaned toward the teensy frog, so unlike the one she had seen four weeks ago with Dirty by her side. That frog had dazzled the dusky jungle with is vivid colors. This creature seemed less intent on being the brightest thing in the forest. Its markings still advertised its power, but in a self-effacing way, as if it knew it would never be the star of the show.

"It's beautiful," she whispered.

Alé gestured around them with the machete. "This jungle is a perfect place to live. It provides everything that this animal needs to survive. Shelter, food, hiding places, mates. This frog would not be happy living anywhere else."

He stood, wiping dirt from his hands and knees. "Are you ready to walk?"

She took Alé's outstretched hand, rising to her feet and glancing again at the frog, still motionless and nearly invisible from five feet above.

Hopping back into position on the narrow path, Alé whistled to the rhythm of his machete.

Between swings, his eyes darted around the forest.

They'd gone no more than a hundred paces past the frog when he stopped walking and raised his fisted hand to indicate that Stella should stop as well. Pointing his machete upward, he turned his head over his shoulder to whisper, "*Sloths.*"

Twenty feet above them, a mother sloth dangled from a branch with one arm while a baby clung to her belly. The mother looked in their direction and then turned back to the tree, reaching lazy arm toward a branch lined with soft, dangling fronds like giant basil leaves.

Stella wondered how many sloths climbed around Corcovado right now, quiet and invisible. Dozens? Hundreds? Were this mother and baby the only ones within eyeshot? If she had some kind of ex-ray sloth-vision, would she see a hundred sloths in this patch of jungle?

She pictured Dirty, lying on the beach by a fig tree… And above him, a sloth hanging by one arm from a branch. Dirty panting hard, whimpering through some kind of pain. Behind him, her father leaning against a tree, sharpening a fishhook with a knife.

As she stared at the baby-carrying sloth, Stella muttered, "Do you think he's waiting for me?"

She bit her bottom lip, unsure whom she was asking about.

Alé nodded. "I know that he is."

A chill overran her chest and arms, shooting up her neck.

It nagged at her, this feeling that something was *wrong*. With Dirty.

She wiped sweat from her forehead. "Let's go."

"Yes," Alé said, dipping his eyebrows as if remembering that they had to stay focused and serious. "It is time to move. We will arrive at the ocean soon."

He whacked forward and Stella followed, huffing and sweating. She concentrated on her feet, stepping cautiously.

If the path had been cleared of debris and her body were in top shape, they could've moved five times faster. The slow pace heightened Stella's anxiety, and she chewed the inside of her cheek until it bled, her mind replaying the image of Dirty whimpering below the fig tree.

Every few minutes, she sucked water from the hose on her pouch, rationing each sip as if she might run out.

When the morning humidity dissolved and afternoon heat deepened, Stella and Alé sat on the thick roots of a tree to eat lunch. She ate granola and apples while he pointed out various species of tree and plant. Tucking the apple core into a baggie in the top of her pack, she swallowed two Ibuprofens to manage the swelling in her ankle.

Standing, she shook out each leg. "How far have we gone?"

"We have gone almost two and a half miles." He took down half his sandwich in three bites.

Two and a half miles? How had they only gone two and a half miles in almost four hours? It would be dark in another five or six hours.

Alé stuffed his lunch trash into his sandwich baggie. "Do you want to rest a little longer?"

"No," she said, picking up her pack. "Let's keep going. I'm moving too slowly."

He stepped in front of her, stopping her with a gentle smile. "You are doing a good job. If you can do it, we will walk for five more hours and then we will set up a campsite. If you get tired, we will stop sooner. You must stay strong so that you are able to hike out when we find your dog."

Behind them, a large-sounding animal bounded through a stand of ferns. Stella jumped, wheeling around, nearly dropping her pack. She scanned the shadows. The jungle was still. Could Dirty be this far away from where she left him?

Without a word, Alé looked at her and shook his head.

She cursed quietly. "Let's go."

As they set off, the path was mercifully clear of debris, and Alé bounced forward. Without looking back, he raised a finger. "Tonight, I will catch a fish for us and we will eat a good meal. You will feel better after you eat the most fresh fish in the world."

The rainforest muffled all sounds, only rarely giving up the distant call of a bird or treetop monkey squabble. Every few steps, Stella looked up from her feet to scan the canopy. Occasionally, Alé lifted his machete to point at a bird, rattling off facts about its life history.

For several more hours, Stella put one foot in front of the other in the blooming heat. The air pushed against her skin hot and thick like a sauna. With each breath, Stella felt like she was inhaling hot coffee.

Inside the stiff new hiking boots, her feet and ankle started to throb as her fragile muscles swelled. Her mostly-healed blisters threatened to punch through her skin again.

The moleskin would do its job, she reminded herself. The ankle would hold, inside its brace. She could handle pain. She wasn't a wuss.

A cloud floated overhead, darkening the jungle, and Alé slowed his pace. He held up a hand to signal that she should stop walking.

The silence took on an eerie timbre.

With his back to her, Alé pointed into the shadows thirty or forty feet ahead, on the left side of the trail.

The remnants of a messy campsite unfurled across a small clearing: a hammock strung between two trees underneath a tarp heavy with leaves and old rain. A muddy green sleeping bag crumpled on the ground. An upturned plastic cup, crawling with ants. An open backpack perched on a tree root next to a rumpled windbreaker. A dozen crushed plastic water bottles, lying on their sides, pooled with dirty rainwater. Two logs, charred from a recent fire, flanked by an empty can of beans, its peeled-back top gaping. Behind the campsite, a pile of muddy trash.

Alé tiptoed forward. "Camping and fires are not permitted in Corcovado. This campsite is illegal."

Stella followed close behind him, heart pounding in her ears.

Alé stuck his machete into the backpack gaping open on the ground and rooted through its contents. "Wallets. Probably stolen."

Dizzied, Stella recalled the man with acne-scarred cheeks, the whites of his eyes gleaming, his voice flat: *Trouble?*

She shivered, noticing her footprints in the mud and side-stepping onto a bed of leaves. A wet candy wrapper clung to the base of a tree beside her.

Alé took her elbow and tugged her toward the trail. "We must be careful. Many tourists have been robbed in Corcovado this year. This man who stays here, I think he is a bad man. Can you hike for one more hour so that we can get away from this campsite?"

Stella nodded, raising one foot like a flamingo to relieve pressure on the nascent blisters. She put that foot down and raised the other.

Clearing her throat, she closed her eyes against the rapid thrum of her heart.

Alé placed a hand on her shoulders, forcing her to meet his eyes. "I see that this is hard for you, mija. You are very brave. We will make a nice campsite on the beach tonight, I promise. It will be beautiful."

She reached up to touch his shoulder, faking a smile.

They tramped forward on the path for twenty minutes, her mind spinning in uncomfortable circles. Could the man with the machete be watching them? Would he find them during the night? Regardless, she was glad that they were going to camp on the beach. Seemed like there was a greater chance

Dirty could find them if they were on the beach. But if Dirty could find them more easily, would the same be true of the man from the illegal campsite?

She cleared her throat again, coughing hard. Was she allergic to something? She stopped walking, squatted, and dropped her head to her hands, taking a few deep breaths.

Alé turned back to squat next to her, placing a hand on her back. "Wait here for a moment. I will find something amazing to show you."

He stepped off the path, putting down his machete and reaching toward a small tree with leaves as long as his arm, drooping on either side of their long stems like umbrellas bowed by a rainstorm. With his fingers, Alé lifted the drooping edges of a leaf and gestured to Stella to look underneath.

She stooped and craned her neck to peer at the underside of the umbrella leaf, gasping. "Are those bats?"

Six or seven critters, each one barely larger than a golf ball, clung to the leaf upside-down.

"Tent-making bats," Alé whispered. "One bat weighs only half of one ounce. This bat spreads fig seeds around the forest, which makes the new trees grow."

Large, funnel-shaped ears grew as long as the bats' muzzles. From the tips of their noses, protruding nostrils flared like stamens. Two delicate white stripes partitioned their faces, setting off tiny black eyes. Their wings folded tight against their bodies as they huddled cheek-to-cheek, jumbled like a pile of kittens.

"Damn." Stella sniffed, twisting her nose at the strong musty smell. "That's the ugliest animal I've ever seen. They're so ugly they're kind of cute."

Alé's lips parted, showing his teeth. "If my nose looked like that, I would not have found a wife."

Stella stood, grunting at her feet and putting a hand on Alé's shoulder. "The bats are amazing. Seeing the jungle with you makes it a lot better."

"There is much beauty here," he said, picking up his machete and using it to point at her backpack. "Don't forget to drink your water."

As she sucked water from her pouch, she stifled a growing urge to call out for Dirty. Could he be this far from where she'd left him? Should she call to him? No, she didn't want the man from the campsite to hear her. She pursed her lips to keep his name from busting out of her mouth.

Anxiety stirred in her gut. She wondered if Dirty would remember her.

Her Dad had gone away for a month, once, for work. Torres had moped around the house with her head hung low, skipping meals, uninterested in walks. Stella grudgingly walked her every morning and evening until the dog broke her leash, tearing down the street, disappearing for two days. After that, they paid the neighbor's kid five bucks a day to walk the dog, and as the weeks rolled by, Torres moped less and ate more, following Stella and her mother around the house despite their indifference toward her.

When Stella's father pulled up in Moby Dick at the end of his trip, Torres howled at the front window, trying to break through the pane. Her father opened the front door, and Torres leapt into his arms, licking his face, yelping, while Stella and her mother rolled their eyes at each other, jealous that the first greeting had gone to a canine.

Dirty would remember her, right? He would leap into her arms?

Moving through the rainforest, Stella felt disconnected from her body. She steadied her breath, inhaling and exhaling with her footsteps. As they got farther from the messy campsite in the jungle, she felt less queasy at the possibility of sharing the jungle with the man she had met on the trail four weeks earlier. Surely, he wouldn't find them.

Late in the afternoon, they emerged from the canopy onto a wide-open beach. Stella squinted up at an azure sky flecked with clouds. The pre-dusk sun blasted Stella hard in the face and she pulled her sunglasses down over her eyes.

Broken palm fronds and tree branches and seaweed rimmed the high-water line, erasing much of the coastline's beauty. Down the beach, a small tree had washed up onto the sand, withered and waterlogged but intact. Twenty or thirty feet past the muddy cram of storm debris, the ocean shimmered turquoise, the same hue it had been on her last day with Dirty.

The place where she and Dirty had spent that last day—it was close. She could feel it.

In some ways, this debris-laden stretch of beach looked nothing like the spot where she had been rescued. But the smells of fish and seaweed, the turquoise water, the clean salt breeze, all of these things were identical.

Dropping to her knees, running fingers through the sand, Stella scanned the vast expanse, half-expecting Dirty to burst around a bend, loping toward her, tongue dangling.

Nothing moved but the waves, slushing up and down the gently-sloping shore. Was Dirty standing in the surf right now? Could he be just around that bend?

She needed to call to him. "Alé…"

Just ahead on the sand, Alé stopped walking and turned around to face her.

"Can I call for Dirty? Are we far enough from the man's campsite?"

He walked back to her and rested a hand on her shoulder. "It is better if you wait just a little longer, mija. The man will not come this far out, but we do not want him to hear us."

Alé squatted next to her. "And we are still too far away to find your friend. We must walk almost three more miles to get to the place where the paramedics found you. When we get there, we will find your friend. He will wait there for you."

Stella stood, wobbling under the weight of her pack. "Can we keep going a little farther tonight?"

Several hundred feet from shore, a pod of dolphins coursed through the water, their backs breaking the surface in soft humps.

Alé dropped his backpack to the ground. "You are tired, mija. I can tell. We will camp here tonight."

Stella opened her mouth to protest, and then closed it. She watched the dolphins glide around the curve in the coastline.

Dropping back down to sit on the sand, she unlaced a boot and gingerly nudged it off. Alé knelt next to her as she pulled off her sock and brace. The ankle looked okay. A little swollen, but not too bad.

She lifted the moleskin protecting her old blisters. The skin ached red and raw, but unbroken.

"Your feet look good. No blisters." Alé surveyed the flat beach, nodding. "This is a good place to camp."

She rolled her ankle and pulled off her other boot. "Are you sure we're far enough from that man's camp? Will he find us here? We could keep walking."

"No, no." Ale pulled a hammock from his pack. "This is perfect. Unless we make a lot of noise, he will not come out this far, because tourists never come this far at night. So he thinks that there is nobody to rob out here. Probably, he made his campsite beyond where the tourists go so that nobody will ever see where he lives and take his things. We are safe here, but we will be even safer if we do not make very much noise."

Not feeling comforted by Alé's rickety assessment of their safety, Stella shuffled to the high-water line and sat with her toes skimming the crests of the waves. The water felt cool and soothing on her tired feet.

Her lips pulsed in the direct sun, and she pulled a tube of balm from her pocket, closing her eyes as the gel cooled her mouth. Just three and a half weeks ago, her raw bleeding lips had awakened her in the night during her hospital stay.

Behind her, Alé busied himself setting up the campsite, calling out, "Our hammocks are built with mosquito nets treated with permethrin—this is the best camping invention! The bugs hate the permethrin so they will not try to come inside our hammocks to sleep with us."

Barely audible over the ocean breeze, she muttered in his direction, "Do you need help?"

Alé swatted the air with a strong, weatherworn hand. "No, mija, this is what you paid me for. Plus, setting up a camp, this is one of my favorite things in the world."

"Thank you, Alé." Stella smiled and turned back to the ocean. If her feet and body felt stronger, she would run down the beach right now for three miles, until she arrived at that triangular peninsula jutting out into the ocean. She would scream through the jungle until she found Dirty, dead or alive.

She lay back on the sand, slapping a mosquito on her chest, listening to the waves.

Her father's voice whispered clearly over the waves: *I will wait for you.*

She shot upright, gaping over her shoulders.

"What the fuck," she whispered, relieved that Alé wasn't watching.

He emerged from the jungle beaming, hurrying toward her, his voice hushed. "Stella, you must come with me so that I can show you something very rare. You will like this thing." He beckoned her urgently with his hand. "Try to be quiet."

Stella glowered at her feet, wondering if she had the mettle to put her shoes back on.

Alé jogged to her backpack and unstrapped the flip-flops lashed to the side of her backpack, handing them to her. "Put these on. We will not go far."

He put his finger to his lips and motioned for her to follow as he ducked between two low-hanging branches and tiptoed into the canopy.

Grudgingly following Alé's soft steps, Stella flip-flopped noisily over and around roots and storm debris.

Just inside the jungle, Alé pointed to a tree crammed with leaves the size of a human hand, and green fig-like fruits rimming long branches that shook erratically.

Stella scanned the treetops to discern what was causing the shaking.

"There! Do you see them?" Alé's mouth hung open as he craned his head backward. "Scarlet macaws. They are making scarlet macaw babies right now!"

Directly above them, two crimson-red parrots stood on a fluttering branch, flapping their vivid yellow and blue wings. One of them bobbed its head in and out, ruffling its long red neck feathers. They grabbed each other's bulky black-and-white beaks awkwardly, like tipsy lovers. Pressing their tails together, they teetered back and forth as their spindly talons strained to balance on the thin branch. When the tail-press had run its course, one of the macaws bowed its head to nuzzle the other's chest, and they tipsy-kissed again, and then started the ritual again. After the next round, one macaw bit onto her lover's foot, forcing the lover to wobble precariously as it struggled to stand on one talon.

Stella held her breath.

"This is very rare behavior," Alé whispered. "It is very lucky to see this."

"Incredible," she said, calm and invisible.

With a hand half-covering his mouth, Alé whispered, "These birds will stay with each other for their entire life, and they might live fifty years. They have babies every two or three years, so they will not do this behavior again for a long time."

As she watched the parrots move through the motions of making more parrots, a fraction of Stella's anxiety melted off of her. She stopped scanning the forest for Dirty, stopped wondering what time it was or when they would arrive at the rescue beach in the morning. Something about these birds, this intimate act, took her out of place and time.

She had found a robin's egg, once, during a late-high-school camping trip with her father and Torres. The delicate blue egg had lain in pieces on the ground.

Stella and her father squatted to look at the remains as Torres leaned in to sniff.

She picked up one of the shells, slightly sticky on the inside. "Do you think the egg fell out of the nest before it hatched?"

Torres leaned in, touching the tip of his tongue to one of the fragments.

Her father picked up another sliver of eggshell. "No, I think it hatched and the parents threw the egg out of the nest to eliminate the smell." Stella put the shell back on the ground, arranging the largest bits in a circle. "Do birds do that?"

Her father shrugged. "I would, if I were a bird."

Stella wished her father were there, in Corcovado, to see the scarlet macaws. She watched them until her neck began to ache from craning back her heavy head, and the twilight swarm of mosquitoes started to rise.

Alé motioned toward the beach, and they left the birds to finish their lovefest in private.

The sun was dropping through pink fingers of clouds as Stella wiggled into her expensive long-sleeved pullover. A gift from her mother, it had been treated with insect repellent that would never wash off. The notion of bug-repellent clothes felt like an impossible luxury.

"Can I text my mom?" she asked, smothering herself in a cloud of DEET.

"Of course." Alé fiddled with the phone and handed it to her. "Type your message there."

"Thanks." She held the phone limply as she watched a gangly pelican dive into the ocean so hard she thought the bird's body would break on impact. Thrashing back to the surface, the pelican flipped several fish into the air and caught them in its floppy gullet.

Stella typed:

Hi Mom. We're safe. Haven't found Dirty yet. Alejandro is a really good guide, strong and smart. Saw scarlet macaws today. It's beautiful here, which feels weird b/c of last time… Hoping to find Dirty tomorrow. Love you. –S

Pressing *Send*, she handed the phone back to Alé as he rolled his jeans up around his knees.

"I will be back soon, with dinner." He gave her a thumbs-up and waded into the surf with a fishing pole.

Stella sank into her hammock underneath the mosquito net. Swaying gently to the music of the ocean, she fell asleep.

The dream came to her again: her father throwing a stick out into the river, Torres jumping in after it. As Torres swam back to shore, the dog's eyes changed from blue to black, and she morphed into Dirty. But this time, as Dirty paddled to the riverbank through swelling rapids, her father was not there to reach out a hand. Dirty scrabbled his front paws on a slick rock. A surge of upstream water barreled toward him, pelting him in the face, ripping him off the rock and carrying him away.

Screaming, she tumbled out of her hammock, pounding an elbow and knee onto the packed sand.

Alé appeared above her in the last fuzz of daylight, holding a fish. "Are you okay?"

"I don't know," she said, wiping sand from her face, scanning the beach. "Dirty. I think he's in trouble. How early can we leave tomorrow?"

Alé strung the fish to a tree and opened his knife's handle to pull out a flint. "The sun will start to rise by five in the morning. We will leave then, okay? It is safer this way. Too dangerous to walk in the dark."

Stella nodded, slapping a mosquito on her neck. She slipped back under her hammock's net, watching the waves as Alé built a fire.

"Building this fire is illegal," Alé said as the first sticks took flame. "Please do not tell anyone I built this fire, okay?"

"Okay." Rummaging in her pack for granola, her fingers slid across a rough piece of cloth, and she pulled it out. A turquoise dog collar, with a silver paw-print-shaped nameplate that read: *Dirty.*

Alé scraped the scales off the fish. "And camping here, also illegal. So we will not tell anyone that either, okay?"

Unbuckling the dog collar, Stella twisted it twice around her wrist and clasped it. "I didn't know you were a rebel, Alé."

He gave the collar an approving nod and dug his knife into the fish's belly, scraping out the guts. "I played by the rules for many years, but it didn't make me happier or richer, so now I just do my life with kindness."

"I like that." Stepping out of her hammock, she held her hands to the fire and admired the bright turquoise fabric around her wrist, hoping it would be big enough for Dirty's neck. "Could the man from the campsite smell the fire?"

"I do not think so. Even if he smelled it, he would not know where it was coming from. And we will put it out as soon as the fish is cooked." Alé flipped the fish lying on a stone at the edge of the fire.

Shadows danced in and out of sun-dried wrinkles that made him look older than his 42 years. He spoke low into the flames, "I took my daughter camping once."

Stella could picture it: Alé pointing out monkeys in the trees as his daughter squealed, and holding her hand as she giggled, toes fidgeting in the waves. "Did she like it?"

He nodded, touching the black shell necklace strung around his neck before pulling the fish away from the fire and shaving its roasted flesh into two bowls. "I took her to a campground by Manuel Antonio National Park and I blew up a mattress in the tent and put in it her favorite stuffed animals and her special blanket. Before she fell asleep, she said, 'Nunca me he sentido tan bien,' which means, *I have never felt this good.* Maybe that was the happiest night of my life."

"You're a good dad." Stella scooped up sand and poured it over her feet, burying them. "I'm glad she got to experience that."

Alé handed her a bowl of fish and rice.

As she took it from him, the bottoms of her arms glowed warm from the fire beneath. "My dad took me camping a lot, and I didn't like it back then, but now I wish I could go camping with him one more time."

Alé kicked sand over the fire, squelching the flames, and then picked up his own bowl of fish as the last tendrils of smoke gasped from the fire. "It is good that you went camping with him. We are lucky."

"We are." Picking off a flake of fish with her fingers, she smelled it and then touched it to her tongue, moaning. "Damn, that's good."

"It is the best food in the world." Alé raised his water pouch. "Cheers."

They emptied their bowls, and Stella sucked down the dregs of water from her pouch.

Alé reached into his pack and handed her the last pouch he'd filled in Dominical. "We will find more water tomorrow. I will make it pure like snow, do not worry."

"Thanks." Stella gathered their dishes and washed them in the surf under a sky pounding with stars. When she padded barefoot back up to the campsite, Alé sat in his hammock reading a book by the light of his headlamp.

She squinted at the title on the paperback, smiling. "Alé, are you seriously reading *The Unbearable Lightness of Being*?"

He held up the book. "This is a very good novel. Have you read it?"

"No." She exhaled with a laugh. "Damn, it's no wonder you speak such good English."

"Thank you. That is a very nice compliment." He smiled and looked back down at his book.

An hour later, as Alé drifted to sleep in his hammock, impervious to the insects' screaming, Stella sat on the beach until the night's chill sent her back to the campsite, where she pulled on her jacket and wrapped herself in the folds of her hammock.

As the minutes ticked toward dawn, she stared down the beach, searching for the shape of a dog bounding toward her in the starlight.

COSTA RICA

Trip Two
Second Day Back In The Jungle

WHEN THE MOON started to fade into the deep blue of morning, Stella wondered if it was too early to wake Alé.

She hadn't slept. The constant night chatter of frogs and bugs sawed at her nerves. She scratched at her skin, imagining bugs that weren't there. Her stomach growled and she started hyperventilating, panicking, although she had consumed no dirty water. Her muscles never relaxed, braced for the inevitable encroachment of snakes and bandits and anteaters. By morning, her body ached from the unnatural crumple of the hammock. She longed for the balm of Dirty's body, his sour breath hot and soft on her neck.

The night had been star-bright, free from the canopy's cloak, and the brightness had been a relief: at least she could've seen the bandit if he'd approached.

Across the span of ocean, the caps of waves popped white through the dawn, and then disappeared. She watched the beach in both directions, wondering how far away a dog could smell a human.

Reaching down to her backpack below the hammock, Stella pulled out the GPS device and sent her mother a ping.

She pictured her mom sitting at the backyard table, coffee steaming in her hand, sighing at her phone as her location beeped onto the screen.

"Good morning, Stella." Alé's voice danced through the darkness, despite the early hour. "This sunrise will be so beautiful that it will break your heart. I can tell."

Like a cat, Stella stretched her arms and back. "Good morning."

Alé sat up in his hammock, swaying. "Are you ready to go and find your dog?"

"I'm ready." She slipped out of the hammock, sinking her toes into the cool sand. Putting weight on her feet, they felt pretty good. No shooting pains where her blisters had raged four weeks ago. The slight ache in her ankle wouldn't be a hindrance.

She tugged off her pullover, stretching her arms again. "This is a nice temperature. It doesn't feel like anything."

"I like that." Alé's wide smile almost nudged off the sides of his face. "This temperature doesn't feel like anything. What a beautiful day!"

She massaged the arches of her feet as she chewed handfuls of granola, and then dropped to the sand to apply fresh moleskin to her heels and toes.

Alé handed her a cup of coffee brewed over his camp stove. "Your feet look good. You brought Ibuprofen, yes? You should take this too."

Stella nodded up at him. "Thanks. I will."

Unaccustomed to coffee, she took a tentative sip, almost spitting it out when the bitter tang rolled over her tongue. But as it slid down her throat, she felt instantly rejuvenated. She took another sip, and another. "This is disgusting—I don't even like coffee—but I can't stop drinking it."

He raised his cup to her. "Everything tastes better on the trail."

"My dad used to say that." She raised her cup to Alé, and then up to the fading moon.

"We will walk mostly under the trees today." Alé glanced overhead. Sinewy branches traced black patterns through a clear navy sky. "It will be too hot to walk on the beach. Close to here, there's a trail that goes inside the trees and follows the beach."

A gigantic bird, some kind of eagle, soared overhead. Stella stopped bandaging her toe to watch it pass. "I know it's going to be hot, but what if…"

Alé shook his head as he packed away the hammocks and camping stove. "I know why you are worrying. We will be able to see the beach almost the whole time. You will know if your friend is there."

Kicking sand over the remnants of fire until no trace remained, he gave the campsite a nod of approval. "And the dog will know that you are there before you see him. He will smell you."

"Okay." Gingerly, she pulled on her ankle brace and hiking socks, nodding at him. "I trust you."

"Good!" He clapped his hands. "Now let's go. It is 5AM!"

Cinching her bootlaces, Stella raised her exhausted body to her feet and strapped Alé's water pouch to her pack. "Let's go."

Alé drifted down the beach pointing at shells and crabs, spewing factoids about what they ate, how long they lived.

Stella nodded with an occasional, "Wow" or "Cool," unable to match his early-morning energy.

They clambered over driftwood—entire trees, washed ashore in the storm—and long knotty jumbles of seaweed. Decaying plastic bags and colorful flip-flops strewed the beach, carried across the ocean on meandering currents.

They moved slowly through this clutter; Alé seemed to relish the slowness, but Stella's skin itched from frustration and impatience.

She scrambled ahead of him, straying into the hard-packed surf to comb for impressions made by dog paws.

Thirty hard minutes into the day's trek, her body went cold. In the sand, a trail of prints emerged from the jungle and then moved along the high-water line.

"Alé." Her voice quivered.

Bent over to examine a fragment of coral, Alé didn't hear her.

When he stood and sauntered up behind her saying something about cauliflower corals, she interrupted him, "Alé."

His eyes went wide and he dropped the coral as he leaned down to look at the tracks. "Qué maravilloso! Un jaguar!"

Grunting under the weight of her pack, Stella squatted to look more closely at the prints. "Jaguar? These are from a jaguar?"

Alé nodded, beaming. "Sí. It is very lucky to see this."

She dropped to her knees and bent her head to the ground, wrenching her fingers closed around damp chunky wads of sand. Grains of grit swirled into her scalp. She wanted to scream, to release her frustrations in a guttural wail, but she forced herself to keep it together.

Still doubled over, she lifted one arm to scratch at a mosquito bite on her shoulder, making it bleed.

Alé put his hand on her back. "You thought it was him."

A breeze puffed Stella's thick brown ponytail off her shoulders, cooling the sweat that pooled around her neck. She sat up and wiped her eyes, the skin on her face stretching tight from heat and thirst.

Stooping, Alé pointed toward one of the footprints. "You see the toes, here? They are round, and there is no mark from the claws. That is because cats walk with the claws inside the feet. If you find tracks from your dog, you will see a small mark above each toe, from the claw."

Her father had tried to teach her this lesson, once, in the Texas back-country. "These are mountain lion tracks," he had said. "You can tell it's a cat 'cause…" and then she had tuned him out, certain that she would never need to know how to identify the tracks of a mountain lion.

She reached into her pocket and pulled out the thin tube of insect-repelling sunscreen lotion, slathering it frantically on her face, shoulders and lips. She took a swig from the water pouch, her belly going soft from worry when she saw that it was only half-full.

Hitching the dog collar higher up on her arm, she kneaded her wrist where it had left indentations in her skin, and then resettled the strap low on her wrist, with the nameplate facing outward.

The tide stretched higher, almost licking her boots as she hoisted herself back to her feet and trudged onto the soft sand with Alé to follow the jaguar's tracks back into the jungle.

Alé pointed at another footprint. "He knows this trail that we are going to use today. Qué maravilloso."

Stepping quietly, Stella whispered, "Should I be troubled? Do we really want to go for a hike with a jaguar?"

Alé shook his head. "Oh, no, do not be troubled. A jaguar does not want to eat you for dinner. You do not taste very good. Plus, a jaguar will see that I have this!" Squatting in warrior stance, he brandished his machete.

As they stepped into the jungle, an itch spread over Stella's thighs and arms. She wanted to pull off her shirt and scratch her whole body until she'd raked off her epidermis. The jungle—how could she possibly be back in this jungle? Her breathing became irregular, noisy inhales followed by choppy exhales.

Looking down, she forced herself to focus the jaguar tracks, analyzing the shape of the toes and the pattern of the animal's gait: left back paw, then left front, right back, right front.

As she moved forward, Stella squinted through the copse on her left to where the beach met the tree line fifty feet away. Though the trees weren't densely packed here, she couldn't make out any beachside details. Dirty could be out there looking for her, and neither of them would know how close they were. Again, his name gathered in her throat and lungs and she had to clinch her teeth shut to keep herself from screaming, *DIRTYYY!*

She bent down to drop her thumb inside one of the jaguar's toe prints, and WHACK, she smacked her forehead on a low-hanging branch, dropping to the ground with a thud.

The world swilled into a lush haze. Opening her eyes, she raised a hand to touch her head where a lump had already risen like a flat marble. Her knee—she must have landed on her left knee—ached, and she shifted her leg out from underneath her to pull the pressure off it. At least it wasn't her right knee, already doing extra work to support the healing ankle sprain.

Alé leaned over her, saying something. What was he saying? His mouth was moving, but she couldn't understand him. Was he speaking Spanish, or English?

"Stella? Are you okay?" His eyebrows dipped.

Jungle smells flooded her nose, sailing through her mouth: leaf mold, muddy water, animal urine.

Alé put two fingers on the knotty forehead swelling, pulling a small bottle from his backpack. "Stella?"

His voice was too loud. She looked down at the jungle floor.

He handed her two pills. "Here, take this Ibuprofen. Drink some water."

She shook her head. "Have to save the water."

"No, you will drink." He shoved the straw from the water pouch into her mouth.

She sucked down a sip, wondering if it was happening again, if the jungle was swallowing her. She wasn't someone who just *fell down* while walking. She'd never been clumsy. This was the second time she'd fallen in two days—not to mention all the tumbles she took a few weeks ago. It felt like this jungle, hell-bent on destroying her, was sucking away her strength and focus.

Alé made her take another sip, and slowly, sounds and smells sank to their normal levels, the pain in her head softened. Her knee stopped aching.

"Do you feel like you will throw up?" Alé made her sip a third time, the water pouch now only one-quarter full.

She searched her body. "No."

"Gracias a Dios. You will be fine," Alé said. "I do not think you have a concussion, but you must not push yourself too hard. It is very hot and you are still recovering. We will walk more slowly."

"No! Not more slowly." She teetered on the verge of a mental explosion. For the past 24 hours, she'd pressed back panic and stress and terror, and she couldn't fucking do it anymore, and the only thing that could fix her right now was finding Dirty.

Bracing her fists on the ground, she raised herself to a squat. Alé clamped a hand under her armpit, lifting her to her feet.

She brushed off her jeans and chewed the inside of her cheek as she waited out a wave of vertigo. When it cleared, she lifted her chin. "I'm fine. Let's go."

The jaguar tracks disappeared into the undergrowth, but Stella and Alé pressed forward on the thin, jumbled trail. Alé whacked furiously at vines and branches, sweat seeping outward from his armpits as he worked to clear the trail.

Though their pace had slowed to a near crawl, each step felt like a hammer pounding Stella's temples. Her mouth grew dry, but she wouldn't let herself drink. Twice, she stumbled, catching herself before she careened to the ground. Alé tried to make her sit and rest, but she refused.

Through the thin stand of trees that separated her from the beach, she could still only see glimpses of ocean and blue sky. The jungle pressed in closer, and she fiddled with the nameplate on the wrist-bound dog collar to keep herself alert, focused.

As the midmorning heat sucked sweat from her pores, she'd had enough of the rainforest. She needed space. Fresh air. She was mustering the energy to tell Alé that she needed to walk out on the open shore, even if meant that they would walk more slowly, when the trail led them out of the canopy onto the beach. Stella staggered, dizzy, onto the blazing sand.

"One more hour, perhaps," Alé said, wiping his wet brow with his forearm. "We are close."

Dirty was close. She might see him any minute. Maybe he could even smell her now. Maybe he was nearby, muzzle raised, nose twitching as he caught a familiar scent.

Her gaze darted everywhere, searching for canine movements. She wanted to call to him. And why shouldn't she? That man from the campsite—he couldn't be out this far, could he?

Boots sinking into the sand with every step, she trudged over to Alé . "The man from the campsite—he wouldn't be out this far, would he?"

Alé shook his head. "No. Almost nobody comes out here. It is too far for tourists, and there are no hostels close by. The man from the campsite would not be here, because there is nothing to steal."

Stella swigged from her water pouch. There were only a few sips left. "I'm going to call for him, okay? Dirty? I didn't want to scare you."

Alé nodded, pursing his lips. "Yes, mija. You call for him now."

Cupping her hands around her mouth, she bellowed, "DIRTY!"

Birds cawed overhead, and the surf rose and fell with a shush.

She turned in the opposite direction and ran a few steps down the beach, blood pounding her head. "DIRTY!"

Something scuttled at the edge of the tree line, and she dropped her pack, running toward it, her throat thickening with anticipation.

"Stella," Alé cautioned quietly after her.

Fighting against the sinking sand, Stella scrambled to the edge of the forest, leaping into the canopy just in time to see the tail of a coati disappear into the thick.

She stood, stunned, listening to nothing.

Holding her head in her hands, she turned to walk back to her backpack on the beach.

With a nod, Alé tucked his thumbs under the straps on his shoulders. "Let's go find him."

Thumping the pack back on her back, Stella steadied herself on her feet and they set off as the sun rose higher, reaching its pinnacle.

Her anxious throat swelled tight, and she wheezed and panted with every breath, trembling, holding back tears. Wiping her eyes so she could see clear, she spun in a full circle every few steps, looking in every direction.

As they tramped around a bend in the coast, a new stretch of beach unwound in front of them. A long triangular peninsula of sand jutted out into the surf.

Stella flung her pack onto the sand and wailed into her cupped hands: "DIRTY!" She ran, boot heels sinking in the sand, toward the tree line. "DIRTY!"

Scrabbling back to the water line, she searched for paw prints in the packed sand and screamed again: "DIRTY!"

Frantic, she turned again toward the tree line. "DIRTY! DIRTY!"

Her voice cracked from the strain. "DIRTYYYY!"

A crab skittered past her boot, disappearing into a sand hole. Farther down the beach, a tall white shorebird probed the bank with a curved beak.

Dropping to the ground, Stella closed her eyes. Her head throbbed and she rolled onto her side, covering her tear-streaked face with her arm. Sand grabbed at her lip and cheek and forehead.

She slitted open her eyes. Right over there, that's where Dirty had waded into the surf, muzzle gummy from fish guts, staring toward the horizon.

Right here, on this exact patch, he had lain next to her as strength drained out of her and leeched into the sand.

And right over there, that's where her father had stooped with Dirty behind the fray of rescuers as she flailed, restrained by hands that didn't understand what they were taking from her.

He wasn't here. She had been certain he would be here.

If he were nearby, he would've smelled her by now. Or he would've heard her. He was probably dead. Or maybe he had wandered to some far-flung part of Corcovado where she could never find him.

Maybe it wasn't possible to find one goddamn dog in a vast wilderness. Maybe her *dead father* had not told her to go back to Costa Rica to find a goddamn *dog*.

She wiped her eyes, shaking.

If she couldn't find him, she didn't know how she would recover. She had staked her emotional recovery on this bond that she imagined she had with Dirty.

She'd been through too much, had experienced hardship and sadness so crushing that she didn't have the skills to move past them. Not without him.

She turned around to look for Alé. He stood by a tree at the edge of the canopy, stringing up his hammock and mosquito net. With a nod, he walked past her to pick up the backpack that she had flung onto the sand.

"Will you be okay here for a while?" As he walked toward her with the pack on his shoulder, his voice barely rose above the waves.

Nodding, she wiped sand from her mouth and cheek. "Can I text my mom?"

He handed her the phone from his pocket. "Your water is gone. I will go find water and come back."

He floated up the beach, walking effortlessly, as if his heels were immune to the sinking sand. Dropping her pack by his hammock, he disappeared into the shade of the trees.

Stella wiped a dribble of snot from her lip and texted her mom:

Hi Mom. We made it to the beach where I was rescued. Dirty isn't here. I need to find him. I love you.

She raised her left arm, angling the nameplate on the dog collar so it glinted in the sun. *DIRTY.*

Cursing, she unlatched the collar from her wrist and flung it up the beach.

Fingers and toes tingling with frustration, she unlaced her shoes, lobbing them up the bank.

Dirty wasn't there.

Her father was dead.

Her body was wrecked.

Her brain felt broken.

Picking up a hefty piece of driftwood, she lifted it over her head, biceps bulging, and bashed it down into the sand. Splinters flew away from the branch. She lifted it again and brought it down hard on the ground, splinters flying over and over and over. The wood scraped rough on her palm, making it glow red. Each time the driftwood hit the earth, she grunted as the impact sent shockwaves through her body, ratcheting up her frustration, her anger, her anguish and helplessness. When the driftwood had been reduced to a thousand woody shards, she clutched her hair with her fingers as tears streamed down her face.

It felt good, this tantrum. Cathartic, and appropriately shitty. Anger and sadness coursed through her, invigorated her. Bashing that stick into the ground, it had made her feel alive.

This wasn't like her. She wasn't a tantrum person. She almost always kept her emotions in check. Aside from the brief outburst at her father's funeral, the last time she remembered having a tantrum, she was five or six years old. She and her parents had gone to Zilker Park in January to see the Christmas lights. Every year, she would stand under the giant illuminated tree, arms outstretched, looking up into the spiral of lights, spinning herself in circles until she tumbled to the ground.

Most years, her family went to Zilker in December, but that year they'd been busy with family visits and work obligations and an ill-timed flu, which they'd passed from one to the other like the pecan pie at Christmas dinner.

"Will the Christmas tree still be lit up next week?" she asked her father as she sweated through a 103-degree fever.

"I think so," he said. "We'll go as soon as you're well."

They made it to Zilker, still blowing their noses, just as the lights were being pulled down for the season. Stella flung herself on the ground, screaming like she was being electrocuted. Her mother told her to "hush" and stepped away to mutter apologies to everyone within earshot.

Her father sat with her on the dry winter grass as she convulsed with sobs.

"This sucks," he said. "I'm disappointed too."

Lying next to her, he rubbed her back. "But I have a feeling that crying isn't gonna be what makes you feel better. You can let me know. If the crying doesn't make you feel good, we could try what I call a 'redirect,' which is doing something else that makes you feel good. Like, replacing the bad feeling with a good one. Let me know when you're done crying and then we can talk about what might be a good redirect."

She sobbed awkwardly for another minute or two, angry at him for trying to manipulate her—she might be young but she wasn't stupid—but she did wonder what the redirect was gonna be. What kind of thing could give her a "good feeling" right now? Without looking up from the ground, she said, "Like what redirect?"

"Hmmm..." He made a show of hard-thinking. "Hut's Hamburger's?"

She sat up, frowning hard, wiping her eyes. She did love Hut's Hamburgers.

Her father brushed dry grass off her face and picked her up, whirling her around until she squealed, laughing.

Now, almost two decades later, Stella leaned back on the sand panting from the tantrum, dry lips splitting along small seams. She imagined her father wiping the sand off her face.

"I found water." Alé's voice floated toward her as he crossed the beach holding a large plastic jug and a toiletry bag. "There's a small river not far from here."

"That's..." She dug her fingers into the sand, opening her eyes. "That's gotta be the river that made me sick."

Alé sat next to her, nestling the jug into the sand. "Maybe, but I walked upstream until I found a small waterfall moving over some rocks. The water there is nicer than it is downstream. And now I will show you how I clean the water."

He pulled a bottle out of the bag and unscrewed the cap, tapping out a few tablets into his palm. "First, I will put these Iodine tablets into the water, and that will kill all of the bacterias."

He dropped the tablets into the jug, shook it, and then held up another vial. "Now I will put in these tablets, which will take away the not very good taste of the Iodine. Then, in thirty minutes, this water will be perfectly good for drinking."

Stella's stomach turned as she remembered the moldy, murky tang of the creek water.

Alé screwed the top on the jug and leaned toward her. "But I am not finished! Just for you, I will also boil this water on my illegal camping stove so that we know that we have twice killed all of the little bacterias."

She liked the idea of boiling the water. Those microscopic shitheads couldn't survive boiling, right?

He handed her a small bottle of pills. "Also, you will take one of these twice a day for the rest of the trip."

Reading the Spanish label, she scrunched her nose. "Oregano? Are you telling to eat oregano?"

"Yes! Oregano kills so many bacterias. This way, we will three-times-kill the bacterias."

He held up a cloth bag, retrieved from Stella's pack. "And then we will also send the water through the water filter that your mother bought for you, so that will kill the bacterias a fourth time."

He handed her his half-full water pouch. "Here, you can finish the water in my pouch. This is the last water from Dominical. Tonight, I will drink the water with four-times-killed bacterias, and you will see that I am not sick in the morning."

"Thanks." She took the pouch from him and swallowed two fragrant oregano pills. It seemed silly to presume that an Italian herb could quash the microorganisms that nearly killed her, but it couldn't hurt to swallow a little oregano.

"One more thing." He pulled another pill bottle from his bag. "This is a powerful antibiotic. Just in case you sneak into the jungle and drink dirty water when I am not looking, I can heal you with this antibiotic."

His hard face glinted like polished leather as he packed the bottles back in his bag. "And you should put on sunscreen. Your nose is pink."

Stella covered her nose self-consciously with her hand and gave him a playful shove. "I'm lucky you're here, Alé. You're a good man. Your daughter was lucky to have you as a father."

Pursing his lips, he cleared his throat.

"That is the nicest thing that you could say to me. Thank you, mija." He stood and offered her a hand as he looked down at the remnants of the splintered branch. "It looks like you had some fun while I was gone. You must be very hot. You should rest in the shade, okay? You still have a bump on your head."

She touched the knot on her forehead as she stood, stretching each arm and shaking out each leg. She turned in a slow circle, squinting down the beach and into the jungle.

"He will come." This time, Alé's voice did not sing with confidence. He gently clasped her hand. "You must get out of the sun so that you are strong for him."

He pulled her to her feet and she shuffled up the beach, dragging her feet so she could watch rivulets of sand gather around and slide off of her moleskin-wrapped toes. As she toed past the dog collar, she stood over it so that it lay in her shadow. The turquoise fabric still shone with the waxy sheen of newness. She had debated which nameplate to choose: the bone-shaped cutout was cute, but a bone was just a reminder of the dead animal that it came from, and that seemed too reminiscent of Dirty's difficult life. So she'd gone with a plate shaped like a paw print. It didn't have fingernail tick marks above each toe, like a dog's real paw print would. This print in the nameplate looked a lot like the jaguar prints she'd seen earlier.

She picked up the collar and re-buckled it around her wrist, sliding the pad of her finger over the name etched into the smooth silver tag.

Standing next to the strung up hammocks, Alé called to her as he pulled something out of his backpack. "I need your help."

Stella squinted down the beach again in both directions before joining him at the campsite.

Alé knelt, handing Stella a pair of pliers and a pill bottle filled with brown liquid. "It is time to test your jungle strength."

Grateful to be shaded by the trees, she tossed her sunglasses into her hammock. Alé rolled up his sleeve, exposing a large swollen bug bite on the outside of his bicep. A hole as wide as a coffee stirrer punctured the center of the bite.

With his other arm, Alé pointed to the bite. "Inside that little hole is a botfly larva. His mother laid an egg inside my skin and the egg has hatched, and now I have a little, how do you Americans say it, a little asshole baby in there eating on me."

"You have got to be kidding me." Stella laughed and looked away, pretending to gag. "That's fucking gross. Does it hurt?"

Alé shrugged, wiping the red swelling with piece of gauze. "A little. It's not too bad. But I want the asshole baby to stop eating on me."

Stella swallowed hard. She looked down at the tweezers and bottle in her hands and shuddered.

Alé pointed to the bottle. "I need you to pour a lot of this Iodine into the hole, and then the larva will stick out his head, and you will pull him out with the tweezers."

"No fucking way." Still holding the bottle, Stella put the back of her hand over her mouth, gagging for real.

With a mischievous smile, Alé crossed his arms, leaving the botfly hole exposed. "You won't do this thing for me? After I came all this way to help you find your dog?"

"This is insane." Stella looked from the tweezers to the bottle, and back to the tweezers. She leaned in to look at the swelling. The opening was deep and dark, and she couldn't see anything inside it. Half-grinning, half-retching, she said, "This is not cool, Alé. I will do it, but we better find my freaking dog. I can't believe I'm going to do this. Is it going to hurt you?"

"Not too bad." Alé shrugged, smiling, pointing at the bottle in her hand. "Put the Iodine on it first, please. You can pour a lot of it."

She unscrewed the bottle tentatively. "This is fucking gross. I might throw up. All over you."

"You will not throw up. You are stronger than you think." Alé braced his arm against his torso, so the botfly burrow was positioned just below Stella's head. "Pour the liquid very slowly onto the hole until it is completely full and dripping on my arm."

She tilted the bottle over the cavity and poured one drop, watching it sink in.

He nodded. "Very good. Now pour a lot more drops."

A seagull cawed overhead, making Stella jump, and she laughed nervously.

She tipped the bottle again and Iodine overflowed into the hole, running down both sides of Alé's arm.

Almost instantly, a white wormy head wriggled out of the hole.

Stella turned her face away and bent down to dry-retch.

Alé's voice went up a notch in volume and pitch. "Good! Now grab the asshole baby before it goes back in! Put the tweezers into the hole, around the larva's head, and push the tweezers in. It won't hurt. Don't worry about me."

He caught her eyes and gave her an impish nod. He obviously thought this was incredibly fun.

Stella shook her head. Even Dirty's wounds, crawling with maggots, seemed less disgusting than this little worm burrowed into Alé's arm, eating his flesh from inside his body. She swallowed again to stave off a wave of nausea.

Dirty had cleaned his wounds' maggots with his own mouth. If he could do that, she could pull one goddamn maggot out of a friend's arm.

Holding her breath, she leaned over Alé's bicep and clamped the tweezers around the squirming white head. It wiggled against the clamp.

"Push down into my skin before you grab it." Alé didn't flinch, didn't move at all. "Otherwise it might go back in."

"Jesus, Alé." She looked into his eyes, disgusted and mesmerized. "I can't."

"You can." Alé stared at her strong and hard, like her roller derby coach before a big match. "Do it. Now."

With a grunt, she opened the tweezers just a hair and shoved them a few millimeters deeper into Alé's arm.

He grunted with her, holding his arm steady as he shouted, "Now grab it!"

Growling, she grabbed the head of the larva and pressed the tweezers around it, sensing the bulk of it inside the metal clamp, pulling, feeling its body dislodge. The worm slid slightly out of the hole.

Alé smiled at her like a proud daddy. "Good work. Keep pulling!"

The seagulls cawed again, and Stella used her upper arm to wipe the perspiration from her brow. "For fuck's sake this is awful."

Alé belly-laughed. "Keep pulling!"

Stella laughed with him, pulling on the larva's head, gagging as it dislodged further. She kept tugging and gagging, and finally the inch-long thing slid out of the hole, wriggling in the tweezers.

She extended her arm, holding it as far from her body as she could, screaming, "Fucking hell! What do I do with this?"

Still laughing, Alé pointed town the beach. "Throw the asshole baby in the ocean!"

She ran, still screaming, across the shore, and tossed the tweezers and larva as far as she could, then doubled over cackling between dry-heaves.

Alé ran across the beach and dropped to his knees next to her, holding his stomach as he whooped. When he caught his breath, he put a hand on her back. "You did a good job, mija."

Sitting back on her heels, panting, she side-eyed him. "I hope you get bit by a snake tonight."

He shrugged. "If I die, good luck finding your way home."

She lay back, her hair mixing with the sand, sun slamming her pupils. Her abdomen hurt from laughing so hard. She'd almost forgotten what it felt like to laugh that way.

Turning her head to the side, she squinted down the beach to her left, then her right.

Alé stood, wiping sand from his jeans and examining his wound. "You will be stronger for him if you stay out of the sun."

Stella smiled up at him. "Apparently I already have all the jungle strength."

He laughed again, bounding back to the campsite.

She reached her arm out, waving it through sand. This is where she lay, that day, when she thought she might die. When she had known how precarious her existence was, but still somehow, she had been filled with gratitude and love for the creature next to her, for the moments they had experienced.

She closed her eyes, remembering the rancid smell of him, that smell that had made her gag. She sniffed the air, checking for that smell.

When her skin began to throb from the sun, she stood, scanning the coastline, and then toddled back to the campsite. Climbing into her hammock, she rocked back and forth in the breeze, struggling to keep her eyes open.

She hadn't slept in so long. Her body was desperate for rest.

Alé would watch for Dirty. The dog would smell her before he saw her. She could sleep for just a few…

The dream came to her again, her father and Torres hiking back toward their car in pelting rain. But this time, it was her father who slipped into the river. He scrabbled at a boulder, straining to pull himself back onto shore. Torres understood that he was in trouble and latched her mouth onto his sleeve, struggling to pull him back up onto the slick rocks. Losing her grip, Torres tumbled into the water too. Her father grabbed onto a scrubby bush with one hand as Torres battled to swim toward him. Just before she reached him, she became Dirty. Dirty stuck his arm in a rock crevice, bracing himself against the flow, grabbing her father's collar with his mouth. Dirty fought to lift her father onto the bank, but the river rose in a rush and carried them both away.

Bolting upright in her hammock, her clothes drenched with sweat, she screamed: "DIRTY!!!!"

He was in trouble. If he weren't in trouble he would be here already. How the hell was she going to find him? She had to find him.

Alé jogged toward her from the beach, carrying two fishes on a line.

"Are you okay?" He squatted, waiting for her to speak.

She said nothing, trying to remember her dream. Was it the same one as always? Dirty had been in this one, right? Hyperventilating, she looked around the campsite as if trying to find something she had lost.

She needed to find Dirty.

Alé waited a few more beats, and then rifled in his pack, pulling out an orange and handing it to her. "You slept a long time. You should drink some water."

Dazed, she turned back toward the jungle, half expecting to see her father.

She took the the orange, cool and smooth in her palm, and picked up her water pouch, sucked down the last few sips of water from Dominical. "How long? Did I sleep?"

Unfolding a small tarp, Alé slapped the fish down on it and unsnapped the knife from the side of his pack. With quick, skilled movements, he scraped away fish scales with the blade. "Two hours, maybe three."

Mid-afternoon sun drummed the campsite with direct light. She had missed half the afternoon. The sun would set soon. She needed to go look for Dirty. Now.

Her stomach growled so loudly that she jumped.

Alé pointed at her with the knife. "Eat the orange. You have not eaten enough."

She scanned the beach, sinking her fingernails into the cool orange peel, prying it away from the flesh, shoving half the fruit in her mouth in a single bite.

She turned around again to look behind her, into the jungle.

Alé flipped the fish over and scraped scales from the other flank. "He has not come yet."

She tipped herself out of the hammock and slid into her flip-flops, stepping just inside the canopy, eyes adjusting to the dimmer light. Leaves fluttered on the fringe of ocean breeze. Two small birds flitted around a short tree and then soared up out of view.

With all her power, she screamed into the undergrowth, "DIRTY!"

Startled by the sound, a small songbird fled its branch.

Stella cupped her hands around her mouth and screamed again, "DIRTY!"

Her eyes skimmed right and left, and she stepped back over to the campsite, sitting in the sand, pulling on her socks. "I'm going to look for him."

"You will be more lucky in finding him if you stay here." Alé flipped the fish onto its back, sinking the blade into its belly and flicking out the guts in one quick movement. "The jungle is big. You cannot find something in the jungle if it does not want to be found. If your dog wants to be found, he will come to you."

"Fuck!" She slapped the hammock's anchor tree with her hand, shards of bark stinging the side of her fist. Alé was right.

She slapped the rough bark several times until her palm glowed red and splintered, and then she grabbed a low-hanging branch, yanking it toward her, ripping it off the trunk. "Fuck fuck FUCK!"

When the anger quelled, she stood, branch in hand, palm burning.

She pictured Dirty's face as he dropped a dead fish in front of her, head on the ground, gazing at her with upturned eyes. How could he not be here?

He probably didn't even remember her. She was never going to find him.

Her body felt so heavy, and her head throbbed, and tears welled in her eyes, swelling her throat.

As she threw the stick onto the ground, her eye caught on a filmy old rope lying in the detritus. Squatting to get a better look, she realized it wasn't a rope. It was a snake skin, white and withered, crumpled around itself. Holding her breath, she reached out and touched it lightly, then yanked back her hand.

"That one is not venomous. Not a worry." Alé picked up a fish and threaded a thin rope through its mouth and gill.

Sheepish, Stella stepped toward her hammock and watched Alé hang the skinned, gutted fish from the tree. He wiped his hands on his jeans and sat down with the second fish.

"Sorry about the outburst." She sat down on the sand next to him, wiping her eyes and picking up the branch she had just tossed down, absently ripping twigs away from its core. "It's just, I have a feeling that Dirty's in trouble. I can't just sit here."

"Stella, I need you to trust me. This is where you should be." Hands slimy, Alé paused his fish-cleaning and looked up at her. "I will go into the jungle to look for him. Maybe I will find tracks. But you should stay here. What if he smells you and comes to find you, and you are not here?"

Flinging the stick away, Stella used her fingernails to pull a splinter out of her palm, wincing.

Alé wiped his damp forehead with the back of his wrist, the knife in his hand catching a glint of sun. "After I clean the fish, I will go into the jungle and look for Dirty's tracks while you wait here. Okay?"

She nodded, comforted by his steady wisdom.

After a few breaths, she pointed at the second fish. "Need some help?"

"Yes, you can clean your own fish today." He handed her the knife, positioning it in her palm, wrapping her fingers around the handle. "Hold it like this, and scrape down the side to remove the scales, like I did the other one."

When she tried to scrape the scales with the bulky knife, its blade sank bluntly into the flank.

"Make a bigger angle, like this." He tilted her hand against the side of the carcass, steadied the fish's head and tail, and she tried again.

This time, the motion sent scales flying, and she repeated with quick flicks of her hand, sticky scales clinging to her fingers and arm and landing on the tarp in glistening piles, like snow.

"Now, you cut from here to here." He pointed to the belly of the fish, from the tail to the neck.

The knife slid easily through the fish's skin and flesh.

Making a scooping motion with two fingers, Alé pointed at the exposed innards. "Do you want me to remove the things that are inside, or can you do it?"

She scrunched her nose and wiped her forehead with her forearm. "I just pulled a baby worm out of your arm. I can do it."

Grinning, he took the knife from her and pointed at the gash. "I will hold the knife. You do not need it for the next part. Use your fingers to pull out the intestines and stomach and then I will give the knife back to you and you will cut out what is inside."

She squelched two fingers into the cavity and yanked out a pocket of guts—the liver and stomach and intestines oozed out in one glop—and took the knife from Alé, cutting the glop away with a few flicks.

He clapped once and patted her on the back. "You are having a very big day! Is it your first time to clean a fish?"

Stella sat back on her heels, looking down at her slimy hands. "Yeah." He strung the fish up from the tree, and gathered the guts and scales inside the tarp. "Your father would be proud of you."

"Thanks." Stella wiped her hands in the sand and looked toward the sea. "He would."

Alé cleaned the knife with a wet rag and stuck it in a sheath on his belt.

As they washed their hands in the surf, Alé said, "Now I will go look for Dirty. It will be dark in about three hours. I will be back before it is dark, and I will show you how to cook your fish. You will be okay here by yourself?"

"I'm good." She nodded, hooking a finger under the dog collar on her wrist, twisting the fabric until it pinched her skin. "Thanks for showing me how to clean the fish."

Her body still felt heavy as she watched him walk into the jungle.

Obsessed by vigilance, she looked to her left down the beach, and then to the right, and then turned back to squint into the jungle, and then looked left, right, behind, over and over and over.

For months after her father had died, she sat on the couch facing the door, glancing up every time she heard a sound outside, hoping that he might walk in holding hamburger bags: *It's dinner time, folks!*

This longing for Dirty, this heart-rending wait, it reminded her of those months after her father's death.

The late afternoon rolled by in a wash of soaring birds, scuttling crabs, waves lolling in and out. Rocking in her hammock, Stella's eyes ached from the strain of searching the forest line for a dog's shadow or a jaguar's slink.

As the sun shimmered toward the edge of the horizon, Alé ducked out of the jungle shaking his head, mouth drawn in a way that made Stella shiver.

"I did not find him, I am sorry." Not meeting her eyes, Alé reached up to unstring the fish dangling from the tree.

Nausea washed through Stella's stomach. "What's that look on your face, Alé?

Alé still avoided her gaze as he sat in the sand and unstrapped the knife from his pack. "I… It is nothing, I think."

"Alé, don't fuck with me." Stella stepped out of her hammock and stood in front of him, forcing him to look at her. "What did you see?"

He lowered the knife and fish to his lap and peered up at her, stone-faced. "I saw the jaguar tracks again, and I saw some tracks that look like a dog, although it could be a coyote."

Stella held her breath. "Okay? And?"

Alé took a deep breath and wiped his mouth awkwardly. "There was some blood near the tracks, and then the tracks left the trail. I followed them as far as I could, but then I lost them."

Stella's body flushed numb. "How much blood?"

Alé turned toward the horizon, took a breath in and out.

Stella stomped her foot, a wave of pain radiating through her knee and thigh, piercing into her abdomen. "Alé, how much blood?"

He cleared his throat, looked down at the fish in his hands, then turned back to Stella. "Quite a bit. But it could be that the dog killed a large prey item. Or it could be that the tracks were not from him."

Stella's knees buckled and she collapsed onto the sand, dropping her head into her hands, tears pushing up and out of her eyes, falling onto the sand. "They're his tracks. He's dead, isn't he?"

For the first time, Alé's voice trembled. "We don't know that, mija."

Body tingling, Stella stood and walked away from the campsite, slowly at first, then faster and faster, tearing down the beach, away from Alé, away from everything. She ran hard and fast, heels pounding the sand, pain thwapping her feet with every step. Stepping on a sharp shell, she cursed and kept running until her feet screamed in pain and she fell to the ground, sobbing.

This was all one big fucking waste of time. *Of course* her dead father hadn't told her to come to the jungle to find a fucking dog.

Drenched in anguish, she breathed hot and fast, sobbing until her body was wrung empty and her breathing slowed. The sun pierced her reddened skin, and she turned her face toward the ground, sand gathering on her lip, a few granules sucking into her mouth as she inhaled.

As the sky darkened and heat evaporated, she stood, turning around, looking back toward the triangular peninsula of sand thrusting into a vast ocean.

Sluggish, she walked back toward Alé as she stared toward the horizon, mourning her dad and her dog and everything else shitty.

When she approached the campsite, Alé sat by a pile of sticks he'd arranged for their campfire dinner. He flipped open his knife handle to pull out the flint.

About twenty feet away from the camp, Stella stopped walking and said quietly, "We can go back tomorrow. He's not coming."

Alé put down the flint. "We don't know this yet, mija."

Stella whispered, "We can go back tomorrow."

Alé nodded. "Okay, mija. If that is what you want to do."

She stood for several more minutes, watching Alé put the flint down next to the pile of sticks, watching him arrange two rocks by the fire, feeling nothing.

He nodded over to her where she stood several body lengths away. "Since there is a jaguar nearby, we will keep our campfire going through the night."

Again, Stella shivered. Her fingertips tingled, and she floated outside her body as she walked the distance back to the campsite and sat down next to her backpack.

Numb, she reached into her bag and rifled through it, unsure what she was looking for. Her fingers knocked against a pair of silver flasks. She stared at them, chewing on her cheek, and then pulled them out, nesting them in the sand.

Alé glanced at the flasks and then handed Stella the flint. She took it absently, turning it over in her hands. A metal rod, a few inches long and just thicker than a drinking straw, was embedded in a small black plastic handle half as long as her pointer finger. She'd watched her father use a flint just like this a hundred times—*my magical ferro rod*, he called it.

"You will light the fire?"

Alé's voice startled her, and she shook her head. She didn't want to light the fire. Didn't want to do anything.

She felt a familiar emptiness, the same emptiness she had carried for more than two years now. She hated herself for allowing this blankness to consume her. Her father wouldn't want this for her. He would want her to live her fucking life, like he had lived his. Stella so badly wanted to become a person that he'd be proud of, but that desire sometimes suffocated her.

Dirty was dead. Now she felt certain of this. Part of her wanted to just give the fuck up on everything. To find the toxic stream inside the jungle and lap up its water once again and then lie on the beach until the bacteria killed her.

But she didn't want to be like her mother, bending and breaking beneath the weight of the world, living only on the margins of human experience.

"Yeah. I'll do it." She nodded at Alé, gripping the flint's handle.

A pelican bobbed in the surf, and farther out, a pod of dolphins quietly moved across the horizon.

Alé showed her how to hold the ferro rod over the bed of dry twigs and shaved wood, and rake the knife's edge along the flint until sparks flew into the tinder. As she raked, Alé leaned toward the first sparks, breathing gently on them until fiery tentacles spread through the kindling and smoke billowed upward.

"Well done." He patted her on the back. "Again, your father is proud."

She ran her hand over the flames, her palm grazing the tops of the tendrils. "I wish he was here."

Alé placed each fish on a rock at the edge of the fire.

Stella ran two fingers over the silver flasks nestled in the sand as she watched the dolphins disappear around the curve in the coastline. She lifted one of the flasks from the sand and handed it to Alé.

He raised it toward the sun to read the words painted on its side: "Emergency Drinking Water. Ha! This is funny."

"My dad and I…." Her voice cracked. "My dad and I made this whiskey. Right before he…"

She pulled the second flask from the sand, remembering the day her dad had given it to her. The summer after her freshman year in college, her father had asked her to go camping with him in hill country.

She had shrugged off the suggestion, finally feeling old enough that she didn't need to indulge his camping obsession. "I'm working every weekend, Dad."

He winked at her and handed her a small box. "I figured you might be too busy, but I had to ask. Anyway, I have a present for you."

He pointed at the twine that tied the box together. "I bound the box with fishing twine. I know it looks ugly, but it's camping-themed." He smiled, elated by his ugly packaging. "This is a thank-you gift for going camping with me so many times. Those are some of the best memories from my whole life."

The corners of his eyes crinkled.

Pulling off the lid, Stella lifted out a silver flask with etched letters: *Emergency Drinking Water.*

Tears brimmed on her lid. "Dad, I can't take your flask."

He smiled so wide that he almost looked like he'd start laughing. "That one's yours, Squirrel. I got you one just like mine. Look on the back."

She flipped the flask over in her hand. On the backside, in smaller print: *You're strong like a tree, Squirrel. Don't ever forget it. -Dad*

This was what he had often said when she'd skinned a knee or failed a test or stood up to a bully. She was *strong like a tree*, and a tree could live for two hundred years, through tornadoes and plagues and wars. *Not everyone is strong like a tree,* he would say, *but you are. You're my Squirrel.*

Running her fingers along the letters, her seventeen-year-old self had known her father didn't intend for her to feel guilty at that moment, but the gift, so thoughtful and heartfelt, filled had her with remorse. She'd wanted to apologize to him for being so complicated, and for being busy all the time. She'd wanted to promise him she'd be a better daughter. Instead, she'd hugged the flask to her chest. "I love it, Dad. Thank you. Maybe I can get a weekend off later this summer."

He waved a hand in front of his face. "I didn't give it to you to muscle you into going camping. I just wanted you to have something special. If you decide you want to go camping, that's great, but it's truly okay if it doesn't work out. I'm just real happy you like it."

She threw her arms around him. "I love it."

Later that summer, her father left her forever.

Raising her flask to Alé in a toast, Stella sniffed and cleared her throat, cheeks wet. "This is the first time I've used the flask. First time I've drunk from our last cask of whiskey. I think he'd want us to have it now. The flask you're drinking from was his."

Alé wiped his eyes. "I am honored, my friend. Thank you for sharing this with me."

They both took a swig.

"Damn. That's disgusting" Stella squinched her face, remembering the first time she'd tried her father's whiskey, seven years ago. This batch was no better. Her dad had loved making whiskey, but he certainly wasn't any good at it.

She blew her nose into her shirtsleeve and wiped her cheeks. "Since my dad died, I haven't really *felt* much. Of anything. About anything. Until I met this goddamn dog."

She took another sip, squinching her cheeks at the taste, forcing herself to focus on the calming throat-burn. "I can't shake this stupid idea that there's part of my dad in Dirty. And now Dirty's probably dead too."

Alé's chin trembled as he raised his flask. "Cheers to your father." Coming up from a long draft, he smiled. "It's not that bad. I have had worse."

Stella took a shaky breath, thinking of her father's biceps pushing out against his t-shirt as he crushed the malt, and the wide-openness in his eyes as he poured the moonshine into small oak casks.

Firelight sent shadows dancing above Alé's chin and nose and eyebrows.

"I have a box of things that my daughter made." He took another swig. "Some drawings, a little writing—she had just learned how to write some words. And some doll clothes. She liked to cut up old clothes that tourists threw in the garbage and put them on her dolls. I have some of those also. I haven't opened the box in more than two years."

Stella swallowed another sip without flinching. "You'll open it when you're ready."

He nodded. "Thank you, Stella. I will."

The fuzzy balm of whiskey softened her fear of jaguars, but the night still pressed in heavy. "I don't think my dad knew how much I loved him."

Light flicked across Alé's eyes. "Stella, I will tell you something that I know is true, and you must believe me. Your father knew how much you loved him. I saw love in my daughter's eyes even when she said nothing to me. Even when she was mad at me. A father knows how much his daughter loves him."

Stella closed her eyes.

As a child, when the heaviness of the world pushed in, her father would sit by her bed and sing his own version of the old children's song:

Hush little baby, don't you cry.

Daddy's gonna paint your face with pie.

And if that pie tastes like a frog,

Daddy's gonna give you an ugly dog.

And if that ugly dog gets mean,

Daddy's gonna give you a blue-faced queen.

And if that blue-faced queen won't play,

You gotta stop your crying now, any old way.

Stella heard his voice singing the song in her mind as she drank the whiskey that her father's fingers had touched.

After dinner, Alé gathered enough wood to keep the fire burning through the night while Stella halfheartedly called Dirty's name into the gathering night.

COSTA RICA

Trip Two
Second Night Back In The Jungle

WELL PAST MIDNIGHT, Stella lay awake in her hammock, hugging the fabric around her chest. A metallic tisk-tisk clinked through the insect opera as Alé sharpened his blade with a stone.

A dizzying palate of stars framed the sliver moon, and Stella stepped out of her swaying bed, pulling on her jacket and walking toward the beach. The Milky Way stretched across the full expanse of night.

Sitting on the cool sand, she shivered.

Near Orion's belt, something caught her eye: a star, shooting across the black, trailed by a long silver tail. Before it fizzled, another streaked across a different span of sky. Two minutes later, another.

Her fingers tingled. It had been years since she'd seen a meteor shower.

When she was eight or nine years old, she'd gone camping with her father on a warm moonless night. From a deep sleep, her dad awakened her and dragged her out of the tent and into a field to lie on a blanket. "Look up," he said, ignoring her gripes and yawns. "It'll be worth it."

There was nowhere to look but up, so she did, just as a tiny white light blasted from one horizon to the other.

"Hey!" She sat up, gaping. "What was that?"

"That was a meteor, Squirrel." He pointed up, to the other side of the sky. "There's another one."

She lay back and he scooted her in close, propping her head inside the crook of his shoulder. "A meteor's a space rock that wants to come to Earth so bad it shoots through the atmosphere and burns real hot, so hot that it almost melts. Watch—there'll be lots more. We are witnessing a meteor shower."

Meteors shot in all directions, across the night's quadrants, and Stella squealed and pointed at each new speck of light.

"It's pretty," she said. "I like a meteor shower."

Still burrowed in his shoulder, she looked up at his face.

His skin shone translucent in the white starlight, like a ghost.

He took his daughter's tiny hand in his. "A meteor shower always reminds me that we're at the mercy of a big, beautiful universe. Some people might think that's scary, but I don't. For me, it's just a sign of all the magic that's around us all the time."

They watched meteors flash across the sky until she fell asleep on the blanket. When she awoke, she was back in the tent, tucked into her sleeping bag.

She'd seen meteors since, but never more than one, and never a meteor shower until she looked up from the beach in Costa Rica, feeling hopeless and lost.

She pulled her jacket tighter against the cool Corcovado air and whispered at the sky, "Daddy, should I go home? Is he not coming?"

Another flash traced across the black, and Stella's chin trembled. She whispered again, through shaky breaths, "Okay. I get it. Thank you for sending him. If he's still out there, please protect him, if you can, Daddy."

She leaned back, propped on her elbows, not daring to lie all the way down with a jaguar on the prowl. When her neck began to ache from looking up, she slipped back into her hammock.

Barely able to raise her voice above a whisper, she said to Alé, "Meteor shower."

He put down his book and nodded. "Yes. Beautiful, no? You can sleep for a while. I will stay awake to watch for him."

"You can sleep. I'm not going to." She sank into the fabric, twisting the dog collar on her wrist.

"Okay. Good night Stella." Alé closed his eyes, seemed to fall asleep almost instantly.

Stella envied his calm comfort with the world, even after everything he had been through. He'd lost even more than she had, but his spirit was still so kind and happy.

Tears gathered in her eyes as she unbuckled the collar, running it through her fingers a few more times before she tucked it in the top of her pack.

Rocking in her hammock, she took another sip from her flask, now half-empty. The night was still. So clear and starry that it made her sad, though she couldn't pinpoint exactly why.

Several hours into her vigil, a clatter arose in the forest behind her, and her body went cold. The fire burned low, sending light only a few feet into the jungle. Pulling the hammock tight around her neck, she craned her head and squinted at the noise. An animal. It was an animal with heavy feet, knocking through the trees, making no effort to hide its sound. Those were not Dirty's footsteps—his paws fell nearly silent through the jungle.

Stella didn't dare wake Alé. She searched her hammock for the pocket-knife, cursing, remembering that she'd left it in her backpack. Her breathing accelerated, and the big animal moved closer.

Stella bit her lip to avoid crying out as the animal plodded fast out of the forest behind her, lumbering into the starlight, nose to the ground, sniffing.

It was a giant pig. Or, maybe it wasn't a pig. What the hell was it? It looked like a cross between a pig and a hippopotamus. It had a long drooping snout like an elephant's, but much shorter. And little round ears like pancakes. Thick-bodied, the animal must weigh several hundred pounds.

It lifted its snout from the ground and stared at her so calmly that she felt no fear. The animal didn't move, didn't charge or bristle. It just *stared* at her for several seconds, like it was trying to figure out what she was. Then, without rushing, it plodded back into the forest, kicking past leaves and sticks with clunky hooves.

Stella shook her head as she checked her phone for the hundredth time: 4:47AM. Alé snored in his hammock.

She didn't want the sun to rise. Didn't want to meet the reality of the day. She wanted to stay here, on this beach, where Dirty still felt alive to her. Where he was still part of her story.

The fire's last cinders snapped, and Stella wondered if she should add another log. Maybe she didn't need to bother. It would be light within an hour, and she didn't really want to get out of her hammock, with Alé asleep and a giant hippopotamus pig roaming nearby. Not to mention the jaguar.

Thin wisps of cloud had slid across the sky, leaving bands of stars visible. Near the coastline's bend, a family of raccoons picked up fallen fruits and chased crabs across the beach.

Stella watched them with exhausted indifference.

Three of the raccoons looked like babies, tumbling over each other while the larger one, presumably the mother, dug holes in the sand.

The chorus of insects suddenly shushed, and the mother raccoon raised herself up on hind legs, surveying right and left with quick, frenetic jerks of the head. Dropping back on all fours, she dashed off the beach and her babies followed as closely as their stubby legs could carry them.

Where the beach disappeared around a bend, something moved. Stella shivered and sat up, gathering the hammock around her shoulders and wondering again if she should wake Alé. She reached down to grab the knife in the top pocket of her backpack, trying to make as little noise as possible. Grasping knife handle, she flicked it open.

In shadows, the thing at the far end of the beach moved closer, slowly, stalking like a predator.

"A… Alé," she whispered.

He let out a long, satisfied snore.

The thing on the beach crept one step closer, low to the ground. It was large.

"Alé," she whispered louder. Again, he snored.

Stella's face drained cold.

The thing inched closer again, and her eyes almost discerned its shape. Was it limping?

"Alé!" This time, her voice rose above a whisper, but he didn't stir.

The thing limped another step closer, and another, the edges of its body haloed by starlight.

Something in its shape—its torso, maybe—made her think it might not be a jaguar. Jaguars were thick-bodied, right? This animal was lithe…

She tumbled out of her hammock onto the sand, bracing herself on hands and knees, eyes locked on the creature. When she moved, the creature stopped, dropping its belly to the ground.

That motion… She had seen that motion before. Hadn't she?

She stopped breathing.

Afraid to move, she waited.

The creature crawled forward, barely raising itself off the ground.

She had seen this crawl. Was she imagining it? Was this just another hallucination? Was she dreaming?

She inhaled sharply, and tears came to her eyes.

Raising up slowly, she moved tentatively toward the creature, and it raised its head.

Slowly, she stood, showing her full height in the open air.

The animal pushed up to a stand and limped quickly forward, its features coming clear in the silver light.

"DIRTY!" She screamed, weeping, running toward him.

He tried to run to her, but fell to the sand, stood again, tried to run again.

"DIRTY!" She yelled again, now close enough for moonlight to catch on his eyes.

He shuffled another step closer, and now she could smell him, and she was tumbling into him.

He bounded on top of her, tackling onto the sand, licking her face. She laughed, face soaked as she repeated his name: "Dirty… Dirty… Dirty…"

Yelping, he leapt onto her repeatedly, licking her cheeks and nose and mouth, now turning his face skyward, howling.

Stella laughed again, burying her face in the filthy, rancid fur on his shoulder. She pulled back to look at him, and he met her eyes as she touched his cheek. "Hi, buddy."

Footsteps pounded up behind them and Alé burst into view, his big teeth glowing. He raised his face to the sky, making the sign of the cross on his head and shoulders. Nodding at her, he watched for a moment and then walked away, leaving her with the moment.

Dirty dropped to the sand beside Stella. She lay on her side and they stared at each other, nose-to-nose. He whined, nuzzling her face with his.

His stench wrapped around her: rotten flesh. He must have just eaten a nasty little carcass.

Panting hard, Dirty's tongue drooped out of the side of his mouth, picking up granules as the tip dipped onto the beach. His eyes looked tired.

She put her hands on his cheeks. "Dirty? Are you okay?"

He licked her nose, whining.

"You knew I was coming for you, right?" She held his face. "I'm always coming back for you, Dirty. Do you understand?"

He tucked his head under her chin, burying his nose into the top of her jacket.

Pressing in close, he reached out a paw and found the palm of her hand. She closed her fingers around his knobby, furry toes, listening to him breathe, draping her free arm around his body and sinking her fingers into his fur. Within moments, they fell asleep, fogging each other's cheeks with their breath.

COSTA RICA

Trip Two
Third Day Back In The Jungle

AN ACHE IN Stella's hip and shoulder roused her from a weighty sleep. The top of Dirty's head pressed into her neck, his paw still resting in her hand. As she shifted the weight off her crumpled shoulder, Dirty opened his eyes.

In the morning light, Stella got a good look at him. Half of his left ear flopped unnaturally, ripped down the middle. Puncture wounds, clotted with dried blood, marred the left side of his face. Worse still, his left front paw was deeply gashed, two of its toes blackened and oozing pus.

She touched his neck tenderly. "Oh my god, Dirty!"

Without raising his head, Dirty opened his eyes and watched her take in the extent of his wounds.

Alé jogged over, calling out, "You found him! Are you happy?"

Stella eased herself out from under the dog. "Alé, he's hurt! We gotta get him to a vet."

Alé squatted to examine Dirty, touching his head. "Jaguar, I think. He is lucky to be alive."

Stella's heart swelled heavy in her chest, and she touched Dirty's face. His breathing seemed shallow—or maybe she was just imagining it? Did he always breathe like this, short and choppy?

Sprinting back to the campsite, Alé called over his shoulder, "I will get my medical supplies."

Stella placed a hand on Dirty's torso, feeling his heartbeat. "I knew something was wrong with you, buddy."

Stella and Alé rinsed his wounds with filtered water and dabbed them with antibacterial cream. Panting, he held his front leg aloft and whimpered as Alé gently bandaged the bloody, festering paw.

"This probably hurts a lot." Alé lowered the dog's bandaged limb to the ground.

Stella kissed the top of Dirty's head. "Alé, I want to walk all the way back today."

The sun beat hard, plastering sweaty strands of hair to the sides of her head.

A week ago, she had been certain she would find Dirty, and then yesterday she'd begun to accept that she might not find him. She'd stayed strong through so many emotional arrows, but now her spirit was too fractured to face the possibility of finding Dirty and then losing him. Again.

"It is very far, Stella. I don't know if you will be able to walk eight miles in one day." Alé packed the supplies back in his bag, squinting down the beach. "It took us twelve hours to get here, with difficult hiking. We will not have to clear the path so much on the way back, but we will be carrying the dog, so we will still go more slowly. You have not slept very much and you are probably still weak from your last time in the jungle."

Stella stroked the dog's back and wiped her eyes with the back of her hand. "I *will* walk the whole way."

Alé looked her up and down, breathed in and out, and nodded. "I packed up the camp and filled our water bottles while you and the dog were sleeping. So we are ready to go."

Flooded with energy, Stella pushed herself to her feet, brushed sand from her hands and jeans. She spoke gently: "Dirty? Can you stand?"

He looked up at her, motionless.

Sliding her hands under his torso, she lifted him to his feet. With drooping eyes, he put weight on three paws.

Stella backed away a few steps. "Come here, buddy."

He didn't move.

She backed away farther. "Dirty, come here."

Still watching her, he lay back down.

Jogging to the campsite fifty feet away, she yelled, "Dirty! Come!"

With head hung low and eyes trained on Stella, he struggled to his feet and limped forward several steps, panting. With a whimper, he dropped to the sand.

"He cannot walk. We will have to carry him." Alé rushed toward the dog with two bowls in his hand. He knelt in front of Dirty and placed the bowls below the dog's mouth. "Here, Dirty."

Sobbing, Stella scrambled to lace up her boots as Dirty lapped up food and water.

Alé stroked the crown of Dirty's head, calling over his shoulder, "He is eating. This is good."

The tide reached higher on the shore, flicking the edges of Dirty's limp hind legs.

Stella dumped out everything in her pack: hammock, mosquito net, jacket, sweatshirt, sunscreen, insect repellent, oranges, granola, peanut butter, water.

With the empty pack, she ran back to Dirty and Alé, out of breath, wiping her eyes. "I'm going to carry him."

"No." Alé shook his head and stood between her and the dog. "Stella, you cannot. You were in the hospital four weeks ago. Your ankle is sore. The dog probably weighs fifteen kilos. I will carry him."

"My ankle is fine." Her ankle—she hadn't even been thinking about her ankle—at that moment, it didn't hurt at all. It was like the pain had evaporated the moment Dirty returned. She bored into Alé with puffy eyes, voice shaking, "Don't fight me on this, Alé. I'm gonna carry my dog."

They stared at each other until Alé's expression softened and he put a hand on her shoulder. "You will carry the dog. I will take my hammock out of my backpack, and I will carry your water and food. I will come back soon to get the things we leave behind. Let's get ready to go."

Alé jogged back to the campsite, dumping a few things from his pack and tossing in Stella's food.

She stooped and put a hand on the side of Dirty's face. "I need you to trust me. I have to put you in my pack and it's probably gonna hurt."

He pressed his head into her palm.

She leaned forward until the wet tip of his nose touched hers. Closing her eyes, she whispered, "I got you, Dirty."

He licked her cheek and nose and eyes and she kissed his head, putting her arms gently around him. "You're a good dog."

He leaned into her arms as she and Alé lifted him from the sand and dropped his hindquarters into the pack. His emaciated frame slid easily into the open cavity.

Stella spoke low and gentle: "Good boy, Dirty. Good boy."

When his bandaged paw bumped against the side of the pack, he let out a quiet yelp.

As they cinched the fabric at the top of the compartment around his shoulders, Dirty looked from Stella to Alé, and back to Stella.

"You're gonna be alright, buddy." She held the tube from her water pouch next to his mouth, squeezing a few drops onto his tongue, and he lapped them up.

She looked into his trusting eyes. "Now I'm gonna put you on my back and stand up. You gotta stay in the backpack, okay?"

She rested a hand on the side of his face and he closed his eyes.

Alé moved around to the back of the pack and grabbed the outside straps. "You stand up, and I will lift this onto your shoulders."

Still feeling adrenalized, no pain in her ankle, Stella planted her feet on the shifting sand. Alé heaved the pack up and bumbled it onto one of her shoulders and then the other, Dirty whining as he jostled back and forth. Stella huffed as the weight of his body pressed her feet deeper into the bank.

With the backpack stabilized, Dirty's whining faded. He leaned his chin forward to rest it on her shoulder, his breath hot and sour on her neck.

Grateful for the feel of him on her back, she leaned her cheek into his and gently stroked the top of his head. "I'm gonna get you home, okay, my friend?"

Alé handed her a sturdy stick, about four feet long and as thick as several fingers. "Do you want a walking stick? I found this one in the jungle."

"Thank you." She took it from him, testing it in the sand and putting a hand on his shoulder. "I looked for a walking stick for three days and never found one. You are the best goddamn guide in Costa Rica. I'm going to make sure everyone knows it."

His eyes glinted. "I know you will."

Stella took her first step of the day, adjusting the straps to distribute Dirty's weight evenly on her back. Her shoulders strained under the pull, and her feet plodded hard, but the wrenching pressure reminded her that she was alive, she was with Dirty, finally saving him like he saved her. She could carry him for eight miles. She would carry him for fifty miles if she had to.

Her father had carried her on his back like this, once, when she was five or six.

She'd been hiking with him along a scrubby creek when she twisted her ankle.

"It hurrrrrrts!" she screamed.

Without complaint, her father shifted his backpack to the front of his body and hoisted her onto his back, carrying this double load toward the trailhead as he sang in his mediocre baritone: "*Ee-i-ee-i-o... And on that farm they had a...*"

"*Giraffe!*" Stella called out. This was their game: she would call out an animal for which her father couldn't possibly know the voice, and he would invent a sound for the animal.

He sang: "*With a BREE-BREE here and a BREE-BREE there!*"

"Dad!" She giggled, clinging to his neck with one arm as she reached with the other toward a clump of Spanish moss hanging from the branch of a live oak tree. "Giraffes do *not* say 'bree!'"

He stopped walking and turned his sunburned face toward hers. "They absolutely do, Squirrel."

Huffing, out of breath, he marched forward through the desert scrub. "We'll look it up when we get home and I'll prove it to you."

Before she and her father got back to the car, her ankle stopped hurting, but she didn't want to let go of his neck.

At age five, she probably weighed little more than Dirty did now. He pulled his bandaged paw out of the pack and placed it on Stella's shoulder.

As they trudged trough the sand, her feet warmed in her boots and her legs limbered.

Giant boulders dotted the beach, like dinosaur turtles coming ashore to nest. She wandered amongst the boulders and driftwood, taking a sinuous path to avoid climbing or clambering over anything.

NOT JUST A DOG

She sipped four-times-filtered water from her pouch and held the tube to Dirty's mouth to dribble on his tongue, soaking her t-shirt from the overflow. Each time she gave him water, he reached up to lick the bottom of her chin. And each time he licked her, she smiled and sighed, her chest swelling from everything she felt for this dog.

With the mid-morning heat slowing them down, Stella and Alé stepped off the beach and onto the jungle path that Alé had cleared two days earlier. All three of them breathed easier in the shade of the canopy.

Seven miles. From this point, there should be about seven miles left. That meant eleven more hours of hiking. Maybe ten, if they hurried.

Alé stopped and turned back to examine Stella's gait and demeanor. "Is it okay for you? Dirty? Is he heavy?"

Stella shook her head. Her body felt strong. "No. I'm fine. Thank you."

Dirty burrowed the crown of his head in the side of Stella's neck, his hot breath misting her chin. With each stride, his body bobbed inside the pack.

A tree root reached out across the trail like a child's bent knee. Stella stepped over it clumsily, her foot thumping heavy on the ground.

Dirty grunted, yelping, and then tilted his face to lick her chin.

"Sorry, Dirty." She would balance her footfalls more carefully.

A toucan flew through the canopy and her eyes followed it for a few seconds.

Dirty lifted his head, his wiry fur brushing oily on her neck as he tracked the bird's passage.

She nuzzled him with her chin. "Remember when we met? I thought I was gonna die, and then you showed up all nasty—god you smelled bad—and you stared at me all night long. Like a creepy angel."

As Stella uttered the word "angel," *BAM,* she kicked a hidden tree root, nearly toppling to the ground, yelping as she caught herself on her weaker foot. Dirty yelped, and she steadied herself, breathing hard.

Turning her face toward Dirty, she cupped the side of his head with her palm, and he licked her wrist. ""You okay? You're okay. We're okay."

An ache rose in her weak ankle, and she shook her head. She would not acknowledge weakness. Dirty needed her to be strong. She turned her head slightly toward him, eyes focused on the trail ahead. "That first night—I feel bad for being mean to you that first night. If anyone told me then that I'd be coming back to this jungle to get you four weeks later, I would've…"

Something fell to the ground beside her—a small green fruit, no bigger than an eyeball. She looked up. A troop of white-faced spider monkeys lazed on branches, clambering over each other as they broke open fruit casks and chewed on leaves and groomed bugs from each other's backs.

The sun slinked through matted branches. Stella held out her arms to watch dappled patches of light slide across her skin. "And remember when you stood between me and that snake? I think that's when I knew you were *my* dog and I was *your* person. I guess you understood that a lot sooner than I did."

Dirty licked salt from the side of her neck.

"Thanks, buddy." She smiled at his cooling tongue. "You know, a month ago, I would've said that getting licked by a dog was disgusting, but actually, it feels pretty good."

He shifted inside the pack, and she paused to lift the chafing straps off her shoulders.

Adrenaline fading, her quads started to burn, and her ankle wobbled. Again, she shook her head to refuse the pain.

Thinking about pain made pain worse. Everyone knew that.

She would keep talking to Dirty. She would focus on him. "So, then, you found me some water, which I guess nearly killed me but obviously that's not your fault. And then you found the beach. I still don't know how you found that beach."

Alé pointed overhead. A sloth clung to the branch of a tree with long shiny leaves. Stella craned her head toward the creature as she passed underneath, soothed by its nearness, but not wanting to slow her pace.

As she refocused on the trail, her hand brushed against the side of a small bush and dislodged a wad of feathery dust clinging to a leaf. The dust wad poofed out over her fingers. She held up her hand to wipe it off, and the dust swarmed across her palm and wrist, each particle crawling on minuscule legs.

"Fuck!" Her voice cracked through the jungle as she shook her right hand violently, slapping it with her left. "What is that?"

Dirty's body went rigid in the backpack as if he might jump.

Alé sprinted back to Stella, grabbing her hand where the rust-colored specks—dozens of them; maybe hundreds—skittered onto her forearm. "Seed ticks. Hold your arm still for me."

Dirty joggled in the pack as she shifted her weight. She held her arm out as far as possible, as if trying to dislodge it from her body. "Ticks? Are you fucking kidding me? We do not have time for this!"

Alé snatched the water bottle from the side of his pack, unscrewed the top, and poured it slowly over her hand and forearm, calmly wiping off ticks with his free hand.

Several clung to her skin, and she yanked her arm away, unable to hold still. Cursing, she thrashed her wrist through the air, slapping and raking it with her other hand. She wanted to set fire to her arm, to slaughter the little fuckers holding up her already-slow rescue march.

Dirty whimpered, confused, raising himself farther out of the pack to assess the threat.

Alé handed Stella the bottle. "Pour water slowly on your arm and wipe them away. They will come off. I have something else to help."

Dirty whimpered and Alé dropped his daypack, unzipping outside pouch.

"Dammit!" As Stella doused her arm with water, she commanded, "Dirty, stay!"

He lowered himself back into the pack.

"Dammit, we have *got* to keep moving." Ten or twenty tiny ticks still scrambled around her skin, searching for a comfortable patch of open flesh where they could sink their teeth. Flailing, Stella wiped off one, then two, then three, cursing.

Alé took her arm and blotted it with the sticky side of a piece of duct tape, picking up a couple of bugs with each blot. Gently, he swiveled her wrist and tape-vacuumed the underside of the arm. Releasing her hand, he pointed. "Look—they are all gone. No more seed ticks."

"Shit. Are you sure?" Panting, Stella lifted her arm and examined her elbow and triceps and wrist and fingers. She pulled up the short sleeve of her t-shirt so she could peer into her armpit, lifted her shirt to examine her torso, and then cursed and squinted at every inch of her arm again, lifted up her shirt again, wiped her hands frantically over her abdomen. She wanted to throw off all her clothes and stand under a waterfall, but even more than that, she wanted to get out of the goddamn jungle, get Dirty to a goddamn veterinarian. She still panted like she'd sprinted for two miles. "That was an actual fucking nightmare."

Dirty leaned forward in the backpack and she held her arm up in front of his face. He licked it intently, washing it clean from wrist to elbow.

Trembling, she shifted from one foot to the other as Alé re-cinched the top of the pack around Dirty's shoulders.

For the tenth time, Stella examined every millimeter of skin on her arms and hands, brushing her neck and face, shaking out her hair, imagining tiny ticks everywhere. "Are there any on my neck? Or in my hair?"

Alé leaned in, squinting. "No, they are gone."

"Let's get the fuck out of here." Stella shivered, tightening the straps on her pack. Suddenly her feet and legs screamed at her, aching, and her shoulders felt Dirty's full weight.

Should she let Alé carry Dirty? No, she could do this. Her body could fucking do this.

Striding forward, Alé spoke without looking back, "Less than five more miles."

As they walked, Stella obsessively searched trailside leaves and branches for rusty poofballs, her mind replaying the image of tiny parasites swarming her hand and arm.

The forest rolled out calm around them as the morning faded to midday. Stella's pace slowed, her chest and armpits and face drenched in sweat, body aching. Again she wondered if she should pass the dog to Alé. But *she* wanted to be the one to carry him out of this jungle. She *needed* to do this for him.

She stopped telling Dirty stories, stopped scanning the treetops to look for animals, reserving her energy for each next step.

Heat gathered, even under the canopy, and Stella wondered if this was the hottest day she'd experienced the jungle, or if her now-fragile body had just lost its ability to stand up to the rainforest's onslaught.

Dirty's gangly limbs clunked against her back. As she tired, her gait became more jarring, but still he rested his chin on her shoulder.

Lowering her voice to a whisper so Alé couldn't hear, she turned her cheek toward him. "Hey. Did you meet my dad?"

As she stepped over a tree root, Dirty's limp head jounced up and plunked down hard on her shoulder bone. He didn't make a sound.

She reached up to cushion his chin, wishing that he would whimper to remind her that he was still with her. His ears felt hot under her fingertips. Was he feverish? Did dogs get fevers?

Ahead, Alé stopped and slid his pack off his shoulders, dropping it to the ground as he turned toward her. "You need to eat."

She shook her head and tried to push past him. She couldn't stop walking. She was afraid she wouldn't be able to move again if she stopped. "No, we…"

He out an arm, blocking her. "If you don't eat, you will faint. You have to stay strong so that you can carry him."

Dirty hadn't moved or whimpered in several minutes, and she did want to get a look at him.

Stepping around Stella, Alé grabbed the outside straps of her pack and lifted it from her shoulders, settling it gently on a bed of leaves, and then tipping the sack on its side so the dog could lie down.

Dirty allowed his body to tumble sideways, half his body still in the pack, the other half splayed on the jungle floor. He didn't try to reposition himself. The bandage on his front paw had started to unfurl, soiled with dirt and pus.

Stella squatted next to him. His eyelids drooped and cheeks hung listless.

They slid the back end of Dirty's limp body from the pack. With barely a whimper, he let them arrange him on the detritus.

Exhaling heavily, his cheeks puffed outward. With glazed eyes trained on Stella, he tried to rise to his feet, legs shaking.

She put a hand on his torso, holding back tears. "Don't get up, Dirty. Stay there."

Again, he placed a trembling paw beneath his weight and tried to push up.

"Oh, god. What are you trying to do? At least let me help you, buddy." She stooped on burning quads, looping her hands under his front armpits and pulling him to his feet. His back legs tremored under his weight. Head drooping forward, he lifted a leg an inch off the ground and let out a long stream of pee that pooled around his back paws.

"Of course," she said, kissing the top of his head. "Good boy."

Dirty staggered back down on the ground, lying in his own urine, and Stella's throat swelled.

His wounds were even worse than she had imagined. His body might be ravaged by infection. With a full-body shudder, she wondered whether he would even make it to the veterinarian—if they rushed, they still had several more hours of hiking, and then probably an hour or more of driving before they could get him to a doctor.

Stella looked in her dog's eyes, trying to assess how much life they still held. He stared into her, trying to tell her something.

Pulling the freeze-dried dog food from Alé's pack, she wetted a few pieces and held them below Dirty's mouth. He sniffed the food and looked away, laying his head on the dirt.

Stella checked her phone—1:13PM. The sun would set in five hours. Shoving a spoonful of peanut butter in her mouth, she turned to Alé. "How much farther to the trailhead?"

He held up his GPS device, his mouth set hard. "A little more than three miles."

They were well over halfway back. Stella shook out one trembling leg and then the next. She choked down a small orange in three bites and sucked water from her pouch, leaning over Dirty, making a tent above his body with hers to give him additional shade.

He opened his eyes and sniffed, trying to lift his head, licking the air.

Alé packed up the peanut butter and orange peels as Stella righted her pack on the ground. On burning quads, she stooped next to Dirty and put her hands on the sides of his face, leaning in to touch his nose with hers. "We gotta do this again, okay, my friend?"

Without moving his neck, he reached out his tongue to lick her chin.

As she whispered reassurances to Dirty, Stella picked up his front quarters while Alé supported the back, and they lowered him, whimpering, into the pack. His bandaged paw grazed the compartment, and he yowled.

At the yowl, Stella's hands quivered and her teeth chattered. She placed a hand on his head and he leaned into the touch. "I'm sorry, Dirty, I'm so sorry. We'll get you help soon."

A muscle in her right quad started to twitch, and her ankle throbbed.

As she stood and reached down to pick up the pack, her right leg buckled beneath her, forcing her to sit.

"Shit." She blinked several times to clear away a blurred black spot seeping into her field of vision. Her body was failing. Again. And Dirty needed help, now. She so badly wanted to be the one to save him, but this couldn't be about *her*.

Wiping her eyes, she looked up at her guide and cleared her throat. "Can you carry him, Alé? I'm slowing down. I don't want to hold us up."

Alé reached for the pack, lifting it easily onto his shoulders. "You can unstrap my daypack from the front of my big backpack. The daypack has everything we need to get home. We will leave the rest here and I will come back to get it."

"Thank you." Unstrapping the daypack and slinging it onto her back, she approached Alé and settled Dirty's chin comfortably on his shoulder. "Let's go."

Dirty turned his body around in the pack so he could look at Stella as she walked behind Alé. His eyelids hung sad and weak, barely open. She didn't know it was possible for a dog to look *sad*. And she had never before seen weakness in Dirty.

Her limbs felt stronger and more limber without his weight, and she was able to move more quickly. Every few steps, she reached out to touch Dirty's head, and each time, he closed his eyes.

"You're a good boy, Dirty," she murmured, stepping closer behind him, nearly treading on Alé's heels. "You hang in there, okay?"

He strained his neck, sniffing toward her.

Overhead, the canopy thinned and cloudless sun blasted over them, oven-hot. Alé pulled a bandana from his pocket and tied it to his forehead.

Stinging sweat trickled into Stella's eyes, and she lifted the collar of her shirt to wipe it away. Dirty's heavy head sagged on the edge of the pack.

The canopy closed in again, providing a welcome shield from the sun.

As Alé stepped past a towering tree with a trunk as wide as five humans, Dirty came alive, whipping his head to the right and letting out a low growl.

Hairs stood up on Stella's arms and neck. "What is it, Dirty?"

The rainforest was thick and still, and they couldn't see more than ten or fifteen feet in any direction.

Alé slowed his steps, looking at Stella over his shoulder. "Did the dog growl at you?"

"No." She swallowed, swiveling her head. "He must've seen something. Or smelled something. He doesn't growl at nothing. And he doesn't growl at me."

Glaring into the dark understory, Dirty growled again.

Alé lifted his machete and held it in front of him as he stepped forward. "Keep moving."

They crept through the jungle, each footfall announcing their location.

Dirty growled in a drone, inhaling quickly and then rumbling through each exhale, until the path led them into a clearing cluttered by the campsite they'd seen two days ago. Fresh cinders lay scattered around a charred log. A roped-up bag of rice swung from a tree branch, and the blue tarp fluttered on its tree lashings.

Turning in Stella's direction, Dirty's growl crescendoed and he bared his teeth. His nostrils flared, and he tipped his nose higher in the air.

"He smells something." Stella shivered, despite the heat, stepping toward Alé so she could touch Dirty's head. The dog yanked his head away from her touch, spanning his neck slowly from left to right.

With the machete, Alé parted the fabric of the limp hammock and pulled out a new-looking Patagonia jacket, shaking his head. "Stolen. We must leave."

They pressed forward, picking up their pace. Stella's exhaustion ballooned as blisters rose under her moleskin and sweat soaked her clothes. Her ankle swelled and legs trembled, and the heat threatened to drag her to the ground.

Dirty whimpered or moaned each time Alé's foot clapped against the ground, jostling his wounds. His head hung over the back of the pack, unfocused eyes no longer locked on Stella as she trailed behind him.

She sucked down half the water in her pouch.

"Two more miles," Alé whispered over his shoulder.

Her head throbbed, skin pulling hotter and tighter. For a beat, she stopped walking to close her eyes, rolling her left calf to relieve a cramp. Her head swam and the jungle danced circles around her. With a light slap on her own cheeks, she pressed on, rubbing her eyes frequently to clear the blurring.

Occasionally, Dirty stretched his muzzle toward her, but his energy seemed to wane. Shifting his weight in the pack, his whimper intoned quieter and quieter.

Alé whispered over his shoulder, "One and a half miles."

Every tree looked the same, and Stella's feet felt disconnected from her body. Only Dirty's head, drooping lower and lower, kept her moving.

Alé stopped pointing out animals in the trees. Stella stopped looking up to measure the sun's progress. She watched the ground, stepping quickly and carefully, frustrated by her body's weakness. She wanted the strength to jog, to gallop.

By the time Alé whispered "One more mile," Dirty had stopped moaning, stopped moving. His head and neck hung limp, his body slumped in the pack.

Reaching forward to stroke his head, Stella looked into the canopy and whispered, *We need your help, Dad.*

Something scuttered in the shadows, and she jerked open her eyes.

Her pupils dilated.

Dirty didn't wake.

Alé stopped mid-stride, holding up a hand.

Stella wiped the sweat from her forehead and touched Dirty's cheek with her fingers. Still, the dog didn't move.

Motioning with his hand, Alé beckoned them forward. They stepped softly on the trail, eyes darting like wide-eyed rabbits.

The silence of the jungle felt unnatural. No invisible paws tisk-tisking through the bushes, no tree creatures swaying in branches overhead. Stella's senses ratcheted up and she scanned the blinding collage of green for irregularities, for dangers whose shapes she didn't know.

Something smelled different here.

Alé whispered over his shoulder, "Cigarette."

Beneath a sheen of sweat, hairs trembled on the back of Stella's neck.

Dirty's nose twitched and he roused, opening his eyes and sniffing the air. He raised his muzzle, scanning the forest.

In the understory off the side of the trail, a distant thumping grew into a loud irregular clatter, crashing closer and louder, barreled toward them, swishing through bushes, jumping over trees.

Dirty snarled, sitting up inside the confines of his pouch. He yanked his bandaged arm out of the pack and twisted around to face the approaching sound just as a small man plunged toward them waving a pistol.

The man's black t-shirt was ripped at the hemline and neck, his hair overgrown. He pointed the pistol at them, yelling something in Spanish.

Fingers of light flickered on one side of the man's face marred by craters carved from acne or disease. This was the same man Stella had seen in the forest four weeks ago.

Leaves trembled in full relief as smells whooshed through Stella's mouth and nose: peat and sweat and unwashed clothes.

The stillness of the air was only broken by the quiet click of the man's hand tightening on the pistol, and the hushed shift of his feet over earth.

Dirty's growl deepened, and Alé dropped his machete.

Time slowed, and Stella held up her hands. Every muscle in her body tensed. Blood pounded thick, and she heard each of her own breaths as if through a megaphone.

Bracing hard against the side of the pack, Dirty placed his paws on Alé's shoulders and lifted his torso so that his head rose above Alé's. Straining toward the man, teeth bared, Dirty opened his mouth.

Stella whispered low and stern, "No, Dirty."

In Spanish, Alé sputtered something nervous and pleading.

The forest's details deepened in clarity, as if painted with the finest brush. The veins in the leaves next to the path. The hairs on Dirty's scruff, standing high. Dirt under the man's fingernails as he cocked the pistol, sending a bright *click* ricocheting through the copse.

The man stepped forward, yelling again in Spanish. Dirty barked, and the man shifted his pistol arm to point at Alé, taking another step toward them.

Stella stopped breathing, clenched her fists, shook her head.

She stared into the man's face. "We'll give you whatever you want," she said, low and forceful.

The man did not look at her. He was looking at Dirty.

Without turning around, Alé said, "He is telling us to tie up the dog and lie on the ground on our stomachs. Do *not* lie on the ground."

The man yelled something else, and Dirty's growl grew in volume until he barked several times. The man stepped closer, now only a body length away.

Alé raised his voice, still facing the man with the gun. "Did you hear me, Stella?"

Stella's breathing raced. "Yes."

A cloud swept away from the sun, and the trail suddenly grew brighter. Speckled light threw itself onto them, illuminating all the shades of green and the dappled pattern on the back of Dirty's head, and for a hundredth of a second, Stella felt heartbroken by the overwhelming beauty.

The man raised a leg to move one step closer, and in a blinding flash of movement, Dirty thrashed out of the pack, flinging Alé to the ground, bounding toward the man as he pointed his pistol at the barking, rushing canine.

The noxious green forest whirled around Stella, and she dropped to her hands and knees, screaming, "NOOOO!!!!!"

Dirty leapt into the air in a blur of teeth and fur, the white bandage on his leg streaking behind him.

The gun went off, and Dirty yelped, leaping at the man's arm.

Screaming, the man tumbled to the ground, flinging the dog off him.

Dirty flew through the air and slammed against a wide tree trunk, slumping in a heap to the ground.

Alé dove onto the muddy path, scrounging for something.

The man pitched forward, lunging at Alé, reaching with one arm…

Alé grabbed something, lurched to his feet, screaming in Spanish.

The gun. Alé held the gun in his outstretched hand.

Stella glanced at Dirty, lying limp on his side at the base of the tree. Blood had seeped through the unraveled bandage on his foot, and his tongue hung slack from the side of his mouth.

Alé waved the gun, screamed something in Spanish again.

The man tripped to his feet, hands raised, sprinting into the jungle, vaulting over ferns and roots until he disappeared into the gloom.

Launching to her feet, Stella scrambled at Dirty, collapsing onto the ground beside him. His glazed eyes were open but unfocused, and he panted hard and fast. She didn't see a bullet wound, but something was desperately wrong with him.

"Dirty? Are you okay?" Gently, she touched his head and torso. He didn't move, so she raised her voice. "Dirty?"

He didn't respond, didn't seem to see her.

She sprinted over to Alé, standing in front of him, stunned. "Are you okay?"

"I am fine." Grim-faced, pistol still extended in his right hand, Alé looked hard into the forest where the man had disappeared. "Let's go."

Grabbing her backpack, Stella threw it onto the ground in front of Dirty. "I gotta get him in the pack."

As Alé uncocked the gun, Stella put a hand on Dirty's chest, checking for the rise and fall of breath. His lungs expanded weakly, and then retracted. He was still breathing.

Alé stepped over to them and leaned down to put his hands under Dirty's torso.

As Stella's eyes drifted to the ground, a flash of red drew her attention, and she blinked, confused. Her eyes followed the trail of red until it reached the bottom of Alé's jeans. Blood seeped through the hemline, trickling into the top of his left boot.

Stella gawked up at him, letting the empty backpack flop to the ground on top of Dirty's still body.

The whites of Alé's eyes showed bright, and his jaw was clenched hard.

She reached out to grab his shoulders. "Alé?"

He shook his head, grimacing. "It's okay."

"Alé, did he shoot you?" She held her breath.

"The bullet only touched the side of my leg." He breathed slowly, raising the bloodied hem of his jeans. She squatted to examine a gouge in his left ankle about an inch long. The skin had been ripped off, exposing the outer layer of muscle. Blood pooled on the leaves beside his boot.

"Oh my god." Her breath caught in her throat. "Did we bring the first aid kit?"

He pointed at the daypack she'd been carrying. "Outside pouch."

Struggling to see through a heavy drip of sweat, Stella yanked out the medical kit. Her fumbling hands dropped it to the ground and she picked it up again. Shaking, she unzipped the pouch and unscrewed the top from the tube of antiseptic cream, smearing it on his wound and looping a messy bandage around the weeping ankle.

Alé didn't make a sound.

Stella looked up at his emotionless face, the muscles in his jaw clenching repeatedly.

Stella put a hand on his shoulder. "Can you walk?"

His eyebrows drew down, pinched over his dark eyes. "Yes."

"I am gonna carry Dirty." She squatted next to her tipped-over backpack. Dirty still hadn't moved, the upper half of his body buried under the sack. Lids drooped low over his glazed eyes.

"No, I can take him," Alé started struggling to his feet, but Stella held up her hand.

"Don't fuck with me right now, Alé. I am taking him." Dirty didn't whimper, didn't even look at her as she eased him back into the pack. Awkwardly, she jerked the straps over her shoulders before Alé could try to help her. "You lead the way."

He hesitated and she pointed down the trail. "Let's go."

With sweat pouring down his temples, Alé limped onto the path. Stella reached over her shoulder with one hand to lift Dirty's limp head and rest it on her shoulder.

Her legs burned, quivering. But if Alé could walk with flesh gaping on the side of his ankle, she could carry a thirty-pound dog on her perfectly functional fucking legs.

Under her breath, she huffed out her team's roller derby mantra: "My body's bruised, my heart is full… My body's bruised, my heart is full… My body's bruised, my heart is full…"

Dirty didn't move, didn't shift in the pack, and his head slid off her shoulder. She was grateful she couldn't see his lifeless eyes. The rotten flesh from his bite wounds festered, stinking.

She grunted with each step, funneling all her energy into the grunts.

Alé tried to mask his limp as he turned around to face her. "Let me take the dog. I can hear you struggling."

"NO." She shook her head. "That is not going to happen. I just need to make noise."

Alé lifted Dirty's head to prop it on Stella's shoulder, and pointed at the pouch on the side of her pack. "You must drink."

"I'll drink while we walk." She sucked from the tube and wiped her mouth. "Let's go."

His limp now more pronounced, Alé moved forward onto a flatter and wider section of trail, now several feet across and heavily trammeled.

A scarlet macaw flitted onto a branch just above them.

The bird—something about the bird made Stella choke on a sob.

Without breaking stride, she inclined her head toward Dirty, whispering. "That's a scarlet macaw. Once she finds a partner, she stays with him for her whole life. Do you see it?"

Dirty's head started to slide off her shoulder, and she braced her fingers around his muzzle to steady it.

Watching her feet so she wouldn't trip, she mumbled to Dirty to keep him focused on the sound of her voice. Maybe Dirty was still in there, listening to her. Maybe her voice would remind him that he needed to stay here, in this life, with her. She told him about her mother's backyard Texas, and making whiskey with her father, and his new friend, Coffee. And she told him about Torres, whom he would never meet. "You're gonna be okay, Dirty. We're almost there. I love you, buddy."

He didn't react.

Scanning the jungle, Alé tucked the gun into his belt and looked at the GPS device. "Half of a mile left."

Stella's lips trembled, either from exhaustion or dehydration or heat, or maybe all three. She didn't give a shit about the trembling in her lips and legs, or the pain and swelling in her ankle, or the wrenching pain in her heels, or her shortness of breath or the sweat pouring from her neck and chest and armpits. She didn't give a shit about the man who had attacked them or the fact that she had nearly perished in this jungle many times over. She didn't care about the predators watching them or the cleanliness of the water she just sucked down. She didn't care about all the pain she had experienced in her past, or the pain she would certainly experience in the future. She didn't feel anger toward her father for leaving her, or her mother for abandoning her, or herself for making so many terrible choices in her life. The only fucking thing she cared about was carrying this goddamn dog out of this goddamn jungle and getting Alé and Dirty to a hospital, and getting Dirty healed so that she could show him the kind of gratitude and love that he had obviously never experienced. The kind of gratitude deserved by a creature who would selflessly risk death for his person over and over and over, with no promise of anything in return. The kind of love deserved by a creature who could crack open a broken soul and fill it with so much love that her wounds would begin to heal.

She would not give up on this fucking dog. She would walk through this jungle that had tried to kill her, with this dog on her back, until her legs fell off.

Tears made runnels down her cheeks, dropping to the dirt below.

Stella looked up into the canopy. The undersides of branches formed black patterns against the ultramarine of a cloudless twilight. Trees waved in a breeze, shifting the day's last shadows. Stella sobbed, holding Dirty's head aloft so his vacant eyes could take in the beauty.

Her legs began to quaver with every step, threatening to buckle and quit entirely. Her breathing became so erratic that she struggled to fill her lungs with sufficient oxygen, and her vision swirled, her brain flicking through blackness, almost fainting. She grimaced, fighting to put one foot in front of another.

She looked up and whispered to her father, "I know you sent him to me. And now my body is breaking again and I don't know if I can do this. Help me, Daddy."

You got this, Squirrel. You're strong like a tree.

His voice wrapped around her, clear and strong. Not like a memory… It sounded like he was right behind her on the trail.

You've always been strong like a tree. You're my Squirrel.

She didn't turn around to look for him, didn't want to know that he wasn't actually there. She just let her father's voice wrap around her, fill her up.

Ahead, the trail widened again and Alé picked up speed, jogging despite his wound. This broad, unbroken stretch of trail—she recognized it. She started running, too, legs in a full tremor, Dirty's body heaving up and down, gravity and fatigue straining to knock her off her feet, but she ran, grunting louder and longer until she barreled forward at full-tilt, screaming.

Thirty or forty feet ahead, Alé called back to her. "We have made it."

Stella sprinted, wiping her eyes to see the path clear in the crepuscular light. She jumped over a tree root, barely catching herself as her knee buckled, catching herself before her body fell to the ground and barreling forward, not slowing her pace.

The soft earth turned to hard-packed dirt, and the dirt opened up around her, and Alé's taxi was there, right in front of her. She collapsed to her knees, wiping her nose and eyes. Lowering the pack to the ground, she slipped her shoulders out of the straps and shoved her arms into the pack, wrapping them around Dirty, lifting his limp body and sliding it through the car door that Alé had opened for her. Carefully, she arranged him on the back bench as Alé slipped into the driver's seat, grunting as he arranged his wounded leg in the footwell.

Dirty's breathing had slowed, his eyes barely open. Stella tugged out his dangling tongue so he wouldn't choke on it.

As Alé cranked the engine, Stella reached forward to touch the back of his shoulder. "Alé, you can't drive, can you? Let me drive."

He forced a smile, his face worn and tired. "Nobody else drives my cab. And anyway, he did not shoot the leg that I use to drive. Close the door."

Energy draining from her body, Stella again nearly fainted as she climbed onto the back seat next to Dirty, reaching out to grab the door handle so she could pull it closed. As her hand clasped on the handle, a movement caught her attention at the treeline on the edge of the parking lot. Someone was there.

Before she could panic that it might be the man from the jungle, she recognized the form, her throat swelling, more tears pushing up onto her eyelids.

Just inside the canopy, her father leaned against a palm tree, locking eyes with her as he reached up to put one hand over his heart. Nodding, he raised his hand and smiled at her, and she smiled back at him, putting her own hand to her heart. Then her father turned around to walk into the jungle, disappearing into the shadows.

Stella let out a wild sob as she pulled the car door closed.

The moment he heard the door latch shut, Alé peeled out of the parking lot, wheels skidding on the dirt.

"We will go to Puerto Jimenez." Alé picked up his cell phone. "The veterinarian Emilia is a friend of mine and her husband is a doctor. I will call her now."

As he dialed the number and spoke to someone in urgent Spanish, Stella wedged herself on the back seat behind Dirty, weeping silently. She spooned her dog, and he rested his head on the soft inside of her upper arm. She held his good paw in her palm and pressed her mouth to his ear as she sang in a whisper:

Hush little baby, don't you cry.

Mommy's gonna paint your face with pie.

And if that pie tastes like a frog,

Mommy's gonna give you an ugly dog.

And if that ugly dog gets mean,

Mommy's gonna give you a blue-faced queen.

And if that blue-faced queen won't play,

You gotta stop your crying now, any old way.

The car careened around curves and thrashed through potholes, suspension squeaking, rusty joints threatening to burst. Alé rolled down his window and a humid blast washed over them.

Dirty's eyelids narrowed to slits. He breathed heavy, gasping.

Stella buried her face in his fur. "Can you hear me, Dirty? I'm not going anywhere. I know you're really hurting, and you're trying to hang on. I hope you know how much I love you. Before I met you, I thought maybe I'd never be happy again. But lying on that beach with you when I was covered in my own shit, knowing I might die, some part of me actually felt *happy*. We were meant to know each other, even if it was only for four weeks. You'll always be with me."

As the minutes unfolded, Alé's taxi growled back onto the paved roads, and Dirty's breathing slowed. Stella pulled him closer, breathing in sync with him, and everything around them disappeared. Nothing existed except the two of them, lying together again, lurching through a chaotic world. She nuzzled her nose in the muddy, crusted fur on the back of his neck, and counted each breath.

Braced by Stella's arm, Dirty almost flew off the seat as the car wheels screeched around a corner, brakes slamming to a full stop.

"We are here," Alé called from the front seat as he tumbled out the door.

Stella vaulted up from the back seat, grabbing Dirty by his torso, lifting him out the door and sprinting across a dirt parking lot toward a small clinic.

A middle-aged woman in surgical scrubs flung open the blue door for her, pointing to a room in the back of the clinic where a young man, also in scrubs, stood waiting under a fluorescent light, arms outstretched.

"Armando will put him on the table," she said to Stella, pulling a clinical mask over her mouth. "Leave us with him and Hector will take care of Alé."

The veterinarian turned to Alé. "Alejandro, Hector will treat you in the operating room. I will take you to him."

"I know where the operating room is." Alé limped heavily toward another door in the back of the room. "You work on the dog. I will find Hector."

As Stella carried Dirty toward Armando, she turned her face toward Alé and sobbed, "Thank you, Alé. Thank you so much. I'll be right here if you need me."

He smiled at her over his shoulder, disappearing through the operating room door.

Stella stumbled into the exam room, and Armando reached out to take Dirty from her. When he held the dog securely, Armando turned around to place the dog on the table, his body forcing a separation between Dirty and Stella. She couldn't see past the vet tech, couldn't see Dirty's face, and she roared, "I don't want to leave him!"

Coming up behind her, the veterinarian put her hands on Stella's shoulders, dark eyes wide and commanding. "It will be better for him if you leave us to do our work. We will take care of him and Alé. I promise."

Stella's body trembled. "Can I say goodbye to him?"

The doctor stepped aside. "Quickly."

Stella bent over Dirty, kissing the top of his head. "We made it, Dirty. You and me. I'll be right outside waiting for you. I'll come get you the second they've fixed you up. I'm always coming back for you. I love you, Dirty."

Without opening his eyes, the tip of his tongue reached up and grazed her cheek.

COSTA RICA

Dominical
Two weeks later

FUCHSIA CLOUDS DROPPED shimmering reflections onto the sea along the wide, flat Dominical beach.

Stella sat on a towel, her right ankle tucked in a soft brace and propped on a beach bag.

Next to her, Alé leaned back on one elbow, his bandaged left leg propped next to hers on the bag. He stuck a finger under the gauze to get a good scratch.

She swatted his hand. "Don't do that."

"I know, I know." He shook his head. "Did you hear? They caught the criminals. Two of them. They robbed more than twenty people in the last two months, and killed one person."

Stella leaned back, propping herself on her hands and resting her head on Alé's shoulder. "I'm glad they got those assholes."

"Me too," he said, slipping something into her hand.

She looked down. In her palm, she held a cream-colored spiral seashell attached to a long black string.

Alé stared at the ocean. "That was my daughter's. I want you to have it."

"Alé, are you sure? I…" Stella's voice caught in her throat. "I can't take this from you."

"You can." He touched the black shell fragment strung around his neck. "I still have this one that she gave me, and I will never take it off."

Stella wrapped her fingers around the necklace. "Thank you, Alé. For everything. You have been so good to me, and…"

He patted her knee. "Thank you, mija. You have been good to me too. With the money you paid me, I can start my guide business in Corcovado again. This is a great gift."

They turned toward the surf, where a three-legged dog stood knee deep in the water, facing the horizon.

Alé shook his head. "He is an extraordinary dog. I am lucky I met him."

Stella's chin trembled as she wiped her eyes. "Everyone who meets him is lucky."

They listened to the waves, and then Alé reached into his shirt pocket and pulled out some folded papers, handing them to Stella. "These are the papers from Doctor Emilia that you will need to get him on the airplane. You have bought his plane ticket?"

She nodded. "Yeah. I can't believe how easy it is to get a dog back to the United States. Seems like it should be harder, but…" Stella shrugged and put a side-arm around Alé. "Thank you again."

"You are welcome! We will have another adventure one day." Grabbing a crutch lying in the sand, Alé lifted himself up on one leg. As he looked down at her, amber light struck his face. He smiled, showing all his teeth. "You will come visit me soon?"

She nodded. "Of course. And you promised to come visit me in Texas."

Pinning the crutch under one armpit, he held out the other arm in celebration. "We will listen to some honkey tonk music!"

She stood and hugged him. "I'll see you in the morning?"

With one arm, he pressed all the air out of her lungs. "Yes, I will see you in the morning for our trip to the airport. And I will not offer to help you carry your bags! I know you can do this yourself."

Smiling, she watched him walk away.

As she sat back down on her towel, she texted her mom: *Looking forward to seeing you tomorrow. How's Coffee?*

Before she'd finished taking a swig from her beer, her mom texted back: *She's good. She's excited to meet her new sibling. Or is Dirty her nephew? Regardless, we can't wait to see you. And Maria has already filled the house with three hundred balloons (quite literally) for your arrival. I told her you wouldn't be home until tomorrow, but she insisted on bringing them today. Coffee is enamored with the balloons—I can't promise that all 300 will survive the day.* ☺

Another text buzzed through, from Gigi:

Can't wait to meet Dirty!

Stella smiled, her cheeks heating. She texted back:

He can't wait to meet you too. Lake Travis sunset when I get back?

Stella glanced up from her phone. Dirty turned around in the surf to make sure she was still there.

She waved at him, and he bounded toward her on three legs. When he reached her, his tail wagged so hard it shook the back half of his body, and he licked her face, her neck, her hands. Lifting his head to the sky, he howled, licking her again while she laughed and buried her face in his neck.

Smoothing out the towel beneath them, she lay down on her side. He knew what to do, curling into the curve of her body, resting his head on the soft part of her bicep. Careful to avoid his scar, she draped her other arm around him and took his front paw in her hand. He breathed as she breathed, cool twilight descending around them.

The final rays of sun vanished into a moonless night, brightened by a blinding spray of stars. Dirty snored warm and calm in the crook of Stella's arm as she searched the sky.

Well after midnight, she finally saw it: a lone meteor, burning its way through the atmosphere in its desperate mission to find a path to Earth.

Stella kissed her fingers and held them to the heavens.

TEXAS

Nine and a Half Years Later

DIRTY NESTLED NEXT to Stella on the couch, his back pressed into her belly. Everyone had left them to finish this journey alone, just as they began it.

Stella wrapped an arm around him, remembering the day she brought him back to Texas. In the car on the way home from the airport, he stuck his face out the window, letting the wind ripple through his jowls. When they got to the house, he tore through the backyard as if it held as much excitement as a Costa Rican jungle. His brain and heart almost exploded when he beheld a gray squirrel. He loved Coffee fully and instantly, and they romped together every day, even after Stella moved into her own apartment.

With the dangers of the jungle behind them, he took it upon himself to protect her from imminent threats like the mailman and the neighbor's lawn mower. He accompanied her to work every day, lying at her feet as she answered phones at the shelter, riding shotgun when she traveled. Every night, he slept with his head draped on her ankle or nestled on her shoulder. He licked her face through good relationships and bad ones. When she got married in Costa Rica, Dirty carried her ring down the aisle to Alé, who officiated the ceremony with a smile so wide it looked like it might break his face. When her son, Michael, was born, Dirty refused to leave his side for months.

And through all of life's fluctuations, Stella had never felt alone because Dirty was her best friend, her heart's partner.

Perhaps Dirty's greatest gift was to teach her how to be fully alive, how to recognize the good around her, and focus on that good. Every day, he reminded her to stop obsessing over things she couldn't control. He taught her that the only thing that matters—truly the only thing—is love, and when a person is experiencing a moment of love, that person is an asshole if she doesn't stop everything and sink into the moment.

Her dad had tried to teach her these lessons, but she wasn't ready for them. Now, feeling Dirty's heartbeat against hers, she understood all of it.

He breathed slowly and moved little.

She stroked his head. "Remember that first night when you lay down next to me? That's when I started loving you."

He pressed the top of his head into her chin.

Kissing his cheek, she whispered in his ear. "You were never *just* a dog to me. You were always so much more to me than just a dog."

He breathed in and out.

"You changed my life, Dirty. As long as I'm alive, you are too." She kissed his head again. "I don't know how I'm going to live without you, but I'll find a way. I know you're tired, and I want you to know I'll be okay. Because you taught me how to be okay."

She held her palm in front of his mouth and he stuck out the tip of his tongue for a gentle lick.

Her fingers sank into his lush, wiry fur. "I just need one more thing from you, okay? I need you to go find my dad and Torres. They're waiting for you."

As he exhaled, Dirty whimpered.

She stroked his head. "I'll come find you some day, okay? Mommy's always coming back, right?"

He tried to raise his front paw, and she knew what he wanted. She took the paw in her hand like she had done so many times before and they lay together, breathing, sinking in to the moment.

ACKNOWLEDGEMENTS

Thank you to everyone who helped me bring this story to life. First, my incredible peer readers: Cindy Luzcando Herron (as I wrote this book, I thought of you reading it), Andy Mitchell, Marcia Wells, Marshall Highet, Andy Dosmann and Lauren Bierman. Thank you, Jen Rees, for your editorial insight. Thanks also to my husband Andy, for encouraging me constantly without pressuring me to do more than I can do. And most of all, thank you to the dogs. You have my heart.